TRIDENT

Published by Boson Books

An imprint of Bitingduck Press
Formerly an imprint of C&M Online Media, Inc.

ISBN 978-1-938463-12-9
eISBN 978-1-938463-08-2

For information contact
Bitingduck Press, LLC
Montreal • Altadena
notifications@bitingduckpress.com
http://www.bitingduckpress.com

Cover art by Johannes Ewers
www.zazzle.com/seawolf

Author's note

This book is a work of fiction with a historical backdrop. I have taken liberties with historical figures, ships, and time frames to blend in with my story. Therefore, this book is not a reflection of actual historical events.

TRIDENT

THE FIGHTING ANTHONYS

BOOK SIX

MICHAEL AYE

Books by Michael Aye

Fiction

War of 1812 Trilogy

War of 1812: Remember the Raisin

The Fighting Anthonys

The Reaper, Book One

HMS SeaWolf, Book Two

Barracuda, Book Three

SeaHorse, Book Four

Peregrine, Book Five

Non-Fiction

What's the Reason for All That Wheezing and Sneezing

Michael A. Fowler and Nancy McKemie

Dedication

This one is for Randy "Lord" Skalla and the entire Skalla family. You have been more than friends.

To:
Kenneth, Michael, Mark, Sebastian, Brayden, and Caed
My Midshipmen

About the Author

Michael Aye is a retired Naval Medical Officer. He has long been a student of early American and British Naval history. Since reading his first Kent novel, Mike has spent many hours reading the great authors of sea fiction, often while being "haze gray and underway" himself. This is his sixth novel in the Fighting Anthonys series.

Acknowledgments

To Nancy and David, my former publishers, for sticking with a novice and teaching him how it should be done.

To Don, David, and Justin—I felt you should at least have your names in print for all the advice and help you've given me.

To HMCM Bob Cornish, USN Retired, former class-mate and still my shipmate. Our thoughts are still one.

CHARACTERS IN THE FIGHTING ANTHONY SERIES

British Officers and Seamen:

Vice Admiral Lord Gilbert "Gil" Anthony – Commands the British fleet in the Caribbean. First son of Retired Admiral Lord James Anthony (deceased) and Lady Anthony.

Captain Sir Gabriel "Gabe" Anthony – Second son of Retired Admiral Lord James Anthony (deceased) and his mistress Maria Dupree.

Bart – Long time cox'n and friend to Admiral Lord Anthony.

Dagan Dupree – Supernumerary on *Trident*; Gabe's uncle and self-appointed guardian.

Jacob (Jake) Hex – Gabe's cox'n and friend.

Rear Admiral Rupert Buck – Recently promoted to flag.

Lord Ragland – British Governor of Barbados.

Lord Skalla – British Foreign Office agent who replaces Sir Victor.

Captain Herschel Chatham – Captain of *Brilliant.*

Captain Stephen Earl –Lord Anthony's new flag captain.

Captain Eli Lamb – Captain of *Stag*.

Captain William Peckham – Captain of *Venus.*

Captain Robert Schoggins – Captain of marines on *Trident*.

Lieutenant John Jenkins – Captain of *Zebra*.

Lieutenant George Jepson – Captain of *Pegasus.*

Lieutenant Peter Parkinson – Captain of *Fortune*.

Lieutenant Joseph Taylor – Captain of *Thorn*.

Lieutenant Donald Campbell – First lieutenant on *Trident*.

Lieutenant David Davy – *Trident*'s third lieutenant; Gabe's friend.

Lieutenant Richard Hawks – Lieutenant on *Trident*.

Lieutenant Justin Holton – Lieutenant on *Trident*.

Lieutenant Mahan – Lord Anthony's flag lieutenant.

Lieutenant Wesley – *Trident*'s second lieutenant.

Robert Cornish – Physician and surgeon.

David Hayes – Master on *Trident*.
Ronald Laqua – Masters mate, acting lieutenant.
LeMatt – Lord Anthony's secretary.
Josiah Nesbit – Gabe's chef and gentleman's gentleman.
Silas – Lord Anthony's steward.
Chen Lee - Rear Admiral Buck's servant.
Crowe – Rear Admiral Buck's cox'n.
Fleming – Rear Admiral Buck's secretary.
Bridges – Lord Skalla's agent in Africa.

The Ladies:

Lady Deborah – Lord Anthony's wife. They met after pirates had attacked the ship Lady Deborah and her first husband were aboard. Her first husband was killed by the pirates before Lord Anthony's ship came to the rescue. The marriage between Lady Deborah and her first husband had been one of convenience; when she and Lord Anthony met it was love at first sight. They later married and had a daughter, Macayla.

Faith – Gabe's wife. They met in HMS SeaWolf where Gabe had survived an explosion but was wounded. Faith and Nanny were walking on the beach and came upon him. They hid Gabe and nursed him back to health. Gabe and Faith fell in love, but with her being an American and with Gabe being a British sea officer it was difficult.

Betsy – Dagan's love. She is the sister of General Manning's deceased wife. She is a young widow who lives with the general. Dagan met Betsy during the time General Manning was being held in Saint Augustine as a paroled prisoner of war.

Rebecca/Becky – Lord Anthony's sister. She lives in England with her husband, Hugh, and daughter, Gretchen.

Maria Dupree – Gabe's mother and Dagan's sister. She was Admiral Lord James Anthony's mistress of many years.

The Americans:

General Manning – America's chief negotiator for POW exchange.

Andre Dupree – Dagan's uncle. He moved to Virginia years ago.

Caleb McKean – Physician and surgeon. Gabe's friend. Loves Kitty Dupree.

Kitty – Andre Dupree's daughter who loves Caleb McKean.

Jubal – Andre Dupree's son. Still a youngster, he appears to have the same "gift" as his cousin, Dagan.

Kawliga – American Indian who lives with Andre Dupree's family and looks after Jubal. Kawliga understands Jubal's "gift".

Ariel – Dagan's ward

Lum – Slave on Faith's family plantation. He kills a man attempting to rape Faith. He spends time with Gabe on board ship as his servant, and then when Faith and Gabe reunite, he leaves the sea to be with her and Nanny.

Nanny – Like Lum, she was a slave on Faith's family plantation. She was a personal servant to Faith's mother and has been Faith's nanny since birth. She loves Lum.

Captain Horne – Captain, American privateer.

The American Privateer

It was seventeen seventy six
The war had just begun
The British had the Navy
With the biggest gun

But the British merchantmen
Sailed the seas in fear
Would their ship be raided by
The American privateer

Now the privateer's been taken
No more convoys will she raid
Her captain wounded and weary
Offers up his bloody blade

But the British captain
Declines and tells him no
How can I take the blade
Of such a gallant foe

-Michael Aye

Prologue

RACK...

"Ahhh..."

The first cry of pain came at lash fifteen. Seaman Paul's back had hardly healed from a previous flogging. It was raw and as red as beef before the present flogging had even started. His back was now a bloody mess. The bosun's mate pulled the bloody tails of the cat between his fingers, untangling the knots as bits of flesh fell to the deck. Taking his time, the mate pulled back his arm, then like a striking snake the cat struck again. Turning muscle and flesh into a raw pulp that was now unrecognizable as a person's back.

"Ahhh!!!"

Sixteen...

The seaman had done his best to uphold the honour of a jack tar by suffering his punishment in silence. But the pain was far too great. His screams were unnerving to both the officers and crew, who were being made to witness the cruel and unnecessary punishment of a good seaman.

Crack...

"Ahhh!!!"

Seventeen...

How much longer he could survive, more than one person wondered; pray God, he would lose consciousness soon.

***

HMS Foxfire, *of twenty-eight guns, rose up and down with the gentle swell in the pre-dusk hour. Punishment usually took place at six bells in the forenoon watch, but Captain Brian, Butcher Brian as he was called by the crew, never let tradition keep him from letting the "cat out of the bag."*

The bosun's mate had piped, "All hands to witness punishment." With hats off, the sullen crew had moved lethargically aft, where the small detachment of solemn faced marines stood tall at attention with their muskets at their sides. They had seen too much of Butcher Brian's savage ways to lift a finger, much less fire on anyone had they risen up in mutiny.

The officers were all present in full dress, sweltering under the hot Georgia sun. Swords hung at their sides as sweat ran down their faces and backs. They were as sick of the captain's brutality as everyone else.

Norton, the first lieutenant, had tried to come to Paul's aid. "Captain, Paul's crime was minimal."

"He cursed a petty officer," Brian retorted.

"Who struck his back with a starter when it was still raw from a previous flogging," Norton argued.

"He shouldn't have been the last one," Brian quipped.

"Twenty-four lashes for saying 'damn you,' Captain, is that not too severe? The bosun's mate, realizing what he'd done, didn't take offense."

"But I heard it, Mr.Norton."

Realizing he was getting nowhere with his argument, Norton changed tack. "Captain, we are carrying a fortune in gold and silver for the forces in Savannah. Cannot punishment wait until after we have safely unloaded our...our cargo?"

"Mr. Norton!" Brian snapped. "We are at the mouth of the Savannah River now, and waiting on the pilot. Our duty is all but complete. Do you think, sir, we have aught to fear? Is not the city under British control?"

"Aye, Captain, but these waters are still teeming with privateers. If the ship or the gold were to fall into enemy hands, sir..."

"Silence!" Brian roared, cutting Norton off, "enough, sir, I've had enough of your ninny ways. I thought better of you, Norton. Truthfully, I did." Turning away from the seething lieutenant, Captain Brian ordered, "Strip."

Two burly bosun's mates tore the shirt from Paul's back.

"Seize him up," Brian barked another order.

The seaman's hands were bound to a grating rigged for the flogging. Captain Brian then made a mockery of reading the article of war that covered Paul's offense, ending with, "so forth and so on."

The order was then given, "Bosun's mate, do your duty."

Brian was one of those captains who made sure he carried both a left-handed and right-handed bosun's mate on board; so that when the cat was applied, the poor sod being punished would have a checkered back.

Twenty-four lashes were Brian's minimum, with thirty-six not being uncommon. When the first dozen had been laid on, a new bosun's mate laid on the next twelve; a new mate for each dozen. When the first bosun finished laying on his twelve, he picked up the red baize bag his cat went in and wiped the gore from his hands. The second bosun had just removed his cat from its bag when an excited cry was heard from the mainmast lookout.

"Deck thar! Deck thar! Boats approaching, sir, they're almost on us."

"Where away," Norton shouted up.

"Close off the larboard bow, sir."

"You waited long enough," Norton replied in disgust.

"I've been calling down, sir, but couldn't get anybody's attention," the anxious lookout responded.

Turning to the captain, Norton was cut off before he could speak.

"Relax, Norton," the captain said. "It's probably the pilot."

"In more than one boat?" Norton asked.

"Most likely the guard boat with dispatches and some bumboatman trying to sell his wares before the others get a chance when we anchor." Brian then ordered, "Continue the punishment."

Again, the cat struck. Time after time the knots biting into the seaman's back until there was not an inch of flesh that hadn't been flayed open and now the white bone of the shoulder blade was plainly visible.

"Ahhh!!!"

The cries of anguish grew louder with every stroke until lash eighteen when there was no sound from the poor soul.

Crack...

Nineteen...

"Stop the punishment." The command was from Cornish, the ship's surgeon.

"What's this?" Brian demanded. "You so easily countermand my orders," the captain screamed.

"It's Paul, sir. He's made no cry with the last few lashes."

"Very well," Brian said, with a sigh. "See to him and let's get on with it... hurry man."

The surgeon made a quick examination of Paul, then turned to the nearest bosun's mate and said, "Cut him down."

Not believing his ears, Brian angrily shouted, spittle spraying as he spoke. "Damn you, sir, you go too far. I'll have you under arrest. Continue punishment. Bosun's mate, do your duty."

"Go right ahead, Captain," Cornish snapped. "Flog away as you will, but Paul will feel nothing. He's died under the lash. Are you satisfied, you maniac? You've ruptured the man's kidney. You murdered another fine seaman, Captain. I will personally see to it you answer for this one. Tell me, Captain, just how many fine seamen do you intend to butcher?"

A silence hung over the ship's company. A long silence, in which time Brian's skin turned ashen. The crew was in shock that someone would openly defy the captain. Suddenly heads appeared over the bulwarks.

A voice spoke out, "Thank you, Captain, for assembling your men and handing me such a rich prize without so much as a sentry's challenge."

Norton whirled around to the marines and crew shouting, "Repel boarders."

The unmistakable sound of hammers being cocked cut short the order. A piercing cry was heard followed by the thud of a body falling to the deck. All eyes moved to the source of the sound. Captain Butcher Brian lay in a heap. Blood was pouring from around the knife sticking in his neck, staining the immaculate deck.

Seeing the look of accusation from Norton, the privateer's captain quickly defended himself. "That was none of our doing, sir. I would look to your own crew for the culprit. But perhaps it's best. Saves a lot of embarrassment and the trouble of a court martial." Then with a salute the privateer said, "I am Captain Nathan Horne and I do hereby claim this ship...and ah...its cargo as a lawful prize of war. To show you I'm not a bloodthirsty devil such as your captain...previous captain, that is, I will give you, your officers, and any crew members who wish to accompany you free passage to Savannah. If you, sir, give your word of honour not to attempt to arm yourselves I will give you time to collect any personal belongings you may wish. I will also give you a brief statement discussing the state of the ship when we took it. It may come in handy should there be any legal proceedings."

"Thank you, sir," Norton mumbled. "You are most kind and thoughtful." He took a breath and made to unbuckle his sword.

Seeing this, Horne shook his head. "No, you've gone through enough. I would not dishonor you by taking your sword."

He then spoke to Foxfire*'s crew at large. "I have given you all the freedom to make your way to Savannah via open boats. However, those of you who wish to remain aboard may do so and will be welcomed to serve our new nation. You will be treated fair and square, like a mate should be treated. The choice is yours, the boats...or to sea."*

The cheers that went up did not surprise Norton. After what Butcher Brian had put the crew through, it was a wonder that any of the men made their way into the boats.

CHAPTER ONE

BANKS OF GRAY CLOUDS moved across the horizon, turning the afternoon sky almost as dark as night. Here and there, lightning streaked across the sky and the distant rumble of thunder grew nearer and nearer. As the wind picked up, rollers could be seen across the anchorage. The rollers turned into whitecaps as the force of the wind picked up. Soon the whitecaps could be seen crashing into the hulls of His Majesty's ships lying at anchor in the Solent. Normally these waters, sheltered between the Isle of Wight and Portsmouth provided a safe anchorage.

Looking at the large sign, shaped like a huge teapot, swinging above the inn's entrance, Rear Admiral Buck felt things might get lively for the ships, even in a safe anchorage tonight. The first drops of rain pelted against the gold braid on the admiral's new uniform as he hurried through the door into Scolfes. The tavern was already busy, and before the night was over it would be packed. The building had been built in the fourteenth century and renovated several times. The outer walls were constructed of thick, grayish stone. The walls not only protected those on the inside from the elements, but also made it easy to keep warm during the cold months and cool when the weather outside was hot.

Scolfes catered to the more well to do in Portsmouth. While not as large as the George Inn on Portsmouth Point it was just as clean, and many swore the fare was much tastier. Once you entered Scolfes, you could go left into the tavern where fine spirits were offered to gentlemen and the occasional escorted lady. To the right was the dining room where a man could bring his wife and family without the fear of some rowdy, boisterous drunk getting out of line. Above the dining area were the inn's rooms. To either end sat a suite or sitting room with its own private bath area, whereas the other single rooms shared a common bathing area. Buck could have had his meals in his room, but preferred the public dining area where he talked with other naval officers. He also enjoyed watching the crowd of civilian diners. A second entrance to the upper rooms was via a staircase that exited onto the street. This was built as an exit in case of a fire, however, it was used more frequently when gentlemen needed to be discreet in regards to the occasional entertainment of unregistered guests.

Scolfes offered a covered, paved walkway lit up by oil lamps. The inn's rooms were clean, and the beds comfortable and relatively vermin free. The staff had proven to be courteous, professional, and showed appreciation for any tips that might be given. In short, Scolfes was a very well run place that would match any in Portsmouth. It was home and headquarters for Rear Admiral Rupert Buck as his newly assembled squadron made ready to set sail.

Thinking of the days to come, Buck felt excited and apprehensive at the same time. The conflict of emotions was due to a message he had received from the port admiral a week ago. His voyage was to be slowed down and hampered by the tedious task of convoy duty. With the ink still wet on his promotion orders to rear admiral, Buck felt it ill advised to complain. After all, had not Lord Anthony's squadron been saddled with the same type of duty when he last sailed from England? Should he damn the American privateers for raiding England's commerce or thank them, as otherwise the promotion to flag rank would undoubtedly still be years away.

It was hard for Buck to realize all that had transpired since he was first lieutenant aboard *Drakkar*. Vice Admiral Lord Anthony had been the ship's captain and Gabe a midshipman. Now, Gabe was commanding officer of the sixty-four gun *HMS Trident*, and Buck's flag captain. Buck's seven-ship squadron included three frigates: two thirty-twos and a smaller twenty-eight. The last three were a ship-rigged sloop of war with eighteen guns and two brigs, each carrying sixteen six-pounders.

Gabe had been discussing the possibility of mounting two carronades on the bow of the ship sloop, arguing that the added firepower of the smashers would more than make up for their short range. *Thorn's* captain was warming to the idea after re-reading the article in the Gazette discussing Gabe's defeat of a larger French squadron that was largely due to the heavier firepower of the carronades.

Buck was to meet with his captains tonight to discuss the convoy assignments. No doubt the topic would come up again. The captain's cabin on *Trident* was not that large. Were it not for the fact that all the ship's officers, starting with the captain and going down, were making room for the admiral and his staff, it would have seemed grand compared to that of a frigate. Buck had been quick to accept her as his new flagship, but had he done Gabe and his officers a disservice by doing so? That was one of the reasons to have the captains' meeting at Scolfes. It would not be so crowded. Looking toward the entrance, he spied Gabe. He always had been punctual. Other uniformed personnel filled the dining room. At a time when most young men were either in the Army, Navy, or Marines, a young officer shouldn't garner much attention. Yet with all the country in an uproar over this dashing young hero, all eyes were on Gabe when he entered. Looking neither left nor right, Gabe made his way straight to the admiral's table. Droplets of rain ran down the sleeves of his uniform as he shook Buck's hand.

"Not a fit night," Buck volunteered.

"Nay, but better in here than out in the anchorage." As if to punctuate Gabe's words, Captain Lamb, of *Stag,* entered the room soaked to the bone.

"You'll get no argument from that one," Buck said smiling.

Soon all the officers of Buck's new squadron had entered. First they had a social hour, and then got down to business. "You want to know a man, you go aboard his ship" – words Lord James Anthony had passed on to his son, Gil, who had passed them on to Rear Admiral Buck. Buck had visited each of the captains aboard their ships and had not been disappointed.

Eli Lamb, of *HMS Stag 32*, was a tall man. He had a ready smile but a quick temper. He was the next senior captain after Gabe but was some years older.

The other thirty-two gun frigate's captain was William Peckham. He was short, starting to gray, and looked like a reverend. He was a thick-set man but not fat, a man who had spent time in the revenue service before the war.

Herschel Chatham was captain of the *Brilliant*, the smallest of Buck's three frigates. Chatham was a young captain in an old ship. He had previously commanded one of the other ships now in Buck's squadron, the *Thorn*. Chatham was the nephew of Vice Admiral Chatham. Buck had, however, got it from one of the man's previous captains that he was a good seaman; he'd been very successful against American raiders when under Admiral Howe in North America.

The *Thorn* was an eighteen-gun ship-rigged sloop of war. She was much like Gabe's first command, which had been a captured American brigantine, the *SeaWolf*. Joseph Taylor was the lieutenant who commanded her. Old for his rank, he'd spent time with the "Honest Johns" until he tired of the India trade. He seemed a likable sort with a vast knowledge of the sea.

The *Fortune* and the *Zebra* were sister ships. They were brigs of the same class, each with sixteen six-pounders. John Jenkins had brought the *Zebra* back to England as a prize from the colonies with the strongest recommendation for command. With the war escalating, the Lords of the Admiralty followed through with the recommendation. Jenkins had been a master's mate, passed the lieutenant's exam and had been the second lieutenant on a frigate. The brig had been British, then taken by the Americans in 1777 and retaken in 1778. Hopefully, she would now serve the king for the remainder of her service.

Peter Parkinson of the *Fortune* looked no older than a school age boy. In fact, Buck doubted he even needed to shave. He reminded Buck of Lieutenant Davy. Like Davy, he was proud and brave, maybe too brave. Buck was glad *Fortune* had a wise old master.

***

HMS Pegasus BOBBED LIKE a cork on a fishing line as the wind picked up. Lieutenant George "Jep" Jepson, the ship's captain, stood as his guest entered the main cabin. Captain Stephen Earl, soon to be Vice Admiral Anthony's flag captain, was drenched from head to toe. His uniform appeared to be pasted to his skin.

Unable to hide his smile, Jepson spoke with a snicker, "I see you didn't get far."

"Hell no," Earl snapped his reply. "We'd no sooner shoved off when the sky opened up and I was soaked clean through."

"Ahem...well," Jepson said, "if you can't get ashore, I could send Parks to pay your respects or possibly even entertain the young lady until the weather moderates. Of course, you would have to advance him a little. The first lieutenant of such a small ship could hardly be expected to entertain a lady in such a lavish manner as would be expected from a post captain."

Chomping on his cigar, Jepson talked out of the side of his mouth, "Should I send for the lieutenant, Captain?"

"No," Earl snapped again, and then added, "but do you know where you can go, sir?"

"Aye," Jepson replied, "to my bed...but only after we've had a wet to warm us up. It's not a night to be out."

Smiling, Earl slung his soaked coat over a chair and accepted the offered brandy. As if in deep thought, Earl stared into the brown liquid. Raising his glass in a toast, he said, "Here's to what might have been."

"Aye," Jepson said as the glasses clinked together. After refilling the glasses, he spoke again. "We got our sailing orders this evening."

Looking over his glass at Jepson, Earl said, "And?"

"We're to set sail ahead of the convoy," Jepson stated. "If weather permits, we can weigh anchor tomorrow if not the following day."

"I see," Earl said. He had thought of sailing aboard the *Trident* to Barbados but didn't think it would be fair to Gabe having the old and the new captain on the same ship. He had enjoyed several evenings out with Gabe and Jepson, and even had dined at the home of Gabe's mother, where Jepson had also been a guest.

Striking up a friendship with the man, Earl had asked Jepson if he'd mind him taking passage aboard *Pegasus*. Since then, he'd taken over the first lieutenant's quarters, refusing Jepson's offer of his cabin. Parks was young enough he could sleep anywhere without the aches and pains brought on by a cramped hammock or cot. He'd not displace Jep, but Parks was fair game.

"Not tomorrow," Earl stated. "Give us a day to say our farewells."

"Aye," Jepson said absently. An extra day would be good. His only thoughts were to whom did Earl wish to bid good-by? Family...or sweetheart? Well, it didn't matter. Hopefully, by tomorrow the weather would clear.

After the men bade each other goodnight, water continued to drip from the soggy uniform coat that Earl had left hanging on the back of Jep's chair. Soon a large puddle had formed. With the motion of the ship riding the swells, the puddle ran towards the bulkhead where Jepson's cot swung. The first thing he'd feel when he arose the next morning would be wet stockings.

CHAPTER TWO

GABE WATCHED THE MEN working in front of his mother's house. A lot had changed since he'd last been home. The improvement commissioners had given approval for the streets to have oil lamps to light them up at night. The street had long been paved with cobblestones, and they now even had a man called a scavenger, who collected rubbish with a cart once a week. It was no wonder Gabe's mom, Maria, did not desire to move to one of the newer suburbs.

Several naval officers had built houses at Kingston. It was a very fashionable area, away from the noise, dirt, and activity that came with the dockyard and naval base. It was close enough, however, that it was just a short horse or carriage ride to Portsmouth.

Gabe didn't think his mother would ever leave the house that she and his father, Admiral James Anthony, had shared. It had taken both Dagan and him to persuade his mother to agree to some new furniture. They had bought several pieces of comfortable upholstered furniture made by Thomas Chippendale and a new clock by James Cox. Because the townhouse was built on three floors, keeping the place up had gotten to be too much. Gabe's mother had denied it, but the housekeeper had said help was a must. Therefore, Gabe and Dagan had set up an interview process. In the last four weeks they had hired two additional maids and a cook. They also hired a man to act as a gardener as well as carriage driver, and had even given the man permission to hire a stable boy to help. Gabe had also purchased a new carriage, an unnecessary extravagance, his mother had protested. Neither Gabe nor Dagan had felt so, and they had argued that it would last for years.

The coach was very similar to the German Landau that had made its English appearance in 1743. Gabe and Dagan had made a pact to never let his mother know how much the carriage had cost.

"She'll know it wasn't cheap," Dagan said matter-of-factly a few days before the coach arrived. "With all the sawing and hammering going on to build a new coach house, she has to know it was, as she put it, extravagant."

Gabe didn't care, his mother was now starting to show her age. She'd been put through enough in her life, and Gabe had decided she'd live as comfortably as he could arrange it for the rest of her years. After his recent victories, he could arrange a lot. It appalled him, however, that some of those who once called her Lord Anthony's mistress or the admiral's kept woman could be so friendly now. He was amazed how at St. George's church the previous Sunday, one of the women, who'd been so critical of Lord Anthony's mistress and bastard son when he was young, had sat on the pew next to his mother and chatted before service.

When Gabe had later discussed this with his mother, she simply said, "Have you never done anything you were ashamed of?"

"Why yes," he replied, "but..." His mother had shushed him before he could finish.

"Have you ever thought of the indignity Christ suffered before he was crucified, son? Christ didn't die so some folks and not others could be forgiven. He died so that we all may be forgiven."

Gabe didn't know what to say to that. His mother then in a soft voice said, "I know how you suffered at times. But you had your father's pride and refused to let anyone see you cry. Now you are the talk of England, my son. How do you think they feel now, embarrassed maybe? Don't be so quick to judge until you've walked in another's shoes."

"That's not always so easy," Gabe mumbled.

"I know, son, but you will be stronger for it."

***

JACOB HEX WAS SITTING at a trestle table in a tavern in Deal. The new cox'n's uniform with his gold braid, purchased by Captain Anthony, made some take a second look, not sure if he was an officer or what.

"Captain Sir Gabriel Anthony," Hex corrected himself as he gave a silent toast. *He was now Sir Gabe, but he was still the captain*, Hex thought, *until he made admiral, that is.*

The tavern had a sign proclaiming it to all as The Baskerville, the finest in Deal. Outside the establishment on a clear day, Walmer Castle could be seen to the south. Hex had grown up playing in the shadows of the castle, but that seemed an eternity ago. He was in a foul mood. His homecoming had been far from what he had expected. He had been away almost four years, but someone could have written and warned him. He'd expected to come home to his widow mother living in their old home place. He thought he would see the place somewhat run down and his mother living off what little had been left after his father had been killed and the debts paid off. None of his expectations had proven true. His mother had married one of his father's previous business associates, meaning a smuggler. She had allowed her new husband to sell their property, lock, stock and barrel. All these changes and he'd not received one letter. Not when he'd been aboard *HMS Rapid*, not when he'd been a prisoner of war, and not after being made Captain Anthony's cox'n aboard *HMS Peregrine*. He'd written letters home from all of those places and not received one letter in return. Well, now he knew why.

She would have had to tell him about all the changes and she couldn't bear the thought of it. He had no animosity that she had remarried, as she was only forty when his father had died. But to marry John Spencer? He'd likely end up much as his father had and she would be a widow again. Spencer was lucky he'd cheated the hangman as long as he had. But for his mother to allow Spencer to sell the property without so much as a by your leave was too much.

"We intended to give you your share," Spencer had said.

"It's well you should," Hex had snapped, "as it was my entire share. As father's only son, I would have inherited it all."

"As you should have once the expenses and debts had been subtracted," Spencer replied, trying to dampen the heat of friction.

"Well, how much am I owed?" Hex asked, not really having a figure in mind but sure whatever it was it would be less than the real value. He was right.

With all the dignity he could muster to tell a bald-face lie, Spencer said, "Your part came to two hundred five pounds, three shillings, and eight pence."

Hex had almost choked on his beer. "Surely you jest," he said. "Just the house and gardens were worth twice that."

"Were," Spencer said. He then added, "Before the debts and loans were paid. Remember you sent nothing home."

"Aye," Hex agreed. "But the solicitor said mother should have been able to live comfortably off the fifty guineas per annum that had been set up by my father."

"Perhaps, had your mother had someone to advise her about her finances. As it was, her standard of living far exceeded the fifty guineas, so loans were made."

"By whom were the loans made?" Hex asked.

"By the bank, sir."

"With your guarantee," Hex stated.

"I was glad to be of service," Spencer said hotly, now that the conversation had turned as it had.

"Well," Hex said, making a sudden decision. "Pay me my two hundred five pounds. You may keep the rest."

"Well, sir, there has been some added expenses..."

"Which you will pay," Hex said, finishing the sentence as his hand fell to the pommel of his sword. There would be no arguing the point.

Realizing he had much to lose and little to gain, Spencer quickly agreed to pay the amount owed.

The money quickly changed hands, and Jacob Hex had left without as much as a farewell. He'd thought to leave his mother with one hundred pounds that had been advanced to him towards expected prize money by Captain Anthony. The hundred pounds along with the promise of another twenty-five pounds per annum to add to what she had been receiving would have been more than enough for his mother to live on. Now, he was leaving on the morrow's coach with a heavy heart, but a full purse.

"Jake. Jake Hex, you ole blade."

Half turning, Hex saw two of his old running mates. Ian Fleming had been an apprentice to his father's accountant, and John Crowe had been one of the boats men, meaning he'd been one of the smuggler's crew alongside Hex. For the first time since he'd returned home, Hex felt joyful.

"Come have a wet," he called to his friends. "We have a lot of catching up to do."

The two men eyed each other then looked at Hex. "Have you been home yet?" they asked.

"Aye, what a surprise that was."

"Good," they replied.

"Good?" Hex frowned.

"Good that you already know," Crowe replied.

"Yeah," Fleming added. "We'd hate to be the ones to break the news."

"Old news now, mates, belly up for a wet," Hex said.

CHAPTER THREE

THE NEXT FEW HOURS passed very quickly. During their time reminiscing, Hex found both men had gone to work for his stepfather. But being the skinflint he was, Spencer had not treated either of them fairly and had in fact cheated them out of their wages, hard earned wages. Now, they worked for Spencer's competitor.

"Ever think of going to sea?" Hex asked.

"We've thought about it," Crowe admitted, "but it'd be our luck to get separated or stuck with some tarter for a captain, who would rather see a flogging than eat."

"What if I could put you on an admiral's staff?"

The two cut their eyes at each other. "Sure," Fleming said, "our old mate is now privately recruiting for an admiral, no less."

"Tell us, Jake," Crowe chided. "Is it for just one admiral you recruit for, or is it the lot?"

"No, just one, and I can't guarantee anything. When I left Portsmouth, our admiral needed a new cox'n and a secretary. You could fill those jobs if...if they haven't been filled and if the admiral likes you. 'Course, I could always get Sir Anthony to sign you on as part of the ship's crew."

"Damme, Jake, but you've taken to associating with England's upper crust. Tis a wonder you'd even talk to the likes of us."

"I've been lucky," Hex admitted. "See this uniform? It was purchased for me by Sir Gabriel. Fact is, I've got a set of uniforms and a few civilian suits so as to be ready for whatever situation or occasion that may arise."

"And pray tell us, what makes Jake Hex so special that Sir Gabriel would go to such expense?"

"I'm his cox'n...among other things."

"Like what?" the two friends asked.

"Well, I'm treated like family when we're not in uniform."

"Family is it?" the two chided with raised eyebrows. "Why would you be treated so highly?"

Hex did not want to reveal he'd saved Sir Gabriel's life so he said, "'Cause that's the way it is with the Anthony's, both Vice Admiral Lord Gilbert Anthony and Captain Sir Gabriel Anthony. Now, no more questions, do you want to sign on or not?"

"We'll think on it."

"Well, don't take too long. I take the coach back tomorrow."

After that the alcohol continued to flow, the stories became more embellished and at some point wenches appeared. Hex had a blonde beauty on his lap with her dress cut low enough that most of her wares were showing when a man burst through the front door, shouting "It's the press gang!" Before the back door could be opened, the Baskerville was surrounded.

"Damme," Crowe grunted.

"Quiet," Hex whispered. "Now go along with whatever I say."

An over-aged midshipman and giant of a bosun's mate entered. "Line up," the mid snapped. Most of the men did as they were told, but not Hex and his two friends.

"You heard the ossifer," the bosun's mate shouted and made to strike Fleming with his starter.

Hex's reflexes were fast and he grabbed the starter. "Easy there, mate."

The bosun's mate tried but could not pull his starter from Hex's grasp. Seeing his attempt was futile, the man said, "The ossifer said line up."

"He's not an officer," Hex corrected the man. "He's a midshipman."

"And who be you?" the midshipman said, taking in the gold braid on Hex's uniform.

"I'm Jacob Hex, Sir Gabriel Anthony's cox'n."

"And you have papers to prove this?"

"Not on me," Hex replied.

"Chain them up," the mid replied.

"I wouldn't do that," Hex said firmly. "I've been sent here to recruit members for Admiral Buck's staff."

"Never heard of him," the mid snapped.

"I'm not surprised," Hex threw back. "But I can promise that if we are detained, not only will you hear from him but you can forget what little career you have left."

Taken aback by Hex's bluntness, but not wanting to back down, the mid said, "You can stay, they go with the rest."

"No," Hex replied with harshness in his voice. Turning to an elderly man who'd been sweeping the tavern floors, Hex said, "Here's a guinea, run to the marine barracks and see if the major might be available."

Hex knew that in all likelihood nobody above the rank of captain would be at the barracks. He also knew it would take an hour for the old man to get there, and even then he might not get anyone to come. He did hope offering a guinea for what would have been done for a schilling might impress the mid enough to back down.

"The marines have no jurisdiction in this matter," the midshipman volunteered, but it was obvious his resolve had weakened.

"You are right, but I'm sure that he will make certain that a message is sent to both Sir Gabriel and Rear Admiral Buck. They will want to know by whom and why I was delayed. Now, sir, if you will be so kind as to spell your name for me so that it will be written correctly?"

A moment passed with the midshipman saying not a word. Finally, he said, "God rot your soul," and stormed out of the tavern.

Waiting a moment to make sure the press gang had moved on, Fleming and Crowe pounded Hex's back. "Bless you, Jake, but ain't you the cold fish. Had 'em sweating you did. What a bluff."

"It wasn't a bluff," Hex replied matter-of-factly. "I would have sent word and his days would have been over, especially if Dagan had've gotten involved."

"Dagan. Who is Dagan?"

"You'll see soon enough. I'm sure that he will be at Sir Gabriel's house."

A sinking feeling came over the two men. "But we ain't said we'd sign on yet, Jake."

"Should I call the press gang back?"

"No," was the feeble reply.

"Good. Now go say your goodbyes and get your bags. I'll expect you back here within an hour."

"Aw, Jake."

"No! One hour. That's it, or then it's the press gang."

As the two walked off, Crowe said to Fleming, "Never expected Jake to be such a tarter."

CHAPTER FOUR

THE COACH RIDE WAS one Hex would just as soon forget. It was too crowded, too bumpy, and too smelly. One of the passengers obviously believed perfume took the place of good old soap and water. Hex would have ridden on top of the coach had it not been for the rain. Still, the wet may have been better than the smell, which not only took his breath, but made his eyes burn. Thank God, he at least sat by a window.

The woman sitting on the middle of the seat opposite of him constantly held a handkerchief to her nose. She was suffering the same effects as Hex. Once when their eyes met, she looked to her left and then fanned her face, letting him know it was the drummer sitting next to her that smelled. The man was fat and sweaty. If the perfume was to cover up body odors, it did a poor job.

Crowe and Fleming were both oblivious to all, as they were sleeping off the abundance of ale consumed prior to leaving Deal. Hex was not sure he'd done the right thing, mentioning the possibility of being on Admiral Buck's staff. But whether it was his staff or just the crew, they'd be better off than winding up in jail if caught smuggling. Hex didn't doubt Spencer wouldn't make an anonymous tip or drop a hint here and there to the revenuers if it might do away with the competition. Each time they went out they were risking their lives; of course, the same could be said about being in the Navy during war.

There was one thing Hex had learned. Captain Anthony...Sir Gabe was not shy when it came to a fight. Be it hand-to-hand or a ship action. What was it Dagan had said? "Stick with the Anthonys and you'll be rich or dead if this war continues." Of course, Dagan and Gabe had survived so there was no reason he, Jake Hex, shouldn't as well. He also remembered another conversation with Dagan when discussing 'loot', "They, meaning the admiralty, don't know what's there when we take a ship. So it don't hurt to hold back a little before it gets inventoried. For your retirement so to speak. They won't miss it and it's us what's risking our neck, not them. I never confiscate so much as to make it obvious but a bit here and there will never be missed."

Of course Sir Gabe, it was hard for Hex to think of the captain as Gabriel, had said don't get caught up in Dagan's larcenous ways. The key to that statement in Hex's mind wasn't to not do it, but just don't get caught. A sudden jolt and lurch as the coach hit a deep pothole threw the young woman almost in Hex's lap.

Quickly gathering herself, the girl looked at her rescuer and said, "Thank you, sir, but I believe it's safe for me to return to my seat now."

The closeness aroused Hex as his hands had accidently brushed her chest and the firmness of ample breast. A knowing look passed between them as his hands took an extra moment to slide back to his side.

"Is Herstmonceux your home?" Hex asked.

"No," she replied. "I will be met there, but I live in nearby Cowbeech."

The next half-hour passed without speaking, but every time Hex glanced her way the woman was looking at him. Was it curiosity or was it more? Once when she was caught staring the woman smiled, looked away, and then back again. The sound of flatulence from one of the sleeping men caused her to giggle.

"One scent is no worse than the other," Hex quipped as the handkerchief had gone back to the woman's face.

Soon the coach slowed. Looking out of his window, Hex commented, "We are here."

A startled shout was suddenly heard then, "Whoa!!! Whoa." The coach slid sideways as the driver applied the brakes hard. The coach tilted as it came to a stop.

"Damn fool," the driver shouted at the man who ran in front of them. Other voices could be heard. Men were yelling and the driver cried out, "Stop throwing those rocks, you idiots. You are spooking the horses." Indeed the horses were rearing up, pawing and whinnying.

As Hex, Crowe, and Fleming hurriedly got out of the coach, they could see three men chasing another, a much smaller man, who had gotten up from the street where he'd fallen and almost been run over. He jumped up and darted around the side of the coach where he collided with Crowe.

"Stop that chink," one of the three men yelled. "We're gonna cut off his pigtail so he can't go to heathen heaven or wherever it is Chinamen go."

Crowe helped the frightened man to his feet. Seeing it was futile to run and already being out of breath, the Chinaman stood his ground. It was very obvious the three men were drunk, but when one of the group pulled out a long knife, Hex stepped forward.

"What's going on here?" he asked.

The man who spoke had breath so hard Hex had to frown and turn his head. "We done told you, mister, we are gonna cut the chink's pigtail off."

"You no cutoff pigtail, me die first," the little man said in broken English.

"Then we'll cut it off after you die," bad breath said.

"Get back in and let's be on our way," said a voice from inside the coach. This was from the fat drummer wearing the perfume.

"Humph!" another voice, that of a woman. "You coward, you'd let three drunken bullies harm that helpless little man."

"Nothing to me, madam," the drummer responded, followed by another humph.

Regardless of what decision Hex may have already made, the woman's comments settled it for him. "Why don't you men just be satisfied with the scare you've already put in the Chinaman. I can see we're on Boreham Street, so the Bull Inn can't be far. Come on down and I will buy you a wet and you can call it a night."

"We ain't calling a bloody thing off, mate. Now stand aside and let us at the chink so we can have our fun. Otherwise, we may have to do a little trimming with you first."

"I wouldn't try that," Hex replied, his voice taking on a hardness and losing the conciliatory demeanor.

"You think you can handle all three of us," bad breath responded with a grin.

"He could if need be," Crowe interjected. "However, he ain't alone and there's no way one Deal boatman would not share the fun with another Deal boatman. That's right, ain't it, Fleming?"

"Right you are, mate. And truth be told I could use a bit of exercise after that coach ride."

A light shone as a door opened from a dwelling on the opposite side of the coach. Taking a quick glance as the light flooded out onto the street, Hex could see a man with an old blunderbuss in his hand.

"What goes on here?" the man said with an authoritative tone.

The driver answered, "It's just Padget and his ruffians, Henry. They are after Chen Lee."

Henry was the local constable. "Padget, I would have thought the navy would have caught up with your black heart by now. However, you've disturbed me for the last time. Get out of Herstmonceux tonight or by all that's mighty, I'll tell the navy myself."

"You do, you old goat, and it'll be the last time you turn anybody in," Padget snarled.

There was no backing down in the leathery old man. He jammed the barrel of his weapon right into Padget's belly, causing him to take an involuntary step backward. "That so," Henry replied. "Maybe I just ought to end it here so's I can get back to sleep."

There was little doubt in anyone's mind that the constable meant what he said. Padget's friends moved away, not wanting to get caught up in any of the blast from the wicked-looking weapon. A gust of wind rocked the blades on the windmill above the mill causing a loud, heavy groan. Otherwise, there was complete silence until Henry spoke again.

"It's your choice, Padget. Git or get blown away." The choice was echoed by the cocking of the blunderbuss' hammer.

"I'm gone," Padget blurted out. "Come on, mates."

"No, you go on," one of the men said. "Trouble seems to follow you like a dark cloud."

"Aye," the other man replied, "I knew we should never have run with that one."

The man's admission of being a deserter caused Hex, Crowe, and Fleming to look at each other.

"You talk too much," the one man said, glaring at the other. "Can't you see he's an officer of sorts?"

Before the man could speak, Hex said, "I knew you for sailors by your garb, language, and tattoos. Now, it makes no difference to me, but the best place for a man who's run is on another ship."

This caused Crowe to mumble to Fleming, "Here we go again."

"We're headed to the Caribbean, then the colonies, with two of the best officers in the navy," Hex said sounding like a recruiter.

"Who they be?" one of the men asked.

Hex went into his spiel and before he finished, the little Chinaman said, "Good, me go. Chen Lee tired of working at the Bull Inn. Work all day, have to run all night to keep pigtail. Chen Lee keep pigtail in the navy?"

Hex paused. That was an answer he was not sure of, but he didn't think there were any rules that said the man couldn't have his pigtail.

"Ummgh!" Henry grunted. "It's a damn fine cook and houseboy the village will be losing."

CHAPTER FIVE

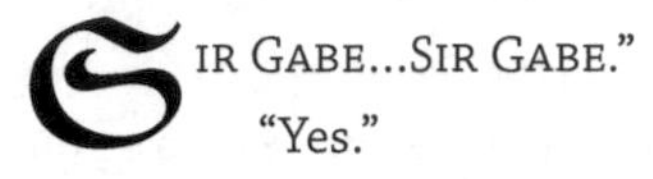

SIR GABE...SIR GABE."

"Yes."

"There's a group of men downstairs to see you, sir."

Gabe rose up from the hammock on the viewing deck. The afternoon was pretty. It was the sunniest day in the last week or so. Watching the lazy clouds overhead, Gabe's eyes had grown heavy and he'd drifted off to sleep. He must have slept for over an hour. He had been thinking of Faith; surely she'd had their child by now. Their son, if Nanny was to be believed. Mother had tried to comfort him and assured him that women bore children every day, so there was no reason to worry on that part.

When he'd spoken of his concerns and worries to Dagan, he'd replied, "I see no squalls ahead."

"Who are they, Mattie?" Gabe asked in regards to the waiting men.

"One of them is that handsome devil...ah, cox'n of yours, sir. I don't know who the rest of them are, but they are a mixed lot to be sure."

By the time Gabe had gotten his boots on and made it to the kitchen, Dagan was sitting at a small table talking to Hex. One of the new maids was taking something out the back door, so undoubtedly the other men had been cast loose while Hex came inside. Seeing Gabe, Hex rose up but was motioned back to his seat.

Dagan volunteered, "Who needs recruiting flyers and a press gang when Jake is out and about?"

Over a glass of bourbon, which Gabe knew was certain to please his cox'n, Hex told the story of his travels, starting with the surprises at home, the men outside, and the handsome lass on the coach. Hex had finally learned her name was Katie Conrad. "She gave me permission to call when we get back to England, and even hinted a letter here and there would be welcomed."

"No telling when we'll get back," Dagan said, and then felt a pang of guilt as his sister, Gabe's mother, passed by. *Stubborn woman*, he thought, *why won't she come with us*?

Thinking of Dagan's words, Hex said, "If we were to get back in the next two or three years, be like she'd already got married, had a brat or two and gotten fat."

"That's possible," Gabe replied. "But it doesn't hurt to consider that she might wait."

Hex then came to the point of coming to Gabe's house before reporting to the ship. "I'm sure Ford and Slade, that's the names they've decided on, can sign on as topmen. Having a note from you will prevent any questions." Gabe nodded his acceptance. Hex then explained about Crowe and Fleming possibly being good candidates for the admiral's cox'n and secretary.

"Would you consider being the admiral's cox'n and Crowe being my cox'n?" Gabe asked, wanting to offer Hex the higher position.

"No sir, not as long as you are satisfied with me."

Gabe smiled. He didn't think Hex would have taken the admiral's job. He'd have been disappointed if Hex had, but just the same, he felt he needed to make the offer.

"Chen Lee is my only concern," Hex said. "I know Nesbit will most likely take care of the cooking for both you and the admiral, but I couldn't just cast off and leave the little fellow, sir."

"Well, you say he was a houseboy and he can cook. It could be the admiral would use him as his servant."

"I think that he'd make a good one too, sir."

Uh huh, Gabe thought. *Damme, if Hex wasn't the wise one. Put just enough out there for me to make a recommendation and then jump on it, knowing full well it was on his mind all along*. Looking at Dagan, Gabe asked, "Remind you of anyone?"

"I don't see any physical resemblance, but he and Bart are two peas from the same pod."

"Aye," Gabe replied sarcastically, but with a grin on his face. "Dagan, if you'll give Jake another glass...a small glass, I will write a note to the first lieutenant and the admiral. If the admiral is not at Scolfes, inquire as to where he may be, Jake."

"Aye, sir."

"Jake."

"Yes sir."

"I can't speak for the admiral in regards to his staff. He may have others in mind."

"I realize that, sir."

"Good. Jake?"

"Yes, sir."

"You did a good job."

"Thank you, sir." After tossing off the last of the warm golden liquid, Hex thought, *now that's a man's drink. Given the choice I'll take Kentucky bourbon every time*. He then had another thought cross his mind. *Given the choice I'd cast my lot with Sir Gabe and Dagan every time. As Bart would say, "And that's no error."*

***

THE SUN WAS UP and starting to shine over England. Jep Jepson had been up before dawn, a habit spawned by being at sea most of his life. Regardless of the time of year or the location, the hour before dawn always seemed to be the darkest, the most damp, and coolest part of the day. To many people it was depressing having to rise up at that time. To Jep it was routine. Something he could live with, or live without when the time came. His first lieutenant, Peter Parks, was already on deck. Jep could hear the lieutenant's voice through the small skylight. The young man was showing the makings of a good seaman and had already shown he was better than average for someone of his experience. A great deal of it had been due to the example his captain had set, though Jep would never consider it.

Parks, Jep had thought more than once, *the young devil will probably be a captain while I'm still a lieutenant*. Not that Jep was sorry for taking his promotion or being given such a fine little command. That's just the way it was. Over-aged lieutenants rarely went beyond such station, but a few had, with some of them attaining the lofty rank of admiral.

Jep had no desire to hang around that long though, truth be told. Of course, with this war with the American cousins, another promotion was not unthinkable. Gabe had risen from midshipman to captain and Lord Anthony from captain to vice admiral. No, promotion was not out of the question for him, all it would take was just a bit of luck on his side. The strong, unmistakable odor of coffee filled the tiny cabin as his servant entered.

Mindful of his captain's ways, Briggs knew that the best way to keep the captain happy was to have a cup of strong brew ready as soon as possible after he crawled out of his cot.

"There's a fair wind coming across the anchorage this morning, Cap'n," Briggs volunteered. "It's going to be a booger getting the sails set 'thout them flogging so loud that the admiral will think the Frogs 'as attacked us with guns ablazing."

Jep couldn't help but smile. Briggs always had been the one for exaggerations. Still in his day he had no equal as a topman. Now with a busted timber, he was glad to have a billet and not be on the beach where he'd be forced to live out his days little more than a pauper.

***

CAPTAIN STEPHEN EARL, HAVING been given permission to stand on the quarterdeck, watched as Jepson's first officer went about getting ready to weigh anchor and set sail. *Pegasus* was a fine little ship with a good crew and officers who knew their business, a testament to the captain.

"Captain." It was the midshipman, Bucklin. The young man was facing the wind as he spoke and his words seemed to whistle. "Mr. Parks' respects, sir. We have the port admiral's boat approaching, sir."

"Gawd," Jep snarled, slipping back into his master's language. Turning to Earl he said, "Probably the port admiral's brother. I hear he has a bumboat business." This made Earl smile as a few chuckles were heard from some of the seamen close by.

"Probably wants to get in a last minute sale, the bloke," one of the seamen volunteered, causing more chuckles.

Soon Lieutenant Parks made his way to the quarterdeck. One of the admiral's staff, a young lieutenant, had delivered a message. Jepson gave a sigh after reading the message.

Handing it to Earl to read, Jepson addressed Parks, "Secure the hands, Mr. Parks. We are to await Lord Skalla from the foreign office. He is to take passage with us to Barbados."

"Aye, Captain."

Thinking back to an incident that happened at Sandy Hook the previous year, he addressed the lieutenant again, "Mr. Parks."

"Aye, Captain."

"Do keep young Robinson occupied when Lord Skalla arrives. We can't have *Pegasus*' reputation soiled by his dumping another foreign office representative into the drink."

Parks' eyes sparkled as he recalled the incident where Sir Victor's man had been knocked overboard by the midshipman, who then threw the man a rope that was not secured at the bitter end. Had the captain not had the sense to stand on the end of the rope, the man likely would have drowned. Smiling, Parks replied, "Aye, Captain, busy he will be."

CHAPTER SIX

GABE HAD JUST SETTLED down to lunch. A sandwich of salted beef, cheese and a sauce made of horseradish. Lord Sandwich, the First Lord of the Admiralty, was reportedly the first person to come up with the ingenious idea of putting meat between two slices of bread. It was said he was such a busy man that he rarely had time for food, and so instead of dining as usual, he'd have the food brought to his desk. *Busy*, Gabe thought, *the man was busy but it was reported he would spend a day at a time at the card table in one of his clubs*. Gil also told of some rowdy times when they were both young men. That was before he became First Lord of the Admiralty. He was just Lord Sandwich. A very wealthy, carousing, gambling Lord Sandwich.

Gabe's mother sat across from him, playing with her food. She ate like a bird, to his way of thinking, but today she had eaten less. Gabe knew what was troubling her. This was his last night ashore. Tomorrow, weather permitting, they would set sail.

He had mixed emotions and felt a pang of guilt because of it. He was ready to be free of the land, and to see if *Trident* was the sailor Stephen Earl had made her out to be. But he was also saddened by the thought that he didn't know when he'd see his mother again. He had no way of knowing when, or even if, he'd be back to England.

Glancing across the table, he saw a packet of papers that were to be delivered to his solicitor. He'd met with his agent, banker, and solicitor. All were friends of his brother-in-law, Hugh. It seemed strange to think of Hugh as a relative. They had become very close since Gabe's return. Hugh had been very helpful in directing Gabe on how to set things up so his mother would be taken care of financially.

"It's better to deal with men of good standing in such affairs," Hugh had said. "Never trust a man who offers you a bargain. Usually he's the only one receiving it."

Finishing his meal, Gabe could feel something between his teeth. He went into the kitchen and pulled a straw from a broom he'd spied. Picking his teeth made him remember he'd ordered a full dozen of the new toothbrushes made from boar bristles. William Addis was said to have invented the new brush while he was in jail for causing a riot.

Admiral Buck swore by the things. By making a paste with water and salt and then dipping the brush into the paste, the teeth could be scrubbed very comfortably. "You can do it every day," Buck had exclaimed. Having a toothache at sea was not something that Gabe wanted. He'd seen men with bad teeth in tremendous pain, their jaws swollen as big as lemons. The ship's surgeon had instruments to pull teeth, but that was just as painful. It took a lot of brandy or grog to put a man out so that he could have a tooth pulled. Even with the spirits, a leather strap was usually in order.

A knock was heard at the front door. Gabe's mother rose up out of her chair to go answer it but settled back down, recalling they had a servant to do that now. It was nice, and Gabe said with the prize money that he'd made these new luxuries were nothing. Dagan had whispered privately that both he and Gabe had put up a "right smart," as he termed it, so she shouldn't be worrying about cost. Dagan had also visited Hugh's banker and solicitor. Should he fall, Maria would inherit his wealth.

Gabe had just drained the last of the tea in his cup when the new servant, Molly, entered the room.

"There's a messenger here, Sir Gabe. Says he's from the port admiral."

This did surprise Gabe. He went to greet the young lieutenant.

"Admiral Webster's compliments, sir, and could you attend him at your earliest convenience?"

"Of course," Gabe replied. Earliest convenience meant now. "Let me change and I will be right there."

"Very well, sir. I shall tell the admiral you are on your way."

Gabe headed up the stairs to change. Seeing his mother, he volunteered, "I don't know what it is." Bounding up the steps he stopped. "Mother, is Jake still out back?"

"I think so, son."

"Would you send Molly to get him, please? I have some errands that need to be done and I'm not sure how long this will take." Seeing the look of concern on his mother's face, Gabe added, "I'm sure it's nothing to worry about, Mother. Otherwise, we'd have heard from Admiral Buck." *Unless it's about Admiral Buck*, Gabe thought but didn't say. *That would be something to worry about*.

***

HEX HAD THE COACHMAN ready when Gabe walked outside. He had forgotten his cloak and thought of going back for it as he heard the rumble of distant thunder. The coachman had his own cloak on already. Not enough time, Gabe decided. As he stepped into the coach, he saw the first drops of rain.

"To the port admiral?" the coachman said.

His mind still on his cloak, it took a moment for Gabe to respond, "Yes, the port admiral." Dagan stepped out of the house. Seeing him Gabe shouted, "I'm off to the port admiral."

Dagan nodded that he'd heard then shouted back, "Good news."

The coach gave a lurch as the horses strained against the harnesses. Gabe automatically put up the window to keep the rain out, but his thoughts were on Dagan's words, "good news."

After a short ride, Gabe jumped from the door of the coach even before it came to a complete stop in front of the port admiral's building, his boots splashing in a puddle of water and spotting up his white breeches. The door was opened by a servant, who took his cocked hat. Obviously, he had a place for it so that it wouldn't drip on the highly polished wooden floors.

Taking a moment for his eyes to adjust to the light, Gabe looked about the room. He realized a number of naval officers sat in chairs or stood in small groups. A couple of the captains he recognized. Most were probably here trying to get the port admiral to agree to something or provide some item or another for their ship.

Another servant had made his way up to Gabe without being seen. He coughed, and once he had Gabe's attention said politely, "This way, sir. The admiral is waiting for you in his office."

"Thank you," Gabe replied, and then grimaced when he took a step and his wet boot squeaked. He flushed as he realized the entire room full of officers was looking his way upon hearing the squishing noise. *Damme,* he thought, *not a good beginning.*

Maybe the scrutiny had more to do with his being allowed to go straight back. Some of the officers had probably been waiting hours.

A small fire was going in the fireplace to take out the dampness and chill brought on by the afternoon rain. Admiral Webster was staring out the rain-splattered window looking toward the anchorage. Admiral Buck, to Gabe's surprise, sat in an upholstered chair with a glass in his hand. *Well, it can't be all bad*, he thought, *otherwise Buck wouldn't be having a wet.*

"The mail packet came in this morning, Sir Gabe, with a letter from your brother," Admiral Webster volunteered as he turned to Gabe.

Damn, Gabe thought, *no greeting, no have a glass, just straight to the point.*

"He entrusted it to the packet's captain, to be brought directly to me upon his arrival."

A sinking feeling came over Gabe. *What was it? Oh God, hopefully Faith was all right*. Seeing the emotion come over Gabe, Webster said,

"Give the boy the letter, Rupert, and pour him a brandy before he has apoplexy."

Taking the letter, Gabe read it then reread it. Without being asked, he sat down in one of the admiral's chairs. He downed the brandy Buck handed him and coughed as the fiery liquid went down, bringing tears to his eyes.

"I'm a father," he managed after he quit coughing. "A boy! We have a boy."

"Did you name him?" Admiral Webster asked.

"Yes sir, before I left. If it had been a girl it would have been named after Faith's mother and grandmother. A boy was to be named after my father and Gil. His name is James Gilbert Anthony."

"Hear, hear," Webster said. "Rupert, pour us another round. I suggest, Sir Gabe, you drink this one a little more slowly."

"Aye, sir. Slowly." Only Gabe's mind was racing. He had so much to do, and so many people he should tell. He needed to buy something for Faith and for the baby. *What do you buy a newborn? Mother would know*, he thought.

"Gabe…Gabe."

"Yes sir." Buck had been calling his name, but he was so caught up in the news he'd not heard. *Damme*, Gabe thought again. "I'm sorry, sir, my mind is adrift," he said, apologizing.

"Yes. Well, I think Lieutenant Campbell can handle the ship another day while you get your affairs in order."

"Thank you…both of you," Gabe replied. "I will get right to it." He was in the coach and headed home when he thought, *I wonder what the officers thought in the admiral's waiting area rushing out as I did.* Well, it didn't matter. What did matter was the coach taking its time getting home when he had important news for his mother. The thought that wet cobblestones might be dangerous never crossed his mind.

CHAPTER SEVEN

THE CANDLES WERE LIT and the dinner table had been set. Gabe, Maria, and Dagan had just returned from shopping. As the three sat down at the table, Gabe asked Mattie if she'd seen Jake.

"He waited until the rain had slacked up before he left, sir. He took the pouch of papers with him but I've not seen him since." Realizing how late it was, Mattie added, "Goodness, late as it is, he should have done been back. He ain't one to miss the evening meal, not that 'un."

A strange silence came over the dining room. Dagan's chair scraped against the floor as he abruptly pushed back from the table. "I'll be back," he said as he made his way out. He'd felt something earlier but didn't act when Gabe had come home with the news of his son.

Taking his cloak down and taking a moment to get a pistol and sword, he hurried out the door. He followed the main street about ten blocks, then turned into an alley between a leather shop, a tavern, and coffee house. Two men were beating a third man with barrel staves. So intent on their victim, they didn't notice another had arrived until Dagan spoke.

"That's enough."

Startled, the men looked up and stopped their beating of the downed man. It was Hex, as Dagan knew it would be. The men still had their arms raised to deliver another blow when Dagan spoke again.

"It's best you be moving along, Gov'nor, less you want some of what he's getting."

"No, Padget," Dagan responded. "It's time you move along. You've already caused enough mischief as it is. But, of course, your kind never seems to learn, do they?"

"You seem to know me mate but I don't recall who you be."

"We haven't met, or else you wouldn't be hurting my friend," Dagan replied. "But your wicked ways have caught up with you. You should have taken Constable Henry's advice. But now you will pay."

Dropping the barrel stave, Padget pulled a pistol from his pocket. "Like as not you will be the one who pays," the rogue responded. "One step and your friend will be a dead man."

"My friend's safety is the only reason you're still alive," Dagan said.

Padget's accomplice spoke for the first time. "I don't know about all this, Padget. I don't mind roughing up a man for his purse, but I ain't going to hang because you killed someone."

"Hush," Padget snapped. Turning back to Dagan, he said, "You talk brave like, but I don't see no weapons."

"I have them," Dagan responded. "But they'll not be needed. Your evil ways have caught up with you and will do you in."

Hex had recovered from the blows that had rained down on him and now was able to focus on the conversation. He'd caught Dagan's eye to let him know he was alert. Still, with a pistol pointed at his head from a foot away, he felt it best to let Dagan continue without any action or interference.

"Come on mate," the other thief whined.

"Listen to him," Dagan said. "Otherwise, death awaits you."

"My arse," Padget hissed. "Not as long as I got this," he said, shaking his pistol.

"You've had your warning," Dagan said, his voice barely above a whisper. As he spoke, he held his arms out to his side, lifting the cloak outward with his arms.

Suddenly, the second thief ducked. "What was that?"

"Nothing," Padget replied.

"Nothing!?" the thief cried out as something knocked his battered hat off his head. "Bats...it's like black bats," the man cried out as he ducked and swatted at the air. "You can't see them," he screamed. "They are everywhere."

Now he dove toward the wet alley dirt. "Get them off me. Oh, Gawd! They're all over me. They're biting me. Padget, help me for God's sake."

"Shut up, you idiot. You'll attract attention," Padget snarled.

"To hell with you," the poor man cried out, his face pale in the early moonlight. His eyes were wild with tears as he tried to stand while ducking to the left and right, all the time swatting at shadows.

"Stand still, you coward, or I'll shoot you," Padget warned.

"Shoot and be damned," the man said. "I should have known better than come with you. Oh, Gawd," he cried again as he swatted at them. "They're everywhere...bats...black wings...they're biting me. Help! Gawd, help me."

"Hush, you fool. I'm warning you. Be quiet or I'll do it for you."

"No," the man said. "I can't stand it. You're the fool. The man was right. You are evil. I'm not going to die for your deeds."

The man turned to run. Crack...the thief stopped and stared at the still smoking pistol barrel.

"They are gone," he gasped. "They're coming for you now, Padget. They are coming for you."

During all this time, Dagan had remained standing, with his arms and cloak held out, not unlike a cape. Now, he let them down. "He is right you know," Dagan spoke softly.

"Not yet they ain't," Padget said. Realizing his pistol was empty, he dropped it next to a puddle left by the afternoon rain. A dagger was deftly drawn from a scabbard on his hip. "Now keep your distance, mate. One false move and I'll slit his throat. I may die but it will be no never mind to this sod because he'll already be dead."

"I don't need to do anything," Dagan responded. "You have already sealed your fate. You're dead and just don't know it."

"Not from the likes of you, I ain't," the man threw back, showing yellow-stained teeth. "Fact is, I am tired of all this talking. I think I'll give your friend a new smile just to see how he looks."

"I wouldn't," Dagan answered.

"I would," Padget laughed...then coughed. A shocked look filled his face. The end of a blade protruded from his mouth almost like someone sticking out their tongue. As he coughed, blood gushed from around the blade as he fell forward, dead.

"Shoot me will you, you bastard," the other thief said, holding his stomach where the ball had entered. "I hope you bust hell wide open." The man then looked at Dagan and said, "You were right. He was an evil man."

The thief then fell to the ground, "Mother..." he cried out as he died.

"Are you okay, Jake? Jake..."

"I'm alright, Dagan," Jake replied, still trying to digest what had taken place. *Were the stories about Dagan true? Did he really have powers? Was he really a soothsayer? Did it matter? Were there really bats flying about or just the thief's imagination? Did it matter? Had it not been for Dagan, I'd been a goner,* Jake thought. *That's what mattered.*

"They jumped me from behind," Jake volunteered. "They clubbed me before I knew anything was amiss."

"Can you walk?" Dagan asked.

"I think so. I am not as dizzy as I was."

"Good. You can lean on me if need be, but let us be on our way."

"I'm surprised that shot hasn't already brought the watchman down on us. Shouldn't we stay and explain what happened?" The look Jake got from Dagan made him say, "Dumb question."

"It will look like a fight between two rogues when the watchman arrives. Why hang around? It will only put Gabe's name in the paper in a negative light. There's always some jealous person ready to cloud matters if they can," Dagan said.

“Let’s be on our way then before the watchman arrives, but keep your eyes open for my hat when we get close to the street. I’d hate to lose it, I just got it today,” Jake said to Dagan.

“I’d worry about your head, was I you,” Dagan growled good-naturedly.

“Oh, I am,” Jake responded, “that’s why I want my hat.”

As several watchmen passed, they noted the two men laughing; one probably worse for wear from drink as he seemed to be supported by the other. *Wouldn’t mind a wet myself*, one watchman thought.

CHAPTER EIGHT

CAPTAIN SIR GABRIEL ANTHONY climbed the companion ladder, stepped over the coaming and out onto the deck of *HMS Trident*. He was a new man. A new father, the flag captain to a new admiral, and captain of a sixty-four gun warship. The smallest in the line of battle, true. The seventy-fours were taking over but still she was a force to be reckoned with. A thought came to his mind and made him chuckle...not unlike Faith. *Did she have her hands full with the little one?* Nanny and Lum would be there, not to mention Aunt Deborah, Uncle Gil, and of course, Uncle Bart, who would be the one to spoil the little one. This made him chuckle again, making several seamen and officers alike look toward their new captain.

"Wonder what 'e thinks is so funny, mate?"

"I don't know," the other replied. "But it can't be the weather."

A fine sprinkle was coming down, more than a mist but not a downpour. Gabe glanced aloft and smiled as he saw blue at the mizzen, Admiral Buck's flag. Looking over the anchorage, the ships in the admiral's squadron and those of the convoy would be getting ready to weigh anchor and make sail. Gabe wiped the rain from his face with a handkerchief. The decks were spotted with the drizzle and would make for slippery work as they got underway.

Lieutenant Donald Campbell walked over to Gabe and greeted him. "Morning, Captain."

"Mr. Campbell."

"The anchor's hove short, sir. The ship is lashed down and all is ready."

"Thank you, Mr. Campbell, have the signal midshipman make a signal to the flag, 'ready to proceed'."

"Aye, Captain."

Gabe felt a pang of guilt. He'd spent so much time ashore getting things taken care of for his mother he'd not spent as much time aboard his ship as he normally would. Stephen Earl had spoken highly of the first lieutenant. "Campbell is a fine officer who has my every trust. He will make a good captain and, indeed, should already be one." From Stephen Earl this was true praise.

Turner, that was the midshipman's name, Lee Turner. Campbell's slight clearing of his throat made Gabe turn. The admiral had just come on deck. Campbell had subtly alerted his captain of the admiral's arrival; this was a good trait for a first officer.

From his spot at the signal halyard, Turner called out, "Flag has replied, sir, 'Congratulations and God's speed.'"

Seeing the puzzled look on the first lieutenant's face, Buck explained, "Our captain is a new father, Mr. Campbell."

A smile broke out on the lieutenant's face. "Let me add my congratulations, Captain. We, the wardroom, will have to toast the little one at the first opportunity."

"Thank you," Gabe replied, and then turned to Buck. "Signal the squadron and convoy to make sail, sir?"

"Aye, Gabe, we've dragged our anchor long enough."

Gabe smiled; there would be some who disagreed. Turning to Campbell, he ordered the lieutenant, "Get the ship underway, please."

"Aye, Captain."

"Lay a course to weather the headland."

Admiral Buck spoke in a whisper to Gabe, "Do you recall the times when Gil was the captain, and we stood back and watched you take us to sea?"

Gabe recalled with a smile. "A few anxious times I'll wager."

"Aye, but not so many either."

The shrill of the bosun's pipe made men jump and sent barefoot seaman scampering in organized chaos.

"Hands aloft, lively now you lubbers."

Swarming topmen made their way up the dizzying heights.

"Move it Taylor, you lazy lubber, or my starter will find your back."

Not an empty threat, Gabe decided. The first lieutenant would not want to be embarrassed the first time they put to sea with the new captain. He had surely warned the bosun he'd tolerate no slackness. The bosun, therefore, had his eyes open and every jack tar knew it.

"Break out the anchor, Mr. Wesley."

Wesley had been the first lieutenant on *Peregrine*. Did he resent being second on *Trident*? Gabe had privately given him the option to stay or leave with a very good recommendation. "Loyalty," Buck had said. "You inspire loyalty. He'd rather stay with you and chance a promotion than cast his lot elsewhere." Whatever the reason, Gabe was glad. Wesley had proved a good seaman and a brave officer who had the respect of his men.

"Heave, you lazy whoreson," a bosun's mate was shouting. "Put your backs into it," he shouted at the forecastle hands. "I declare, you whimper worse than a whore who spent her last schilling and has no more for drink."

Crack! Somebody's back just tasted a starter. "Don't be shirking, Kent, I got me eyes on you."

Clank...clank...clank. The capstan turned slow at first and then faster as the hands put their backs into it. Soon the dripping cable made its way inboard. A flapping sound was heard from above immediately after Campbell ordered, "Loosen head sails."

The topmen were catlike as they made their way along the swaying yards, seeming to pay no mind to the wind, rain, and flapping canvas.

From forward, Wesley cried out, "Anchors aweigh, sir," and Gabe could immediately feel the shift of the ship as it moved with the current, the deck canting slightly.

The forward group set to catting home the anchor. "Amidships," Campbell yelled out, "Man the braces, look alive now, the admiral's eyes are on us."

I wonder which admiral he means, Gabe thought, *the port admiral or the one here on deck.*

Slowly, the yards swung around with a groan as the hands heaved with all their might, trying to get a grip on the wet deck. The sails flagged a time or two, and then filled with the wind. They billowed out with a snap like a gunshot. Like an animal released from its cage, *Trident* reacted; the land quickly fell astern in the gray clouds and rain. Admiral Buck remained on deck until the last ship had weathered the Isle of Wight.

"You have a good ship and experienced crew, Captain," Buck said in a voice so that all near could hear his comment. "I look forward to a successful voyage."

"Thank you, sir," Gabe responded to the admiral's praise. "*Trident* will do her best to bring honour to your flag."

A cheer went up, "Huzza...huzza for the admiral!"

"Thank you," Buck replied, "that was well said." Then plucking at his sodden uniform, he said, "I think I'll go down and see if Chen Lee has unpacked something I can change into."

As the admiral's head disappeared down the companion ladder, Gabe motioned for his cox'n. "How is the admiral's staff coming along, Jake?"

"Nesbit has taken Chen Lee under his wing and he seems to be coming along nicely. Dagan and I have gone over the cox'n duties with Crowe. He should have it all down. I can't say about Fleming. Your secretary, Mr. House, is going over things with him. Of course, Fleming has always been good with figures. He might have made a good purser were he not so honest."

This brought a chuckle from the master. "Well, there's one that probably agrees with you," Gabe responded. David Hayes was the ship's master. His face was like leather from years at sea, facing all the elements. Crows-feet gathered at his eyes when he smiled, which seemed often. He was slim and wore his graying hair shorter than most of his kind. From the few times he and Gabe had talked, he seemed very knowledgeable. *A true professional*, Gabe thought. *A good ship and a good crew indeed. Hopefully, I will not fail her as a captain.*

Out of nowhere, Dagan appeared. "A promising command," he volunteered. *Was he reading my thoughts*? Gabe wondered. Very little had been said when Dagan and Jake had come home the night Jake had been waylaid.

"Trouble?" Gabe had asked as the crumpled package of toothbrushes was handed to him.

"Jake had some problems keeping up with his hat but all is well now," Dagan replied. Gabe had not pressed. He would hear the story when the time was right.

"Captain, sir," It was one of the young gentlemen.

"Yes."

"Admiral's compliments, sir, and would you care to break your fast?"

Gabe's growling stomach punctuated his answer. "I'd be grateful. I will be down directly."

"Yes sir."

What is his name, Gabe wondered. *Brayden, that's it. Humm, I'll know them all soon enough; maybe too well for their liking.*

CHAPTER NINE

LIEUTENANT JOHN BERRY PULLED his watch cloak tighter about his neck and shivered in spite of the coat. It was soaked from the constant spray as the ship dove and reared as it cut through a rolling sea. *Pegasus* was a good ship and not so cramped now that they'd gotten rid of one of their passengers. Captain Earl was a nice enough chap and appeared to be a good seaman. Otherwise, he'd not have been chosen to be Lord Anthony's flag captain. Of course, they still had one passenger, the foreign office man, Lord Skalla. He'd gone ashore with the captain and Captain Earl.

The next thing Berry knew, the captain was back with new sailing orders. *Pegasus* would be putting to sea as soon as she could be made ready. *Damn the luck*, Berry had thought. He'd looked forward to having his cabin back and a few days ashore. There had been a planter's daughter who had shown interest in the young officer. Now that he was back, he'd fill her with tales of their dashing exploits and having his and the ship's name in the Gazette. He even had a copy to show her. In truth, his name was only mentioned in one sentence but it was there just the same.

Captain Jepson was an old tar who had made it to being captain of his own ship. He seemed to be in good with Lord Anthony, and the foreign office gentleman certainly could have had a larger ship take him to Savannah. So the captain, though only a lieutenant, was a man with influence. The time would come when one of his junior officers would be needed. Therefore, it stood to reason, being with a captain such as Jep Jepson would see him promoted or dead before too long.

Berry peered at the compass. This was more from habit than need. One of the helmsmen stretched one arm and yawned. Not much longer now and they'd be relieved. Berry turned and walked down the weather side of the deck. He could see himself in command of a fine ship like the *Pegasus*...to start with. But a frigate, that's what he longed for. A thirty-two would do. He'd rather have something with a bit more iron like a thirty-six or even a thirty-eight. But they would come later. No, a thirty-two would do well to start with.

As Berry made his turn and closed with the helmsman, the seaman spoke out. "The wind seems to be dropping, sir. Feels a bit colder, I believe." The helmsman was an old hand. His comments were to alert the young lieutenant to stop daydreaming and pay attention to the pull of the sails.

They'd have to rouse out all the hands if the wind dropped any further. He glanced once more at the needle on the compass, still on tack.

Bucklin, the midshipman, was moving his arms back and forth over by the rail. Was it to stay awake or stay warm? It always seemed coldest in the pre-dawn. Pacing back and forth it dawned on Berry that he could now see the bow of the ship clearly. The watch would soon be over and he'd have a chance to get a cup of hot coffee and get out of these damp clothes. He'd have some bread and butter as well. A fresh supply had been brought aboard at Barbados. A spoon of the preserves would be nice. *Damn*, Berry thought as his stomach growled. Thinking of food had awakened his innards.

"Deck thar! Sail on the larboard bow."

Well damme, Berry thought. *Breakfast just got postponed.* "Mr. Bucklin."

"Aye, sir."

"Up you go, lad. Tell me what you see."

"Aye, sir. A right report it will be, sir." Bucklin seemed almost glad to have something to do, even if it was nearly time for the watch to end.

"It had better be a good report," Berry snapped, "or Mr. Hacket will see you kissing the gunner's daughter."

This only made the mid smile as he slung the telescope strap around his shoulder and bounded up the shrouds, shunning the lubber's hold, he climbed up and over onto the platform. The lookout, glad for the company, smiled a toothless grin and moved over, pointing toward the sighting.

It only took Bucklin a moment to call down, "Two ships, sir. One, a small frigate, looks French and the other one is a cutter."

Stout, the toothless lookout, spoke to the mid, "She be French all right, Mr. Bucklin. I seen the likes of her before."

Looking once more at the distant ships, Bucklin snapped the glass closed grimacing with the sound of the snap. Break the glass and he'd be kissing the gunner's daughter every evening for the entire voyage. Taking a deep breath, he called down, "The ships are crowding on all sail, sir."

"Very well," Berry answered. "Come on down."

As Bucklin turned to make his way down, Stout spoke again, "Look sir, the flags."

Bringing his glass back to his eye, Bucklin could see the British flag over a French flag. Humph...grabbing a backstay, he took the faster route down. He could feel the burn in the palms of his hands and was glad when his feet touched the deck.

After hearing his report, Berry ordered, "My respects to the captain, young sir, and we have two ships in sight."

"No need, Mr. Berry," Jepson volunteered. "A French ship, a small frigate, perhaps a corvette and a cutter. With our colors over French colors...here in the Caribbean. A British cutter and a French warship, does that not make you suspicious, Mr. Berry?"

"The flags," Berry sputtered.

"A possible ruse, Mr. Berry, to get us to drop our guard."

So much for command of a frigate, Berry thought. "I'm sorry, Captain," Berry began, but the apology was waved away.

"Experience, young sir. We may be seeing two friendly ships. I hope so, but I'll prepare for the worst." Taking a glass from the rack, Jepson climbed a few feet up the shrouds. He stared out across the gray horizon until he found the ships. Focusing the glass, he watched for a minute and then climbed down.

A corvette and a cutter, why here? He didn't think they were British. The cutter had been at one time. *But not now*, he thought. Probably privateers. No signs of any other ships on the horizon, so that increased the likelihood. Picturing his charts in his mind he positioned them somewhere between Montserrat and the islands of St. Kitts and Nevis. None of which were British.

"We still have an hour or more, Mr. Berry. Let's get the men up and fed, and then we will quietly go to quarters."

"Aye, Captain."

"Mr. Berry."

"Yes sir."

"A double measure of grog for your lookout. He has given us an edge, I'm thinking."

"Yes sir."

CHAPTER TEN

QUIETLY, THE SHIP WENT to quarters. No drums beating and no shrill of the bosun's pipes. Men still dazed from being roused out earlier than usual made their way to the stations for quarters. At least they had a belly full of burgoo, hot coffee, and ship's biscuits that were still fresh enough to be weevil free. The other vessels made a fine sight as they approached. Even without the glass it was obvious that it was a French ship, a corvette. *Twenty guns at least*, Jepson thought.

"A ruse de guerre you think, Captain?" This was from Lord Skalla. Jepson had come to like the man. He was small in stature, with black hair that was starting to turn gray above the ears.

Once at sea, Lord Skalla had stopped wearing his powdered wig. "Too damn hot for my taste," he'd declared. His lordship always had a smile on his face and eyes that seemed to dance in the lantern light. He was a very shrewd man who knew his business and would tolerate no mediocrity; a most capable foe, yet a man with a big heart.

Jepson had seen that when dining with Governor Ragland and Lord Anthony's family. Gabe's little man was fussy and Lord Skalla had taken the baby from Faith and whispered, "Come to Uncle Randy." Instantly the child quieted down.

"Must be a papa in his own right," Bart had exclaimed.

"Aye," Uncle Randy acknowledged, "granddaughters."

"They may be as they appear," Jepson replied to his lordship's comment about a possible ruse de guerre. "They will be upon us in another quarter of an hour so we'll know. Mr. Parks."

"Aye, Captain."

"We are no match for the corvette's metal so our only chance is to surprise them, if indeed it is a ruse. Have all the guns double-shotted with a measure of grape. Fill all the swivels with canister and have the last gun on either side ready to fire on the cutter if she joins the battle."

"Which side shall we load, sir?"

"Both sides."

A smile crossed Parks' face. He'd have bet the captain would want to have both sides ready.

"Mr. Parks!"

"Aye, sir."

"Do not open the gun ports. As soon as you are ready have the bosun sound quarters." Seeing the look on the lieutenant's face, Jepson added, "It's time for morning quarters, sir. I'd not want yonder ship to think something is amiss. A trifle slovenly perhaps, but not amiss."

"Aye, Captain."

"Your weapons, sir," This was from Zachary Taylor. He was one of Bart's mates and was recovering from a knee injury.

"He'll do you well," Bart had said. "Time is yew'll need a good man and there's none better I'm thinking." Who could say no to Bart? Lord Anthony never had. So who was he to turn down his old friend?

"Thank you, Zachary. How's your knee today?"

"Its mending, sir. A little tricky going down the ladders, but otherwise it's doing well."

Jepson strapped on his sword and stuck his pistol in his waistband.

"They're loaded, sir."

Smiling Jepson replied, "I was sure they were."

From overhead the lookout called down, "She's going about, sir."

Almost immediately Bucklin called out, "Signals sir."

"Well, are we to wait?" Parks growled. "Or do you need to consult with Robinson?"

"No sir. They say, heave to, have dispatches"

"Acknowledge," Jepson replied. The larger ship completed its maneuver and was now bearing down on *Pegasus*.

"If she comes any closer she'll not need to send a boat across the master," John Jones snorted.

The corvette's bow started to swing as the yards turned and the ship altered her course.

"She's shown her intention by damned," Jepson growled aloud.

Almost in unison, the French flag flew up the halyard as the British flag came down and the gun ports opened. *A minute to soon*, Jepson thought. Had the Frogs waited another minute, they could have fired a complete broadside before Jepson and *Pegasus* could have reacted.

"Open the gun ports and fire as you bear, Mr. Berry. This has to be quick work if we are to win the day."

Survive would be more like it, Zachary thought. What had that damn Bart gotten him into?

BOOM!...BOOM!...BOOM. *Pegasus* was speaking with all the authority she had.

"Mr. James."

"Aye, Captain."

"I intend to cross the Frogs bow, hopefully."

A cheer went up. A lucky shot had hit something so that the Frenchie's anchor broke loose from where it was catted. The anchor fell far enough it was halfway in the water when it stopped. This caused the bow of the ship to slew to starboard.

"Now, Mr. James, helm down."

Lord Skalla had to grab hold of a rail as the deck canted.

"Mr. Berry," Jepson yelled. "The cutter is to starboard. If she opens a gun port pour a broadside into her, if not aim for the mast and riggings." Turning back to the master, Jepson ordered, "As soon as we clear the cutter bring us about and we will engage the larboard guns."

"Do you intend to continue the attack, Captain?" Lord Skalla asked.

"Better to press the advantage now," Jepson replied. "If we don't, sir, they will be on us in an hour at most. They have bigger guns with a longer range. They would chase us down and pound us to pieces before we could get in range. They thought that we'd be an easy prize, otherwise..."

Another cheer! A lucky shot had brought the cutter's mast down.

"Well, that's one puppy we won't have to worry about nipping at our heels," Parks declared.

"Now, Mr. Jones," Jepson ordered. "Bring us about."

Pegasus' crew had been well-trained in both sail drill and gunnery. *Would that be enough*, Jepson wondered. They were overtaking the corvette fast.

"Be ready, Mr. Berry."

The young lieutenant saluted with his sword. One of the corvette's aft guns had been brought to bear. Flames belched out of the cannon, its ball plowing through the forward rail. It missed the gun but flying splinters had several men down, and one was dead. Jepson could see a piece of the rail had gone all the way through the poor soul. He lay in a fetal position as his blood poured onto the polished deck. Another seaman had a splinter a foot long sticking from his shoulder. Others less injured helped the man below.

The deck gave a shudder as more balls struck, but Jepson couldn't see any visible damage. "Above the water line, I hope," he muttered.

"Sir?" Zachary asked.

"Nothing," Jepson snapped. Sorry about his bluntness, he apologized. "Just thinking aloud, Zach. Forgive my ill mood."

"No worries, Cap'n."

Jepson could feel the vibration of the deck as *Pegasus* fired her guns. One after another, the guns roared, only this time they were not only giving but also receiving. Enemy balls plowed into the bulwark and rigging, bringing down a spar and overturning two guns. A flash was seen amidships as a powder boy was hit and his charge ignited. A fast thinking seaman threw a bucket of water on the burning sack and body. The boy was dead. *Its best,* Jepson thought. The pain from the burns would have been unbearable.

"We can't take much more of this," Lord Skalla muttered as he looked about at the destruction.

"Come about, Mr. Jones," Jepson ordered. "Let's engage on the starboard side."

Looking aloft, the master replied, "Aye, Captain, if it holds. They're still trying to take us as a prize, or their gunners don't know what they're about and are shooting high."

"Captain!"

"Yes, Mr. Parks."

"Mr. Berry is in a bad way. Mr. Drake says we don't have enough men left to fight both sides."

"Very well, send every available man to Mr. Drake. If possible, I intend to try to cross her stern if we can make it through one more pass."

"Aye, sir."

The two ships were now converging. *Pegasus'* guns had made their mark upon the French ship but had not done anything to damage her sailing abilities now that the loose anchor had been cut away. The corvette fired first again, and this time there was a sickening crack as a ball hit the forward mast. Jepson was never sure if it was the enemy ball or the shudder of *Pegasus'* deck as the starboard guns fired a broadside, but the mast came down, falling to larboard and causing a list. It brought the ship to a halt as it fell to the sea. Almost at once, grapnels began to fly from the corvette.

"Cut the mast away," Jepson ordered.

Men grabbed axes to chop away the wreckage and chop at the grapnel lines.

"Mr. Hacket," Jepson called to the bosun. "Keep a party busy clearing the mast away. Mr. Parks, stand by to repel boarders."

"Aye, Captain."

Men were firing down from the sides of the taller corvette. These were quickly silenced as one of *Pegasus'* marines fired a load of canister from the tops down onto the Frenchie's sailors. *Good*, Jepson thought. Sergeant O'Malleys got his men deployed. There was another bang from above...sharpshooters. Suddenly a thought came to Jepson: *they'd never expect us to attack.*

"Mr. Parks," Jepson yelled. "Mr. Parks." Finally the lieutenant looked his way. Jepson pointed toward the enemy ship with his sword and yelled again, "Boarders away."

The swivel barked again and a swath of lead decimated a group of enemy sailors. Climbing up and over the enemy rail, Jepson was not surprised to find Lord Skalla at his side. How they made it onto the enemy deck without being cut down was something of a miracle. Men were yelling, cursing, and crying out in pain. It was blade on blade with blood flowing onto the corvette's deck, making it slippery. An officer lunged at Jepson, the tip of his sword just missing Jepson's eye but cutting into his cheek. As Jepson fired his pistol at point blank range, the officer's chest turned crimson and he fell to the deck, grasping the hot pistol barrel in his hand. Jepson clubbed another enemy sailor who was fighting with one of his men. Lord Skalla was locked in combat with a big brute. The larger man seemed to have the leverage but didn't react quickly enough as Lord Skalla dropped his hand, quickly pulled a dagger and drove it into the man's kidney.

Without realizing it, *Pegasus'* men had driven the corvette's people back to the quarterdeck. Above the din of battle a voice called out, "Surrender, surrender."

"Hold your fire," Jepson ordered his men as a few more shots were fired.

The corvette's crew was beaten. Looking about the deck, bodies were strewn everywhere. O'Malley's marines had accounted for a number of them, but the blood lust was upon his seamen after seeing so many of their mates fall to the enemies' guns.

Walking up to the officer who had surrendered, Jepson asked, "Are you the captain?"

"No sir, I'm Blake. I am the second officer."

"You sound American."

"I am."

"On a French ship?" Jepson asked.

"The war makes for strange bed fellows, does it not, Captain?"

"That it does," Jepson agreed. "Where is the captain?"

"Dead," the first officer replied. "I believe you killed him, sir."

Jepson now recalled the officer who'd gouged him, blood was still dripping from the facial wound. "Mr. Parks."

"Yes, sir."

"Secure this ship, and then send Robinson across to the cutter with a few marines and take charge of our prize."

"Aye, Captain."

"I would like to be the first one to congratulate you, sir, if I may. You take on not one but two enemy ships and carry the day, one being a much superior ship, as well. Lord Sandwich will hear of this. I'll even send a letter to his Majesty," Lord Skalla said.

"That's not necessary, your Lordship."

"Nonsense Captain," Lord Skalla replied. "England needs more officers like you."

"Thank you, sir."

"Nay," Lord Skalla answered. "It is I who thanks you."

CHAPTER ELEVEN

GABE WAS STOMPING THE deck trying to get his foot into a rain and sea soaked boot. Nesbit appeared through the doorway and announced, "The admiral is up and about."

Damn Buck, Gabe thought, *he always was an early riser*. "Has Chen Lee gotten over his seasickness?" Gabe asked.

"Aye, Captain. He seems to have recovered fully."

Nodding, Gabe continued to dress. It had been a terrible beginning. No stranger to convoy duty, this was the first time Gabe had been given sole authority and responsibility, not only for his ship, but also the rest of the ships in Admiral Buck's squadron and those in the convoy.

The weather had not helped. Foul weather that had drained the men's strength and tested every ounce of their resolve. No sooner had a watch been dismissed and weary men made it below decks to their hammocks, when one of the bosun's mates would fill the air with the hated sound of his pipes.

"All hands, all hands. Shorten sails, repair foul riggings."

It never ended. Men, stiff, torn and bleeding, would climb aloft from the swaying deck to dizzying heights to accomplish the urgent task. Once back on the deck, they'd be dismissed and would stagger back to their berth decks where the foul stench of the bilges greeted them.

Old hands encouraged the newer ones to eat when they could, in order to keep up their strength. Otherwise, they'd never be able to answer the twitter of the bosun's pipes when they sounded again.

Chen Lee was not the only one to suffer the ills of seasickness. On the dark mess decks the sour odor of vomit made following the recommendations to eat almost impossible.

A poor soul groaned, "I wish I was dead."

Listening to the howl of the wind and feeling the crash of the mighty Atlantic's waves against the hull, one of the old hands replied, "If you don't eat so's you can keep your strength up, you might get your wish."

It wasn't just the men whom the elements harassed. Campbell, the first lieutenant, was on deck at all hours as was the midshipman. Signals were constantly passed in attempts to keep some of the grocery captains from lagging too far behind. As it was, the convoy was stretched out for miles, in spite of every effort by the convoy escorts to keep them on station.

Captain Lamb, of the *Stag*, had even threatened to put a ball amidships of one of the convoy ships if they didn't respond to his signals. Admiral Buck had tried to stay out of the way of things. He let his officers, especially his flag captain, do their jobs without having to worry about the admiral looking over their shoulders. It was a lesson Buck had learned from Lord Anthony. "You have enough to do without worrying about bumping into me at every turn," Lord Anthony had said.

Buck gazed out the large stern windows, feeling the dampness on his palms as he leaned on the sill to get a better view. He now realized how hard and lonely it was to stay below...out of the way as it were. Looking through the glaze created by the salt spray on the window, the ship's frothy wake was bright under the gray skies. Voices could be heard from the forward part of the cabin, several conversations in fact. Nesbit was trying to get a point across to Chen Lee, and Hex was giving instruction to Crowe.

Of his new entourage, Fleming seemed to be coming along the fastest. However, as Hex had stated, pushing paper was pushing paper regardless of the forms. Sums add up or they don't, the same at sea as it is on shore.

Crowe was a good seaman and knew how to handle a boat. It was the ceremony and tradition that was so much a part of the Royal Navy that he was having difficulty with. But it would come. Buck could see the man's determination and his desire to please. He would become a good cox'n.

Gabe seemed pleased with his ship, its officers, and crew, with one exception...the surgeon. He was newly appointed after *Trident's* previous surgeon had decided to retire. Thus the port admiral had posted the first one that came available. The first night at sea, the poor man had scared the watch half to death screaming at the top of his lungs, naked and holding his wedding tackle in his hands as he ran back and forth along the deck until he was subdued. Wright, the senior surgeon's mate, was perplexed by the man's behavior.

"He reminds me of a man who's in his final days of the pox. I have seen one such at the Bedlam Asylum in London," Wright volunteered. "I was interested in the treatment of the black bile, which is said to cause a person to go insane. It's one of the four humours: blood, phlegm, yellow bile, and black bile. One of the mad doctors at Bedlam took me under his wing and I was able to spend a fair amount of time learning to care for the insane."

"Did you say mad doctors?" Buck queried.

"Aye, sir. That's the term they give the doctors who treat the insane or mad patients. Dr. Munro was who I studied under. He had a physician friend from the Royal College of Physicians who got the pox. Dr. Munro treated him until the poor fellow died. Toward the end he acted just like our surgeon does now. Dr. Munro said he wasn't sure if it was the pox that caused the ill humour or the mercury the doctor used to treat himself with. Either way he died."

"Are you certain?" Gabe had asked.

"No, Captain, I'm not."

Since that night the surgeon would have periods where he appeared as sane as anyone but those periods were getting less frequent. The crew avoided the surgeon if at all possible, which wasn't an altogether bad thing as it weeded out the sick and lame from the merely lazy.

***

GABE FINISHED DRESSING AND made his way on deck. Lieutenant Davy had the watch but Campbell, the first lieutenant, was already on deck as well. A sleepy-eyed midshipman, Brayden, tried to hide his yawn as Gabe walked past. It was not so long ago that he couldn't remember such mornings.

The pre-dawn sky was starting to give way to the faint light of dawn. The sea was starting to take shape and rolling waves could be seen before they crashed into the ship's hull, sending spray on board. Glancing aloft, Gabe could see the sails were pulled taut in the morning breeze. The master was by the helmsman, peering at the compass needle.

"Morning, Captain." Campbell and Davy greeted in unison.

"Morning," Gabe replied tugging his watch coat closer against the early morning nip.

"Too much haze for a clear view, but the lookout has reported several sails in sight."

"Your lookout has a fine set of peepers," Gabe responded. He could just make out the men at quarters on the bow of the ship.

The master ambled over to where Gabe was. "Morning, Cap'n."

"Mr. Hayes."

"Promises to be a clear day, Cap'n."

"I hope so," Gabe replied. Looking to his first lieutenant, Gabe spoke, "If the weather is as the master predicts, let's get some of the hammocks on deck and see if we can't dry out."

"Aye, Captain."

"Mr. Davy."

"Aye, Captain."

"Quick as its light enough, signal the squadron to count the convoy ships. Hopefully we haven't lost any of our sheep." This brought a smile to the group.

"We'll soon be getting into the Wolf's Lair," Hayes volunteered.

"We'll be hard pressed to keep the American privateers at bay. Insurance premiums being what they are you'd think you wouldn't have the stragglers you do," Davy added.

"Ah...Mr. Davy," Campbell responded. "You've a lot to learn about grocery captains. Half of them are sailing ships with hulls so ripe it's a wonder they don't just fall out. Some of them do. I will bet you a good many of yonder ships are insured for far more than they are worth, ship and cargo to boot. They hope they get taken. Within a month or so they make their way back to England, file their claim and suddenly they are rich men."

"They aren't held as prisoners of war?" Davy asked.

"Lord no. The Americans will set them adrift close to somewhere like Antigua or Barbados and hope they will be back with another ship before long. Some have even become guests until they can suitably be passed on to some British port. I heard tell one captain's son married the daughter of the privateer that took them. Big wedding it was. Some way to fight a war, if you ask me."

Thinking on Ariel, Davy said, "Well, there are some Colonial ladies that will turn your head, and that is a fact."

Smiling Gabe said, "Mr. Davy is speaking from experience, Mr. Hayes. As I recall, one of these Colonial girls has captured Mr. Davy's heart."

Seeing the bewildered look on the first lieutenant's face, Davy said, "Aye, Dagan's ward," as if that explained it all.

***

CHEN LEE, WITH NESBIT'S help, had prepared an evening meal that had Buck and Gabe wishing they had room to let their pants out another inch or two.

"Navy dinner pretty good, but soon Chen Lee make you fine Chinese meal. Me see how you like. You like me fix navy meal sometime and Chinese meal sometime," the little Chinaman said in his broken English.

As the dishes were cleared away, Buck lit a cigar and Gabe his pipe. Gabe could hear Hex plucking at his mandolin topside through the skylight that was open for the first time since sailing.

Calling to Nesbit, he said, "Have Jake come down here with his instrument." As an afterthought, Gabe added, "With your permission, Admiral?" Buck seemed to be half dozing but motioned with his hand that it was alright.

Gabe had learned during the past few months they had been in Portsmouth that in spite of claims otherwise by Hex, he did have a good voice and was a master musician with any stringed instrument, it seemed. Once Hex made his way to the admiral's cabin, a glass of bourbon was poured for him. Gabe and Buck each sipped on their wine.

"Was that a new tune you were playing?" Gabe asked.

"Aye, Captain, a little something I've put together thinking on your little one."

"Well, let's hear it."

"I've not completed it," Hex admitted. "But here is what I have so far." Taking a moment to tune a string and then taking a pull from the glass of whiskey, Hex sang:

Somewhere in the scheme of things
Man's placed his hopes and dreams
In the thought that one day
He'd have a son
A boy who could carry on
His name would live
Tho he was gone
A ray of sun for the autumn days ...

"Well damme, Jake, but that is good," Buck swore.

Gabe felt emotions building up as he took a sip of his wine to steady himself before he spoke. "I agree with the admiral, Jake. I want to hear it all when it's finished. I'm sure Faith will want to hear it as well."

Sitting topside, Dagan took a pull on his pipe. He'd been listening to the song through the open skylight. How much change would having a son bring to Gabe? Until the war was over, very little, but after...

Sighing, Dagan thought, *maybe it's time for me to be making some plans as well*. A woman in Virginia was foremost in his thoughts lately. Thinking of Gabe's conversation with Davy and Campbell, he said to himself, "Those southern girls from the Colonies know how to turn a sailor's head...and his heart."

CHAPTER TWELVE

"He's dead?"

"Aye, Captain. Stiff, blue, and cold. He's a dead one all right."

Gabe stared at Wright. Recalling the surgeon's screaming fits, he couldn't help but think the poor sod's demons were finally put to rest. They'd be in Barbados within the week and hopefully another surgeon would be available.

"Be nice to have Caleb back, wouldn't it?" Dagan volunteered.

"You think," Gabe started but stopped in mid-sentence as Dagan shook his head no.

"I was just saying it'd be nice."

"Aye, that it would." Turning back to Wright, Gabe said, "You've done a wonderful job thus far and I will make sure your record reflects it, Wright. If you need anything let me know, and if a surgeon is needed we can signal *Stag*. Captain Lamb says he has a good one."

"Yes, sir. Dr. Miller, he's actually a physician who wanted to see what medicine at sea was like firsthand. A gentleman from a well-to-do family I'm told, sir."

"Yes, well I hear Captain Lamb is from a rather well-to-do family, so maybe there is a family connection somewhere."

"Possibly, sir."

A knock at the door brought the conversation to an end. "First lieutenant, sir," the marine announced.

Gabe had been expecting Campbell. There had been a fight and Campbell had asked for permission to handle it unofficially rather than getting the captain involved. Gabe had agreed, knowing the captain's punishment would be a flogging. Campbell's method would bring respect as well as appreciation. If not, the cat could still be let out of the bag.

***

LORD GILBERT ANTHONY SAT in a padded chair watching as his wife, Lady Deborah, and Faith, Gabe's wife, were playing with the new baby. He had forgotten how giddy women could get when it came to children, especially newborns. Gabe had a fine son. "Looks just like his daddy," Faith had proclaimed. *Damned if I can see it*, Lord Anthony thought. Women...mothers must have an eye men lacked. While the boy was a cute little fellow, Lord Anthony failed to see any resemblance to anyone he could think of. He had blondish hair, which was from Faith, as Gabe's hair was black. His face was red, wrinkled, and chubby. How could that be considered to be the spitting image of Gabe?

Oh well, maybe Bart was right. "Best you smile and agree, otherwise your wedding tackle will rust before it's broken out again."

Perfect advice, Anthony thought as he realized the noise he'd been hearing off and on was Bart snoring. An empty glass of wine sat on the table between the two chairs. The flickering flame from the candelabra made shadows dance across Bart. His legs were stretched out and his pipe lay in his lap. At least it had gone out, otherwise an ember might have resulted in damage to Bart's wedding tackle. The thought caused Anthony to smile. He could just see Bart jumping up if an ember had burned through his britches.

Laughter made Anthony look back at the women. Faith was handing the baby to Nanny. They must be getting ready to go home. Unable to stifle a yarn, Anthony realized it was getting late. Deborah and Anthony had tried their best to have Faith stay with them, at least until the baby was bigger, but she had declined.

"Thank you both, but I have Nanny and Lum, as well as Ariel, with me. Lum can come get you when it is time for the baby," Faith had promised Deborah. After the baby had been born Anthony had asked Nanny how Faith had done.

"She did fine, suh. Shucks, that girl was made for child-bearing. I just wish her mama was here to see her, course she's looking down from heben right now."

Lord Anthony had asked about the baby's name but Faith had been coy, stating she and Gabe would tell everyone when he got home. Anthony hoped that wouldn't be long. Knowing the navy as he did, it might be months or even years before Gabe returned.

Jepson had said Gabe would be underway as soon as the convoy ships had been made ready. Captain of a sixty-four, damned if Gabe hadn't moved up fast...maybe too fast; even if England did need brave captains to sail the ships necessary for this war. It was not that Gabe hadn't proved capable, he had. It was the responsibility that went with being a flag captain. Buck, however, would not let him flounder, Anthony was sure of that.

Jepson also had stated that Gabe had a good first lieutenant in Donald Campbell, and a master in David Hayes. An old seadog like Jepson who'd been a master himself would know.

***

A STRONG WIND PUSHED the convoy, though now the sky was clear and bright. For twenty hours the ships sailed at five knots or so, where previously three knots had been only something to wish for.

"How long do you think our grocery captains will keep this up before they start to lag?" Campbell asked his captain.

"I would not venture a guess, Mr. Campbell, as I'm of the opinion it's already lasted longer than I hoped for."

Approaching the captain and the first lieutenant, the master still held his sextant in his bony hand. He had just completed the noontime sighting. "By my reckoning," Hayes said, "we have crossed the thirtieth parallel."

Gabe understood the master's unspoken meaning. They were now over three thousand miles from England and effectively in the waters of the American privateers. The American Navy was so small it did little to cause concern for the British, but the privateers were a different story. They frequently hunted in packs of two or more and had done more to win the war for the Colonies than Washington's army. Half the supplies sent to keep the war going had been taken from the British by rebel ships.

Now the Frogs were out in force with the Americans. This caused the British navy to be stretched so thin that many felt it was better to end the war with the Americans than risk a French invasion of England.

***

GABE HAD JUST DRAINED his second cup of coffee while Hex was shining his sword and taking care of his pistols. Careful to wipe all the salt spray from the weapons, Hex then applied a fine coat of oil to each pistol and then the sword. He then turned his attention to the sword sheath. A knock at the door roused Gabe, whose thoughts had been on Faith and his new son.

"The purser, suh," the sentry announced.

"Good morning, Mr. Gibbs," Gabe welcomed the purser.

"Good morning, Captain, I'm afraid I've a problem, sir."

When the timid man failed to continue, Gabe prompted, "A problem with what?"

"Some of the cask of beef in the lower storage has sprung a leak, sir."

"How did you discover this?" Gabe asked, wondering if the recent storm was not an opportunity for the purser to claim damages to the ship's stores so they could be cast aside and he not be held accountable.

"The bilges smells...ah rotten, sir...quite foul." The little man turned green just thinking of the smell.

"Are you well?" Gabe asked.

"I'm sorry, sir, I have a weak stomach and do not tolerate such humours."

"Well, be that as it may, sir, I'm sad to say you must show me this cask," Gabe informed the purser.

"Cannot the first lieutenant do it, sir? He knows the location."

Gabe could see what it cost the man to admit to his weakness so Gabe relented. "I will see if Mr. Campbell is available."

"Thank you, sir, you are most gracious."

"He is an odd one, Captain," Hex said. "More honest than most. but I've heard sometimes he gets sick when there is weevils in the biscuits."

"And he's in the Navy?"

"Aye, Captain."

Lieutenant Campbell led Gabe and Hex down the hatchway and into the aft steerage. Hex held the lantern high to light up the darkness. The smell was apparent from a distance. The sounds this deep in the bowels of the ship were much different than those on the deck. The clank of the pumps was much louder, as were the groans of the ship's timbers as the keel flexed as it cut through another wave. Water sluicing around the rudder made an eerie sound. Sounds that were not heard topside.

As the proximity of the cask in question grew close, Gabe put his handkerchief to his nose. "Damme, but that's foul. No wonder the purser was reluctant to return down here."

The cask was soon located.

"It looks like the line securing the tier has parted allowing these casks to slide and fall."

"How many are there?" Gabe asked.

Holding the lantern high, Hex quickly counted. "Three maybe four casks are ruined, sir. A fifth may be saved. We can tell better once it's on deck."

"Very well, Mr. Campbell. Check with the surgeon's mate and see if he has any recommendations about cleaning this area and helping with this...this foul odor."

"Aye, Captain. Too bad we cannot run down a Frog. I'm told their officers carry unlimited quantities of perfume."

"Well, don't wait on that possibility, Mr. Campbell. Otherwise, we'll not be allowed in port...anybody's port."

CHAPTER THIRTEEN

THE SUN WAS DIRECTLY overhead and blazed down, making the deck of *Trident* ooze at the seams. The bright green hillsides of Antigua were now in sight. This meant the journey was over for a number of the convoy ships. A few would be headed to the Colonies and on to Halifax, but they would be escorted by ships from Antigua. There would be a handful that would continue on to Barbados under the protection of Admiral Buck's squadron. The voyage had been uneventful other than for the weather. A few strange sails had been sighted, but when Admiral Buck sent a couple of frigates to investigate, the ships scurried away. One island coaster had made a nuisance of itself, its captain thinking he could turn a profit selling his wares to the ships of the convoy. He was almost swamped for his troubles.

A moderate wind meant the convoy should anchor by sundown; the prospect of reaching port created an element of excitement among the men. If nothing else, a few days of relaxed routine would be welcomed.

Admiral Buck mounted the poop and approached Gabe. "I never get tired of Antigua," he volunteered.

"Would that be due to the willing arms of a few rich widows?" Gabe asked jokingly.

"Aye," Buck smiled. "As I recall, you never lacked for attention from the beautiful young ladies who attended Commodore

Gardner's parties. You were a dashing young middy then, and now you are a captain."

"And you an admiral, sir."

"Have you wondered what we'd be, were it not for this damn war?"

"I try not to," Gabe admitted then added, "It's because of the war that I met Faith."

"That's true," Buck responded.

"Think the commodore will be about?" Gabe asked, speaking of Gardner.

"If not, we will take a ride to the plantation," Buck answered. "He is still overseeing that for Lady Deborah, is he not?"

"I've not been told otherwise," Gabe replied.

"Well, you have your ship to work, Captain, so I will leave it to you," Buck said, meaning *I'll get the hell out of your way.*

"Aye, sir."

***

ENGLISH HARBOUR WAS A busy place. Having made his way back on deck after a quick sandwich and glass of lime juice, Gabe took in the impressive sight of so many ships at anchor. It was proof of the growing importance of naval bases in the West Indies. With the French out, the islands had to be constantly on alert for possible attack. Yet their importance as Caribbean bases was of the utmost if the British were to continue to carry the fight to the Colonies and their pesky privateers.

Within minutes the Caribbean sun had caused sweat to run down Gabe's back, sticking his shirt to his skin. Campbell was busy rigging awnings and windsails to help provide shade to the quarterdeck and funnel as much wind as possible below decks. Gun ports were opened to help as well. Boats plied back and forth from the anchored ships to the shore. Tomorrow the activity would increase, as Admiral Buck's squadron would also be busy gathering needed supplies and fresh stores. Water hoys were already making their way to two of the sloops.

Lieutenant Davy approached Gabe and saluted. "A boat has put off from the flagship, sir. In fact, it appears several boats have put off."

Within minutes a young, darkly tanned lieutenant reported himself to Gabe. "Admiral Moffit sends his compliments, sir, and wishes to invite you and your first lieutenant to dinner tonight."

"Moffit?" Gabe asked. "Dutch Moffit?"

"I understand the admiral has been called Dutch at times," the lieutenant replied, consternation on his face.

"The admiral used to be my brother's, Vice Admiral Lord Anthony's, flag captain," Gabe explained.

The lieutenant relaxed and said, "I've had the pleasure of meeting Lord Anthony some months back. He was a most gracious host."

"It was my understanding Admiral St. John had this station."

"He did until last week when he was taken back to England an invalid."

"I'm sorry to hear it," Gabe responded.

St. John was known to be a voice for the common sailor, always arguing for better pay and better conditions at sea. His departure from the service would set back the cause. Yet new voices had taken up the fight, including that of Vice Admiral Anthony.

Admiral Buck had not returned to the ship, but Crowe had returned with a note stating that Buck would see Gabe that evening.

***

Believing in punctuality, Gabe stepped through the entry port of Moffit's flagship, *Thunder,* at exactly seven p.m. As the shrill of pipes faded, Gabe removed his hat to show respect. Moffit's flag captain was Charles Abbott. He had made a name for himself as a bold frigate captain.

Abbott stepped forward and greeted Gabe, "Welcome aboard, sir, I hope you had an uneventful voyage."

"A spell of peevish weather, but nothing to speak of," Gabe replied, shaking his fellow captain's hand.

Gabe was introduced to the ship's officers while the drummers and fifes played a brisk little tune.

"Captain Anthony...Sir Gabe it is now, I'm told." Stepping forward, Admiral Moffit shook Gabe's hand vigorously.

The trio made their way to the great cabin where Moffit called to a servant to bring a glass of hock for his guest.

"I saw your brother some weeks back," Moffit stated. "He told me of your recent exploits and being knighted. Now you are Rupert's flag captain."

"Admiral Buck was most gracious in his offer, sir, greater that I deserve."

"I think not," Moffit stated matter-of-factly. "I will admit being a frigate captain was a happy time for me, but being Lord Anthony's Flag Captain was also rewarding."

Gabe remembered the times and the battle of Nova Scotia when Moffit had been his brother's flag captain. It had been a hotly contested battle that had been touch and go for a while. The loss of men and destruction of ships had been severely felt. Gabe gave an involuntary shudder as he recalled the fierceness of the battle.

The dinner was a huge success, with the guests swapping sea stories and embellished stories of derring do. Both Buck and Moffit told of Gabe's accomplishments with the ladies when he was a young blade.

By the time the loyal toast had been given that evening, the effects of fresh food and fine spirits had taken their toll on most of the officers. When Admiral Buck finally thanked Admiral Moffit for such a fine feast for all the captains and first lieutenants of his squadron, Gabe was in deep thought. He was wondering how many would make it back to their ships without falling into the warm harbor water. Hex had instructed Crowe on the need for extra precaution after such dinners. However, his admiral had other plans for the evening and had drunk surprisingly little. If he were drenched, it'd likely be in deep passion and not the Caribbean Sea.

"I shall be ashore tonight," Buck informed Gabe with a wink just before making his way through the entry port.

"Old acquaintances renewed?" Gabe asked, knowing the answer before his admiral replied.

"Aye!" Buck responded. "I will send word tomorrow where we can meet and hopefully have a wet with Commodore Gardner."

CHAPTER FOURTEEN

LAZY CLOUDS FLOATED ABOVE a blue sky, occasionally blocking the sun and casting a fleeting shadow over *Trident's* deck.

"It's like a young lass," Hayes swore. "Showing just enough of her wares to make you want more, then she moves along, only to return just about the time you've got your humours settled down." The master's comment caused chuckles from several in close hearing.

"You've 'ad 'perience in 'at area 'as you, Mr. Hayes?" one of the helmsmen asked, grinning from ear to ear.

"Aye, Rogers. In my day, I had the run of many a young lass."

"More like running away," Lieutenant Davy quipped, ribbing the master.

"When I was a young buck such as you, Mr. Davy, the lasses fought for the right to be at my table."

"'E must of 'ad a bit of prize money don't you think, Mr. Davy," the helmsman braved a comment.

"I'm sure it was all our good master could do to fight off the attentions of many a wench," Davy joked.

"Aye," Hayes agreed. "But there comes a time when you just get too tired to put up much of a fight and you let the poor lasses take their pleasure with you. A man's job it was at times, I'll admit," he said with a sigh. "And not for those with a suspect constitution, as some I know," Hayes continued, glaring at the helmsman.

"Well, I'm sure you were a rutting buck in your day," Davy offered. "However, age takes its toll on all of us at some point."

"Nay," Hayes threw back. "I'm still the cock of the walk."

Davy snorted. "You mean to tell me, Mr. Hayes, that you can still do it all night long."

"Aye."

"Mr. Hayes, I've heard some sea stories in my time but..." Davy didn't finish the sentence; he just shook his head in disbelief.

"Well, I admit," Hayes said, "that what I used to do all night now takes all night to do...but they enjoy it just the same."

All within hearing burst out in laughter, including Gabe, who'd been standing on the weather side talking with Lieutenant Campbell.

Shaking his head and smiling, Campbell said, "It's hard to get the upper hand on the master."

"Aye," Gabe agreed. "I know another from the same mold," he said, thinking of Bart.

Clearing his throat to get Gabe's attention, Campbell made a motion with his eyes alerting his captain of the admiral's presence.

"I thought I'd enjoy one of these cigars that Commodore Gardner gave me," Buck volunteered. "Would you care to join me?"

"My pleasure, sir," Gabe answered, falling into step with the admiral as he made his way toward the stern. "The ships of the squadron are all on station, sir, but there's not another sail on the horizon."

Buck bit the tip off his cigar and spit it into the white foamy wake created as *Trident* cut through the blue Caribbean Sea under a full press of canvas.

"It was good to see Greta and the Commodore," Buck said, once his cigar was lit.

"Aye," Gabe agreed. "I believe the life as a retired gentleman and planter suits him well."

"That and Greta's cook." Buck joked.

"She was imported from South Carolina before the war," Gabe volunteered. "She cooks a good meal, what Faith says is southern cooking."

"Well, whatever it's called it was a welcome change from Chen Lee's fare. He is a good cook and servant but rice with every meal gets old."

Gabe smiled, "Nesbit said he has tried to make Chen Lee understand that variety is the spice of life."

"Aye," Buck agreed. Taking a puff on the cigar and exhaling a white plume of smoke, he spoke again in a sheepish voice. "I tell you, Gabe, if I could steal away Gardner's cook I'd do it in a heartbeat."

The two had been served fried chicken, yams smothered in butter with cinnamon and sugar, creamy white potatoes, carrots, and hot biscuits. For dessert, apple pie was served with a thick cream poured over the pie. A dessert like neither of the officers had ever tasted before. Breakfast the following morning was eggs, more hot biscuits, a local honey, and oatmeal with a choice of butter or cream.

They had played whist, with Gabe as Greta's partner. During the card game a number of cigars were smoked and several bottles of wine were consumed, with Greta preferring sherry. Gabe and Greta won most of the hands during the game of cards.

"Private signals, that's what it is," the commodore swore good-naturedly. "By gawd, sir, this young officer has worked out signals to cheat me in my own house with my own wife. Ye gads...I can only guess what else they've got schemed up."

Greta leaned over and pulled Gardner to her and with a kiss said in a coy voice, "Makes you wonder, don't it?"

Soon the conversation turned to the war, with Gardner saying, "Well, it's been good for some in the navy...Gil's a vice admiral, you're a rear admiral, and Gabe a captain. I remember sitting on his board for lieutenant."

"You would have been made a flag as well, had you not retired," Buck said.

"Aye, I've no doubt, but I've no stomach for it. I have too many friends in the Colonies and I'm too much in agreement with their cause to fight my friends."

“A great number feel as you do, sir,” Gabe offered.

“Yes well, those in Parliament that did should have stood their ground and put Lord North in his place.” The commodore continued to rant for some time. Many of his comments could have been considered treasonous.

Finally, Greta was able to change the conversation. By that time the commodore was much in his cups. When it was time to retire for the evening, Greta winked at Buck and Gabe as she spoke to her husband.

“Come dear, take me to my bed chamber where you can keep guard over me. My honour must be protected with these randy naval officers in our house.”

Grinning, Gardner replied after a very unromantic belch. “No worries, my dear, I will be most diligent in my husbandly duties.”

“Thank you, dear. I understand there is some whose chamber has recently been invaded.”

“Damn,” Buck swore. “Is nothing kept a secret on this island?”

“Let’s hope they don’t have a system to spread the word all the way to Barbados,” Gabe said.

“The only way that information can get to Barbados,” Buck growled, “is if some busybody in whom I’ve put forth my trust was to run his mouth. We don’t know of such a person do we, Captain?”

“No sir, not that I can think of.”

CHAPTER FIFTEEN

THE AROMATIC SMELL OF tobacco filled the early morning air. Lieutenant Wiley had the deck with Midshipman Sebastian. The group of young gentlemen was a lively lot. More apt to mischief than the usual group, but they were well liked by the crew. More than once Gabe had seen an old hand take time to show one of the mids the proper way of doing things. Thomas was the senior member of the berth. He was ready to take the lieutenant exam.

"A rare one," Campbell had said. "No tyrant, mind you, but not one to tolerate sloppy work."

Hayes approached Gabe, his pipe in his mouth. A small plume of smoke rose as he took a quick puff before speaking to his captain. "We should make landfall about mid-afternoon if the wind holds."

"Aye," Gabe replied. "I could feel a change in the current this morning at quarters."

This comment caused the master to cock his head slightly as he eyed his captain. His respect for the man as a seaman rose a notch. "You are familiar with these waters, I recall," Hayes volunteered.

"Most of my days as an officer have been spent in these waters from the West Indies to the southern Colonies, all the way up to Nova Scotia and back. Not much time in the East Indies, however."

Gabe's shirt was already wet with sea spray and sweat and clung to his skin. As Gabe pulled the uncomfortable shirt away from his body, the master noticed and said, "It'll be a warm one today, I'm thinking. But I'll take the heat over the damp cold North Atlantic."

"You've spent time there?" Gabe asked.

"Aye, Captain, a year in the Baltic. Swore I'd retire before going back. Damn cold near made a cripple out of me. Rheumatism in me knees and hands. Knees popped and crunched so bad I'd have trouble sneaking up on a deaf man."

This caused Gabe to chuckle. He'd heard his father and brother make similar comments.

Seeing the smile on Gabe's face, Dagan, who'd been standing nearby spoke, "Smile if you like, Gabe, but the day will come when you will remember this conversation."

"Are you speaking from experience?" Gabe inquired.

"Aye, I'm starting to notice an ache on a cold morning. You will too, so pay mind to your elders."

Gabe was glad to see Dagan on deck. He had been morose of late, though he did spend time with Gabe and Buck and even played cards with them at times. He'd also spent some time with Hex and Crowe, but he'd not been his usual self. *He's thinking about mother*, Gabe thought and had even made a comment to Hex to that effect.

"Maybe Cap'n, but I would think it's a woman on your uncle's mind."

So that's it, Gabe thought, understanding the feelings well.

***

"Land ho!" Excited sailors rushed to the rail to see the distant island, only to be harried back to their duties by the first lieutenant. The island of Barbados was a welcome sight as it sat under the blazing sun.

Gabe couldn't help but feel excitement at the thought of seeing Faith and his son. "Mr. Campbell."

"Aye, Captain."

"My brother, Lord Anthony, is the commander in chief of this station as you know. He has a sharp eye. I'd not want to embarrass our admiral by a poor showing to Lord Anthony."

"Deck thar! Sails to starboard, sir," the lookout called down interrupting Gabe.

The ships were not yet visible from the deck, but it did not surprise Gabe. It was likely some of his brother's ships returning from patrol. No doubt, a ship would be sent to investigate if the appropriate signals were not given, even if the ship was recognized. All ships stood the possibility of being captured and used to gain advantage for the enemy. The squadron lay on a port tack and made their final leg into Carlisle Bay. Most of the midshipmen suddenly found a need to go aloft. Gabe watched as they made their way up the shrouds.

Everything was different in the West Indies. The sun was brighter, the beaches whiter, and the vegetation was thick and green.

"Deck thar! Ships at anchor, one is a flagship, sir...vice admiral's flag flying, sir."

"Ready to wear ship, sir," Hayes said, interrupting Gabe's thoughts.

Gabe gave a nod to Hayes. The sails were clewed up.

"Stand by to fire the salute, please."

"Aye," the gunner acknowledged.

"My glass if you please," Gabe said to Hex. Focusing in on the flagship, Gabe could see his brother never changed when it came to thinking of his men. The gun ports were open to take advantage of any offshore breeze. An awning was stretched across the wide quarterdeck.

"Do you see Lord Anthony, Gabe?" Buck had approached and if Gabe had been warned his mind had been elsewhere. Seeing the look on Hex's face, he realized he had been warned but not heard.

***

Lord Anthony was on the deck of his flagship watching the approaching ships of Buck's squadron and the few remaining convoy ships make their approach.

"Makes a fine sight does it not, sir?"

"What would you expect, Bart?"

"I 'spect he'd better do it right or I'd give 'em a taste of me boot. And that's no error," the cox'n replied.

The salute began and echoed across the bay.

"Captain Earl."

"Yes, my Lord."

"Let's not let Gabe and Admiral Buck outshine us. Return the salute if you please."

***

ON BOARD *TRIDENT*, BUCK spoke. "I'll leave you to your ship, Captain, while I go change and get ready to meet with Lord Anthony. As soon as you feel all is secure, Gabe, feel free to go ashore. If you are needed before the morrow I will send word."

"Thank you, sir," Gabe replied.

Humph, Dagan thought. *I'd not get between Gabe and the entry port. Not unless I wanted to take a swim, that is.*

"Tops'l sheets, clew up. Ready, Captain?" Campbell inquired. Gabe nodded his acknowledgement.

"Helm a'lee," the first lieutenant ordered.

Glancing forward, Gabe could see Lieutenant Davy. That was another one who would be glad to go ashore. Gabe had started to speak to the first lieutenant but didn't want Campbell to feel obligated because the captain had said something. He had told the first lieutenant the hands would be allowed ashore watch-by-watch once the ship had been properly anchored and everything secured. Campbell had nodded his approval.

Gabe watched as the wheel was put over and the ship began to turn as the rudder gripped, swinging the bow as *Trident* turned into the wind.

"Handles like a frigate," the first lieutenant swore proudly.

"Let go the anchor," Gabe ordered, and an immediate splash was heard, along with the rattle of chains.

Buck then appeared in his shiny new admiral's uniform. "Call away my launch if you please, Mr. Wiley."

"Aye, Admiral."

"Gabe."

"Sir."

"I'm sure it would not be amiss if you were to accompany me to the flagship."

"Let me get my coat, sir." Gabe already had his dress uniform on except for the coat. He had avoided that until the last minute.

"Here, sir." Hex held his coat ready for him. Crowe must have made the cox'n aware the captain would be invited.

"Thank you, Hex."

"Aye, sir."

Dagan was also turned out in his best, ready to accompany Buck and Gabe to the flagship. Gabe turned toward the entry port then stopped and spoke again. "You may go ashore, Jake, and I'll expect you at my house later."

"Aye, Captain."

"Lucky bloke, bloody pet is what 'e is," one of the newer hands spoke.

"The cap'n is a gentleman, you sod," one of *Peregrine's* old hands replied. "Hex saved the cap'n's life once. The cap'n ain't one to forget, not this 'un, he ain't."

CHAPTER SIXTEEN

GABE CRUSHED FAITH TO his chest as they embraced. He'd never been immune to her beauty. The nearness of her body to him made him groan as the pent-up desire for this woman he loved so was on the verge of exploding. Faith pushed her slender body close to her daring sea captain as Gabe lowered his lips to hers for a long passionate kiss. He was intoxicated with her fresh woman's scent. He could smell her sweet breath as her fiery, hot lips responded to his. He'd not forgotten how good she tasted. He'd also not forgotten how she had made love to him just before he'd set sail for England. The memory had been burned into his mind just waiting for the time he'd be with her again.

When they paused to catch their breath, Faith whispered, "Damn, I have missed you." And she quickly claimed his mouth with hers again. Desire soared as the two lovers clinched. Faith let go a soft moan as Gabe fondled a breast, feeling the racing beat of her heart in his hand. Near bursting with passion, Gabe scooped up his wife...his lover from the floor and placed her on the bed a few steps away. Clothes were discarded within the blink of an eye. The first coupling was a frenzy of unleashed passion, each unable to prolong the need to satisfy the fires of desire for one another. When the initial fire was quenched, the two bodies convulsed and collapsed together, falling into the contented slumber neither had enjoyed in months. Faith woke up first and began to trace lines on her man's body with her fingers. She then leaned over his body and moved her head back and forth with her hair just touching Gabe's skin.

He awoke with a smile and said, "You little vixen."

"Should I stop?" Faith asked as her hand drifted below his waist.

"Not when you've got my cannon primed," he responded.

"More like a pistol, me thinks," Faith naughtily replied.

"I'll show you the difference between a pistol and cannon," Gabe bragged.

This time their lovemaking was slow, long, and loving.

***

THE TWO LOVERS HAD taken a bath and were getting ready for guests that evening for dinner. Gil and Deborah were coming, along with Macayla and Bart. Of course, Dagan and Hex would be there as well. Gabe was amazed at how quickly he felt completely at home ashore. It was due to Faith and his new son, yes, his son. They planned to announce his name that evening.

Thinking back on the afternoon, Gabe was surprised at how quickly the meeting aboard his brother's flagship had gone. Once in the admiral's quarters, handshakes, back slaps and even a few hugs were given. They were drinking a toast to the squadron's safe voyage, when his brother's flag lieutenant entered.

"Pardon my interruption," Mahan said and then reported. "Captain Jepson is returning to port with a couple of prizes." His voyage to the colonies had taken a turn it seemed.

Jepson's sudden return to port provided the perfect exit for Gabe. Gil understood the need for his brother to be with his wife and meet his son after being away so long.

Admiral Lord Anthony addressed Buck, "With your permission, Admiral, I will put Bart and my barge at Gabe's disposal for the time being while I greet our victorious Captain Jepson."

"By all means, my Lord," Buck readily agreed. After paying his respects to Lord Ragland, the governor of Barbados, he'd planned to renew his acquaintance with the widow, Livi.

Not forgetting his manners, Gabe invited Admiral Buck and Stephen Earl to dine that evening. Both politely declined, understanding this was to be a family night. Gil had undoubtedly sent word home that Gabe's ship had been sighted. When his barge grounded ashore, Gil's carriage was waiting. Along with it were Faith, their son, Lady Deborah, Lum, and Nanny. Gabe embraced his wife and Deborah, and then took his son from Nanny's arms.

So this was his son, a miracle from heaven. He could see some of the Anthony features. But the little turned up nose was Faith's. The little fellow had a full head of hair and a healthy set of lungs, as he let everyone know it was time to eat. The temper was no doubt Faith's, Gabe decided, but refrained from saying it.

"He's sho' a sight ain't he, Mistuh Gabe?" Nanny declared. "A handsome little devil he is too, jus' like his daddy...but he sho' nuff got his mama's temper." *Ah...like minds,* Gabe thought.

"Amen," Lum chimed in. For once Faith didn't protest.

Once back at their cottage Gabe was greeted, more or less, by Sampson. *He likely tolerates me for Faith's sake*, Gabe thought, *the ungrateful whelp. Had he forgotten it was Gabe and Dagan who had saved his mangy hide*? Rubbing the big beast between the ears, Gabe was glad he had. It was Sampson who'd saved Faith from the rogue, Montique.

***

DAGAN WAS HOLDING HIS great-nephew while Hex looked on. It was hard to recognize the man holding the child as the same one who'd confronted the two villains back in Portsmouth, Hex thought. Would the child inherit some of Dagan's abilities? Gabe had spoken of it one night while at sea. It appeared Dagan's uncle who lived in the Colonies had a son who had the gift. Was it a blessing or a curse? A blessing, Hex decided, otherwise he'd probably be dead.

Dagan had already been told the name of the little one. He had been present when Gabe told his mother she had a grandson and he was going to be named after his grandfather and brother. Holding the child, Dagan so wished Maria could see her grandson.

He favored Gabe...and yes he had Faith's nose, but he was Admiral James all over again. Feeling melancholy, Dagan wondered why his sister, Gabe's mother, wouldn't visit for a few months; thinking if she'd come she would never want to go back. But her home was in Portsmouth. That's where she had lived with and loved her man. Most likely that's where she'd die. Well, maybe Gabe could take the little one to Portsmouth before that happened.

***

IT WAS TIME FOR dinner and everyone had seated themselves around the table. Nanny had promised one of her southern dinners to Gabe before he left, and she more than delivered. Baked ham with raisins and a sweet glaze, yams with a buttery sweet sauce, green beans, creamed yellow corn, and both hot biscuits and cornbread cooked until it had a golden brown crust. Fresh butter was on the table for the bread. Nanny had baked an apple pie, which Dagan loved, and a blackberry pie for Gabe. The family devoured the meal and Gabe swore with cooking like this it'd be hard to put to sea again.

Bart declared, "If we don't put to sea fairly soon 'is lordship won't be able to pass through the entry port. He will soon need a bosun's chair as it is."

"You're looking a little portly yourself," Lord Anthony declared.

"I'm just thick," Bart said defensively. "The women say I'm thick like a real man...not fat, like some."

"I ought to have you flogged, you ungrateful old sea dog," Lord Anthony snarled.

Hex was amazed at the banter. The admiral's cox'n still looked fit enough to bust a head or two should the need arise. He could see a touch of gray in Lord Anthony's hair but while he'd developed a little belly, Hex had no doubt he could still take care of himself. The two together would be a force.

After dessert the group retired to the small setting area. Almost on cue, Nanny got the baby and handed him to Faith while Gabe poured glasses of wine for everyone. Seeing he was short, he excused himself and came back with two more. He handed out the glasses and then taking the last two, he gave one each to Nanny and Lum.

"Tonight," Gabe said, feeling emotion build up and tears come to his eyes. He wiped his eyes with a linen napkin that Nanny handed him, then he continued, "We are here tonight, family and friends...nay family, a big loving family to celebrate the birth of our son." Pulling Faith close, Gabe put his arm around her and said, "A toast to James Gilbert Anthony. I pray he will continue to bring honour to the family name as his grandfather and uncle have."

Deborah reached over and took the napkin from Gabe and handed it to Gil. "You honour me, brother," Gil said humbly. "I'm so proud we have shared our lives for these last few years. I just wish I'd known you long before I did."

After a while, Nanny took the baby to change him. Faith excused herself shortly after, stating it was time to feed the baby and put him to bed. Deborah joined her, leaving the men to cigars, pipes, and brandy.

"You still have your lotz?" Gabe asked Lum.

"Yes suh, I still pick it up from time to time. The little man likes a tune now and then."

"Well, get it and let's have one of your tunes."

Lum's ability with the lotz impressed Hex.

"Hex plays several stringed instruments," Gabe told the group. "Hopefully we can all get together and play a few tunes."

"Sounds good," Bart volunteered, "as long as some don't try to sing." He didn't mention any names but cut his eyes toward Lord Anthony.

"Well, I don't sound like a cat with his tail under a rocker like some," Anthony responded, not mentioning any names either.

***

DAGAN HAD A ROOM at the cottage, but as the night wound down he decided he'd sleep on *Trident*. Before he went back, he, Bart, and Jake made for Bart's favorite tavern for a few tankards and a hand or two of cards. As they sat down at a table, the tavern wench, seeing Bart, automatically brought a deck of cards and rum for the three. Her reward was a coin between her breasts and a slap across her rump.

"I caution you," Dagan said to Jake, "we are friends, but expect no quarter from Bart when it comes to cards."

Sounding hurt, Bart responded, "Pay no mind to 'im, Jake. 'E's a poor loser is all it is. Now tell me, lad, how much did yew bring with yews tonight?"

"Hummph," Jake grunted. "I've little enough."

" Well, no worries," Bart replied. "Iffen yew lose it all, I'll take a marker on yew's prize money."

"Not while I'm sober you won't."

Looking at Dagan, Bart said, "Smart lad yew 'ave 'ere, Dagan." And then he called to the tavern girl, "Dottie, be a good little doxy will yew and fill my friends' tankards. They've been at sea for months and 'ave a powerful thirst. Aye, a powerful thirst."

CHAPTER SEVENTEEN

THE SUN WAS ALREADY high in the Caribbean sky as the hands went about the last of their duties on board *HMS SeaHorse*, flagship for Vice Admiral Lord Anthony, commander in chief for his Majesty's ships in the West Indies. The ship's bell had just rung seven times. Only one hour left in the forenoon watch.

Silas, Lord Anthony's servant, along with help from a couple of the wardroom servants, was busy putting the finishing touches to his lordship's dining area. A meeting was to be held with some of his lordship's officers, including Admiral Buck, his lordship's brother Captain Sir Gabriel Anthony, Lord Skalla, and even Lord Ragland, the governor of Barbados. Such meetings were not uncommon. His lordship liked his captains to be well informed, to know what he was thinking, and was open to suggestions when a captain had a particular thought or idea.

If it all went as expected, his lordship would offer cold refreshments, usually sweetened lime juice, or even tea during the meal. There would be a glass of wine after the meal, along with cigars and pipes being lit. Lord Anthony usually called for his pipe and that was the signal for the others to smoke if they pleased.

After the meal, and after most of the captains and guests had departed, the bourbon would be offered. This was only for a limited few, as the Kentucky bourbon was a precious commodity. A case, in the way of a gift, was occasionally brought to his lordship by some captain from a neutral country. There was little doubt that such 'gifts' had been sent by General Manning in the Colonies or some member of

Dagan's family. However, no one spoke of it and if any type of gift was returned it was a secret...to most.

Silas was more than aware of the amount of good English tea that went missing on occasion, not that it mattered to him. The frequent taste of leftover liquor was more than enough for him to send a ship full of tea for a few cases of the fiery brown liquid called bourbon.

Lieutenant Mahan entered the cabin and waved as he walked past Silas and made his way to where his lordship was sprawled out on the cushions below the stern windows. Bart was polishing Lord Anthony's sword and cussing the damned humidity that created the damn rust that made him have to oil and polish his lordship's swords and pistols every damn day or so.

Looking up at his visitor, Lord Anthony welcomed his flag lieutenant. "Patrick, come in and have a seat." Even with the stern windows open there was little in the way of a cooling breeze.

"Captain Earl has informed me, sir, that Admiral Buck and Sir Gabe are approaching."

Anthony nodded; he'd ask them to come a few minutes early to give them a heads up on the news Jepson had brought back and the recommendations made by Lord Skalla. They were sound recommendations...but not ones that would make Gabe or Faith happy. Still, this was war. War made worse by the Frogs taking a hand in it. Better to inform Gabe ahead of time so he wouldn't feel blindsided. God only knew how Faith would take the news.

The shrill of pipes and roll of drums alerted his lordship that Buck and Gabe had arrived. "Patrick, you and Bart go welcome our guests."

"Aye, my Lord," Mahan responded and made his way out of the cabin.

"Yew wants me to tell Dagan?" Bart asked.

Anthony shook his head. Bart slid the sword back into the scabbard. Damn this rust and damn this war.

***

LIEUTENANT JEPSON ARRIVED WHILE Buck and Gabe were in Lord Anthony's cabin. Stephen Earl greeted Jepson and the two killed some time talking until Mahan stepped through the companionway and onto the deck.

"His lordship will be glad to see you now," the flag lieutenant informed the two.

It was a solemn cabin that Earl and Jepson entered. No doubt, Gabe had been informed of the pending assignment. It dawned on Jepson as he entered the cabin how everyone addressed Gabe as Gabe. Not Sir Gabe or Captain Anthony...just Gabe. Well, anyone of equal rank or seniority, that is.

In all the years he'd known Lord Anthony, he'd only been called Gil by a very few people. It was lieutenant or captain, then admiral, and now Lord Anthony. But all who knew Gabe called him Gabe and no one seemed to mind, least of all Gabe. If Jepson had thought further, most of his friends and fellow officers addressed him as Jep.

One by one, the captains and their first lieutenants in Admiral Buck's squadron arrived, followed at last by Lord Ragland and Lord Skalla.

"I've asked Silas to serve cold meats, fruit, and a cobbler for lunch, gentlemen. In view of the heat, I felt it would be better for digestion. I hear our First Lord of the Admiralty, Lord Sandwich, frequently dines thus."

Several of the officers had also heard of the first lord's custom and laid waste to all Silas had put out.

After the meal, Lord Anthony stood. When the noise died down he said, "I'm glad to have Admiral Buck, my old and dear friend, back from England. It is always a pleasure to share your company." Raising his glass, Anthony said, "A toast to Admiral Buck."

Once the toast had been completed, Anthony said, "To Captain Sir Gabriel Anthony, Knight of the Bath. I'm very proud to have Sir

Gabe as a brother, and even prouder that he has not only chosen to name his new son after our father but also include me in the name as well. Gentlemen, a toast to a future naval officer, little James Gilbert Anthony."

Hearing the toast, Gabe grimaced. Once Faith learned what was in the wind, his son might never set foot on a ship.

"Gentlemen...." Lord Anthony spoke again. "I believe at least a few of you qualify for the title."

This brought a laugh, as Lord Anthony knew it would. Once the laughter died down, Anthony continued, "We all have heard of exploits by brave captains who have beaten the odds and won victories over our enemies. Our brave Sir Gabe recently won a battle under Admiral Buck's flag over superior enemy forces. He was given a knighthood for his victory. Captain Jepson was one of the ship captains in that battle. Well, Captain Jepson on his brig, *Pegasus*, took on and defeated a twenty-four gun French corvette, *Revenant*, which was also in company with an armed cutter. Lord Skalla has informed me that *Revenant* is French for 'ghost'. The ship is sound and seaworthy. Therefore, I have decided to buy the ship in and Lord Ragland has assured me she is making her way through the prize court in an expedient manner." This brought more applause and back-pounding from those closest to Jepson.

Clearing his throat Anthony continued, "*Revenant* is a post ship and cannot have a lieutenant command her. Therefore, I have decided to promote the man who captured her to captain. I also wish to say this decision was highly recommended by Lord Skalla, who was present during the battle. Gentlemen...Captain George Jepson."

When the congratulations subsided Anthony said, "I will now turn the meeting over to Lord Skalla."

Thanking his lordship, Skalla addressed the officers before him. "We recently lost the payroll for the army in the southern colonies. Most of it was a result of poor judgment and neglect on the part of a ship's captain. Not only was the payroll lost, but the ship was taken without a shot being fired. In fact, the only fatality was the ship's captain. Rumor is he was killed by one of his own men. If what we are being told is true, it's probably good that he was killed. Otherwise, he would have been an embarrassment for the country. As most of you know, with the French joining the Americans the war has not gone well. But that's a different topic. When our ship was taken, a good amount of the crew went over to the American side. I understand the captain was a tartar given to flogging a man to death."

Skalla paused, letting the men digest his comments, then he continued, "Several of the ship's officers were allowed to go free. They had been given passage back to England on a transport, but as luck would have it this ship also was taken. One of the ship's boys on the *Revenant,* which had a mixed crew of Americans and French, says our ship and our people are being held captive in a dungeon at the Danes Fort in the Port of Christiansted on St. Croix. The Danes are supposedly neutral but they allow the Americans to come and go as they please. We know they supply the American ships and provide a ready market for the plunder brought to the island by American privateers. I have asked Lord Anthony to assign a squadron to attack St. Croix, free our people, and burn or take back our ship."

This brought forth another round of applause.

"Bloodthirsty lot, I declare," Lord Skalla said jokingly to Lord Anthony.

***

AFTER THE GROUP HAD taken their leave, Bart came back down to the great cabin. Pouring his cox'n two fingers of the Kentucky bourbon, Lord Anthony asked, "How did things go with Dagan?"

"'E knew before I told 'im. 'E said we're going after our ships and people, aren't we?"

"Aye," I said. "'E said 'e'd 'ad a feeling since Jepson's first lieutenant came in to the tavern where we was 'aving a wet and playing cards.

Bloke carried on about taking the corvette and such. Course, soon as the bugger spied us 'e closed 'is trap quick like. But aye, Dagan knew something was in the air."

"Any thoughts on how Faith will react?"

"Not peaceful like, yew can bet," Bart answered, and then picking up the glass of bourbon he sniffed it and then downed the drink in one swallow. "Tolerable," he admitted.

"Tolerable," Anthony repeated, not believing his ears. "You ungrateful dog! I pour you some of the finest liquor made and all you can say is tolerable. You just don't know fine liquor."

"I know's what I like. Now, yews welcome to yew's 'pinion and I's got mine. I might see if Dagan can get some of the St. Croix rum when they go. Now, that's fine rum...what a man drinks."

"Humph," Lord Anthony snorted. "Some folks never learn."

"Aye," Bart responded. "No matter 'ow 'ard I tries to teach 'em."

Stormy Day at Sea

It's a stormy day at sea
The sky is gray it's killing me
Not knowing what to do
'Bout this loneliness and you
The wind is howling
The thunder crashes
My soul sinks lower
With every mile that passes
It's a stormy day at sea

Michael Aye

CHAPTER EIGHTEEN

THE SHIP'S BELL RANG four times in the middle watch. It was two a.m. and Gabe had been up pacing the deck for the last hour. Lieutenant Wesley was the officer of the watch, but all the officers were up. Most of them were down in the wardroom enjoying a quick cup of coffee to chase away the cobwebs before the planned action started. The first lieutenant hovered over the compass in conversation with the master. The admiral was up but had not left his cabin to come topside. The crew, those not required for the watch, were eating a hurried breakfast, if that's what it could be called: cold salt meat, cheese, and ship's biscuit.

Gabe continued to pace. He and Faith had never departed on harsh terms. They'd never even fought. Maybe it was the sudden call to duty when they had expected a month or more together. Maybe it was because of the baby. Who knew? But the words had been said regardless, and the sting was still there.

"Then go…go the hell on and see if I give a damn. Go on your precious ship."

"Faith, we are at war," Gabe had pleaded.

"Oh yes, the King must punish the colonies for wanting their freedom and independence from tyranny with taxes so high we can't eat if we pay them. We are at war alright, but you are on the wrong side, Gabe."

"Faith," Gabe replied, trying to reason with his wife. "You don't mean that."

"Hell I don't, Captain Anthony, and the first ship going to the colonies will find me, the baby, Nanny, and Lum on it." With that, Faith slammed the bedroom door, leaving Gabe to stare at the painted wood.

"She's got a temper worse than her mama ever did," said Nanny. "But don't you worry, Mr. Gabe, she'll cry and come to her senses by tomorrow."

Turning, Gabe murmured, "I'll be gone by then, Nanny."

As Gabe walked out of the door of their cottage, Dagan was sitting on the steps. Rising, he placed his arm around Gabe's shoulder and said, "Sudden squalls usually pass over quickly."

However, Faith hadn't showed the next morning as Gabe departed.

***

ONE OF THE PEOPLE on the corvette captured by Jepson was the first mate of a merchant ship recently taken by the *Revenant*. He had been to St. Croix many times and was well aware of the waters around the island as well as the geography of the island. Using his knowledge, a plan was devised in the great cabin aboard *SeaHorse*. Admiral Buck and his captains, as well as Lord Skalla, Lord Anthony, and Captain Earl were all present. It was decided that a group would be landed ashore. A small vessel could enter St. Croix's Salt River where Christopher Columbus once anchored. It would only be a short march up a road to Christiansted and Fort Christianvaern.

The Danes were breaching their neutrality by keeping British captives locked up in the fort. Lord Skalla wanted the people freed, taking whatever action was required but avoiding as much bloodshed as possible. Therefore, he felt the person leading the assault on the fort needed to be someone of rank and position. Consequently, it fell on Gabe to lead the action.

Lieutenant Campbell had protested, "It's my place to go, sir."

"Aye, Donald, I don't disagree," Gabe answered. "Were I in charge of the operation, you would be the leader, but I'm not." Gabe understood his first lieutenant's feelings and didn't want the man to believe he was not trusted. However, he was reluctant to say anything that might be considered negative about Lord Skalla.

"We don't need to cause more of an international uproar than necessary," Lord Skalla had explained.

Gabe understood...if only Faith had.

***

LIEUTENANT JOHN JENKINS, CAPTAIN of *HMS Zebra*, watched as Gabe stepped through the entry port. There were no drums, pipes, or side party. Marines and sailors making up the shore party were brought aboard the sloop with as much silence as possible. Gabe, Hex, and Dagan were the last to board.

"With your permission I will get underway, Sir Gabe."

Gabe acknowledged the lieutenant with a nod. How strange it had sounded, in the wee hours of the morning, off an island where death might come at any minute...to be addressed as Sir Gabe.

The deck heaved as the sails filled with air. Caught off guard, Gabe stumbled into Hex. Catching his captain, Hex remarked, "Lively little sloop isn't she, Captain? Not steady like *Trident*."

"Aye," Gabe replied, glad he'd not busted his arse on a canting deck.

"It's a good night for the action, sir," Jenkins said as he returned. "Moon is bright and the master says the weather will hold."

"They usually know," Gabe agreed, trying to not let personal problems foul his relationship with this energetic young officer.

Jenkins' ship was one of the three sloops in Admiral Buck's squadron. It had been chosen to land the shore party, while *HMS Fortune* and *HMS Thorn* would enter the harbor at first light. Men from the two ships would retake, if possible, or burn any British or American ships at anchor. Gabe was to take the fort by land assault and row the freed prisoners out to the ships. If the assault failed they would return to the Salt River and be picked up by *Zebra*.

"How will we know if you've taken the fort?" Peter Parkinson, captain of *Fortune*, asked.

Before Gabe could reply, "We'll send up a flare," Joseph Taylor, captain of *Thorn,* said, "If you get buggered by a big thirty-two pound ball, hot off the furnace, you'll know they ain't." This brought a chuckle from the group.

***

GABE SAT IN THE wet stern sheets of the cutter as it heaved under a swell. When the men pulled with their oars they left a trail of phosphorescence in the dark, murky waters. The men had to be hushed as they whispered about such an unusual phenomenon. Even in this early hour, the humid heat had drenched the men in sweat. In the semi-darkness of a full moon the shadows of trees towering above the edges of the narrow Salt River could be seen. Huge nests of great white birds filled the trees.

Gabe whispered, "Caution." To disturb the birds would bring warning to everyone within miles.

A reek of decay from the swamp's edge filled the air, insulting the nostrils, at times almost gagging a few of the men. Making a turn in the river, a small island stood out, full of mangrove trees whose great tangled roots seem to crawl out into the brackish water. A faint sound carried to Gabe as he heard the surf washing up on a small beach. They bore to the left slightly and soon the hard-packed sand grated underneath the boat.

The men piled out of the boats and gathered along the narrow beach, tiny seashells crunching beneath their feet. Marine Captain Schoggins had his sergeant check the men's weapons, and wrap them in cloth to muffle any sound, before they started out.

The fort lay a little more than a league, some three to four miles, away, Gabe had been told. There was a road of sorts that stretched from Christiansted to Frederiksted at the other end of the island, some twenty-eight miles away. There would be little, if any, movement on the road at this early hour, but to get to the road they had to travel down the spongy wet path of a rain forest and mangrove swamp.

Leaving a few men with the boats, the party marched off. By the time the men made it to the road they'd been eaten alive by insects.

Pausing to rest a few minutes before starting down the road, Hex swore as he scraped a blood-swollen leech from his lower leg. "Between the mosquitoes, ticks, and leeches, I believe I've been sucked dry of blood."

Dagan sympathized with him. His body itched from head to toe from countless insect bites.

"I feel like I've been in a steam bath," Gabe swore as he tugged at the damp coat he'd worn. It had helped prevent some of the insect bites but the increased heat made him fill weak and exhausted.

"Captain." It was one of Schoggins' marines.

"Yes, Sergeant."

"There is a fresh water stream just up the trail. Probably not fit to drink, but might do to pour over yer head the cap'n says."

It couldn't hurt, Gabe thought, as he used a damp handkerchief to mop his face.

***

THE TOWN WAS ASLEEP in the predawn hours and there didn't seem to be any activity this side of the fort. A type of sea oak grew on the grounds between the warehouses, wharf, and the fort. Hex had recommended to Gabe that they bring along a couple of old poachers, Thorpe and Morgan. It was these men that Gabe sent out to see if any sentries were patrolling. The two were back within a quarter hour with two prisoners. One apparently had tried to resist and found a belaying pin bounced off his head for his troubles.

Trying to communicate with the Danes was difficult, but Gabe finally figured that a company of soldiers stayed inside the fort with one officer, who usually stayed in his quarters, frequently with one of the young ladies from town. The general lived in town and was probably at a festival being held in Frederiksted. The British prisoners were locked up in the dungeon except for the doctor, who was allowed to stay in the small hospital quarters.

Gabe looked at the sky; it was almost dawn. They had to hurry... hurry, but carefully and quietly. At the other side of town a dog barked...at what? Not his men, Gabe knew, but it wouldn't take much to set off the alarm.

"Robert," Gabe spoke to the marine captain, using his first name. "Are you ready?"

The tall marine smiled, "Whenever you are, sir."

"Mr. Hawks," Gabe spoke to his fifth lieutenant. "You are to set up a rear guard at the fort's gate in case we have to make a hurried departure. If you need me, send Mr. Thomas."

"Aye, Captain."

"Dagan, Jake," Gabe spoke to his uncle and cox'n. "Keep your heads down and your guard up."

CHAPTER NINETEEN

THE MEN MOVED LIKE a pack of wolves across the clearing between the warehouses and the fort, taking advantage of the oaks to provide cover as they ran. One-hundred fifty yards, one-hundred yards, fifty yards, and finally they were at the fort's back wall. No alarm had been sounded. Grappling hooks had been brought, but Thorpe and Morgan were nimbly up and over the wall. A thud and grunt was heard from inside.

Just as the gates were flung open, a shout rang out followed by a gunshot. Gabe and his men poured through the gate. From a parapet, a sergeant barked orders and a volley of muskets cracked out, while off to the side a trumpet blared.

"Forward, move damn you," Schoggins was shouting at his men.

Finding targets, the marines were firing, then kneeling as their comrades stepped around and fired. The soldiers on the wall, fewer in number now, fired a scattered volley at almost point blank range. Several of Gabe's men were cut down, which enraged their mates. The sounds of blows and curses were heard as those firing the muskets were quickly and savagely struck down. A pistol was fired almost in Hex's face. He turned sharply as the ball missed, but the powder singed his hair. Striking out with his blade, Hex took his foe down. Now men were pouring from the barracks, their muskets with bayonets fixed, joining the battle. The Danes may have woken to a great surprise but they had recovered quickly and fought like demons.

Snatching at Hex's arm to get his attention, Gabe shouted to be heard. "Take some men and spike the big guns...don't let them be used on the ships or us."

Hex nodded and was off, grabbing men to assist as he went. Gabe quickly lost sight of Hex's group as a man bellowed like a bull and charged at him with a musket and bayonet in his hand. Gabe struck at the barrel of the musket with his blade and then, like a dancer, did a quick side step. The move saved him. The bayonet passed a hair's breadth from his face. With a backhanded slash, Gabe cut his attacker down. The fighting continued but was ebbing as the British sailors and marines overwhelmed the Danes.

"So much for limiting bloodshed," Schoggins shouted.

"Aye," Gabe replied. Seeing Dagan, he shouted, "Get some men and free our people from the dungeon."

Dagan raised his sword in acknowledgment and was gone. Advancing to the front wall of the fort, Gabe could see Hex's men were busy with the cannons. The last pocket of resistance seemed to be contained, when out of the melee a smallish man with flowing blond hair leaped at Gabe. Startled, Gabe parried the man's blade out of instinct. Cursing and calling Gabe an English dog the man moved like a true swordsman.

"Surrender," Gabe called. Seeing his opponent was an officer, Gabe stepped back and tried to reason with the man. "Sir, the battle is over. Surrender and your life will be spared."

"Never," the man snapped, his chest heaving as he breathed. Several of Gabe's men had now surrounded the officer. "Sir," Gabe tried again. "Drop your weapon and you shall live. You have fought a brave fight. There can be no shame in an honourable surrender."

The officer's reply was to spit in Gabe's face and shout, "English bastard."

The outburst was followed by a pistol shot. The man's eyes seem to lose focus and glaze over just before he fell to the ground. It was Thorpe, still holding a smoking pistol.

As if to explain his actions, Thorpe volunteered, “I don’t let no man spit on me cap’n that way. Not respectful, ’ad no respect at all, the bugger didn’t.”

A flash from the parapet meant Hex had sent up a flare. It was now dawn. How long had the battle lasted? Not near as long as it had seemed.

“Sir.”

Gabe turned to face a man of short stature but who had a commanding voice. “I’m Doctor Robert Cornish. I will be glad to tend to your injured men if you will get them to my small facility.”

“Thank you, doctor,” Gabe replied. He then ordered Thorpe to assist the wounded to the sick quarters.

Hex returned and reported, “Our ships have entered the anchorage, sir.”

It finally dawned on Gabe the reports he was hearing were the cannons on the British ships entering the harbour.

“Good.” Gabe looked about the grounds then ordered, “Hex, find all the boats you can and get our people to the ships. Captain Schoggins, if you will assign a few men to gather our dead I want to move them out of the fort if we can.”

“That should not be a problem, sir. We’ve only lost a handful. I did take the liberty of having the fort’s people placed in their dungeon. See if they enjoy it any more than our people did.”

“You’re a devilish man, Captain…but I like it.”

“Thought you would, sir…gives them a taste of their own medicine.”

It took less than an hour to get everyone on boats and rowed out to the waiting ships. Midshipman Thomas had reported that a group of men were approaching the fort with a flag of truce.

“Have you or Lieutenant Hawkes spoken to them?” Gabe asked.

“No sir.”

"Then don't, but fire a shot over their heads. Well over their heads, mind you, and then report back to me."

Turning back to the marine captain, Gabe spoke again, "Captain Schoggins, I don't want anything left behind that can be used as evidence that the British navy was here."

"They've heard our voices, sir; surely they'll know we are English."

"They'll know we sounded like English," Gabe corrected. "But tell me, Captain, did you go ashore on St. Croix?"

"I don't know that I've even heard of the place, sir."

"Good man," Gabe said. "Now let's be off."

***

THE RENDEZVOUS BACK ABOARD *Trident* was overwhelming. Even Captain Sir Gabriel Anthony, who thought at this point in his career that nothing about the officers and men in his Majesty's navy could surprise him, was amazed. While the attack on the fort had caused more of a fight and casualities than desired, the attack on the ships in the harbor was nothing short of miraculous. The British merchant vessel had been retaken, and a small American gunboat had been set afire. Then Lieutenant Davy had a master's mate steer the retaken merchant ship close to a small Colonial privateer ship. He and a handful of tars were able to board and take that ship as well. A nifty little schooner of ten guns, the name *Tomahawk* was painted across the stern. Someone with a mind for the dramatic had emphasized the name by painting an Indian war ax with blood dripping off the blade. Her battery was made up of four six-pounders per side and two four-pounders on the fo'c'sle. She would need a complement of seventy to seventy-five hands.

Lieutenant Davy had not wasted his time after sailing out of the Danish harbour. By the time he reported aboard the flagship, he had made a fair inventory and inspection. "She is, in all aspects except for water, ready for sea," he reported with a boyish grin on his face.

The presence of a British surgeon at the fort had been fortuitous; he could be assigned as *Trident's* surgeon. Gabe would talk with the man after Lord Skalla had finished interviewing him about the incident in which *HMS Foxfire* had been taken and her captain killed… possibly murdered by one of the ship's own crew.

Norton, the *Foxfire's* first lieutenant, was one of those the doctor had been caring for in the small sick quarters at the fort. He'd tried to put up a fight when the merchant ship was taken. Hopefully, he'd survive. Most of the freed prisoners would be entered into the books on the ships in Admiral Buck's squadron. Those merchant seamen with certificates of immunity would be given passage back to England at some point.

After most of the business had been completed, Gabe sat finishing off the last of his wine when Admiral Buck spoke, "Gabe, I'm speaking to you as a friend and not as my flag captain." Surprised, Gabe nodded his understanding. Buck continued, "I remember when little Midshipman Davy reported aboard *Drakkar* looking like a drowned rat, but ready to fight at the drop of a hat. He's come a long way since then." Gabe continued to listen without interrupting; sure that he knew where this was going. "I'm tempted to put Davy in charge of his prize and recommend his Lordship confirms the appointment. My only question is what about Mr. Wiley?" The admiral then motioned for Chen Lee to fill their glasses and leaned back, letting Gabe catch his thoughts.

"As your friend, I think Mr. Davy is the right choice. As his captain, he has more than proved himself capable and I will support your decision whole-heartedly. Mr. Wiley is senior and is a good officer but lacks the experience Lieutenant Davy has gained these last four years or so. Battling the elements and the Americans, Lieutenant Davy showed initiative, sir. Seeing the schooner was ripe for the taking, he decided to take her. I don't think Lieutenant Wiley would have acted so quickly and decisively. He will make a good captain soon. Mr. Davy is ready now."

"Aye," Buck said, leaning forward to take a pull from the recharged glass. "Our thoughts are one and the same."

A knock at the door interrupted the conversation as the marine sentry announced, "Lord Skalla, sir."

CHAPTER TWENTY

GABE WATCHED AS THE little schooner, *Tomahawk*, disappeared from sight. Lieutenant Davy now had his own command. Gabe had little doubt his brother would confirm the appointment. Davy was to escort the merchantman back to Barbados with all dispatch. Lord Skalla was a passenger, so Davy had little to worry about in regards to the merchantman's captain grumbling about being pushed along so. When Admiral Buck had spoken with the man, he quickly reminded the fellow he could still be in the Danes dungeon at the fort.

Lord Skalla had found out by interviewing several of the prisoners that the American privateers were to join a French squadron under French Admiral Suffren to prey upon British shipping as they traveled from the Indian Ocean back to England. The intelligence suggested the French would send out scouts from Ile de France. The American privateers would be based on a small island off Madagascar known as St. Mary's by the English and Ile Sainte-Marie by the French.

The Indian Ocean was a vital route for the British economy. East India Company ships sailed from China, India, and Arabia loaded down with millions of pounds worth of trade goods. The loss of these ships would devastate the British economy.

Lord Skalla had been most convincing, "I know your orders were to the Southern Colonies, Admiral, but we must act now. Time is not on our side."

Now Lord Skalla sailed with Lieutenant Davy to make sure Lord Anthony and England were made aware of this very real threat. As Davy and *Tomahawk* vanished over the horizon, so did Gabe's hope of making things right with Faith. He had given a letter to Davy who'd promised to deliver it personally.

"Marry Ariel first chance you get while I have Dagan occupied," Gabe had joked.

"He's already given his blessing," Davy responded. "But we'll wait until you return."

As the two shook hands at the entry port, Davy fought back emotion. "I never would have made it without you, Gabe. You and Dagan, that is. Now this, my first ship. The admiral told me you had given your strongest recommendation."

"You've earned it," Gabe replied, his voice cracking with emotion. "Now be off with you."

Davy paused once more before starting down the battens into the waiting boat. "Take care of yourself, Captain, and God speed."

"To you as well, Captain Davy," Gabe replied.

Hex broke Gabe's reverie when he spoke. "He'll be fine, Captain."

"It is not Lieutenant Davy I'm worried about, Jake."

"I know, Captain...it's time for your talk with the new doctor," Hex reminded his captain.

"Thank you," Gabe replied absently, taking one more look at the empty horizon before turning away.

"Got a lot on his mind," Hex volunteered as Dagan walked up.

"Damnable war," Dagan cursed as he ducked down, almost colliding with Mr. Sebastian, the signals midshipman, who was returning flags to their locker.

"My apologies," the youth blurted out.

"On with you, youngster," Dagan replied as he lit his pipe. He was rewarded with a glow from the pipe bowl. Sending the smell of aromatic smoke into the air, Dagan rose up and spoke to his friend, "Faith will see the error of her ways, given time. I just hope Gabe's mind is on his business when the fighting comes."

"We're in for a row then," Hex stated.

"Aye, Jake, a big one if my feelings are right." Hex sighed; he'd not known Dagan to be wrong yet. Seeing Hex's despair, Dagan smiled, "No need to worry, Jake. A Frenchie's ball is no different than that of a jealous husband."

"Aye, but there's a mite of enjoyment that usually comes along before the jealous husband," Jake replied.

***

MIDSHIPMAN BRAYDEN TAPPED ON the door of Gabe's cabin. "Mr. Campbell's respects, sir, and we have sighted several sails on the horizon."

Gabe had heard the cry of "sail ho" but was determined not to rush on deck. He wondered if Buck had found enough to keep him in his cabin or if his curiosity were too great to control and he would find a reason to go for a look.

The youth continued to stand so Gabe prompted, "Is there more?"

"Looks like a whole company of 'Honest Johns'," the boy blurted. "Ere, that's what Mr. Campbell thinks, sir."

"Very well, tell the first lieutenant I will be up directly."

"Aye, sir, directly it is."

It was a full ten days since the squadron had set sail in search of the French and American privateers. A single sail had been spotted. The wind had been contrary at times, making the master, David Hayes, question his recollection of the trade winds from the Caribbean to the coast of Africa. The course lay south-by-southeast toward Africa. And then following the coast of Africa, around the Cape of Good Hope they'd sail to Madagascar, which lay approximately two hundred fifty miles off the eastern coast of Africa.

The privateers were said to have their main base at St. Mary's or Ranter Bay, both of which were on the northeastern side of the island. Ranter Bay was an enclave of the main island, while St. Mary's lay about five miles off Madagascar. In the 1720's, pirates preyed on Britain's East India Company ships, using the same island for bases, so what the French and Americans were attempting was not something new. The British navy had dealt with the problem then and would do so again. The question was how much help Admiral Buck's small squadron of ships would be given, if any, and could the problem be dealt with before the British were bankrupt?

"It's the pirate round revisited," Hayes stated.

"You were there back then?" Midshipman Caed had asked in all innocence, hearing the master talk about the pirates in their heyday. This brought a chuckle from all.

"Not even our master was around back then," Lieutenant Wiley chided.

Admiral Buck had the squadron change tack to intercept the East Indiamen. The captain of the escorting frigate seemed glad to have a diversion from the monotony of convoy duty. Taking advantage of Gabe's offer of refreshments, the captain went aboard *Trident* and enjoyed a wet with Gabe and Admiral Buck.

"No, I've not heard of the combined French and American forces but am not surprised to hear it," the captain said to Gabe and Buck.

They'd had a small warship, likely a French corvette, follow them for a day after they rounded Cape of Good Hope. During the night the ship must have come about, as it was nowhere to be seen at dawn. The convoy was scheduled to lay over at Barbados, taking on water and supplies. They'd then use the trade winds to sail north until they hit the westerly winds. A voyage Gabe had made several times. *I'd like to make the first leg of it now*, he thought. The captain agreed to carry a few personal letters to Barbados along with Buck's dispatches.

That night, Gabe dined with the admiral as usual. The skylight was open and a faint zephyr stirred. The sky was cloudless and the stars were bright with a full moon shining down, lighting up the main deck and reflecting off the smooth sea. Dr. Cornish had also been invited to dine that evening, and upon hearing the shanties and music being played on deck remarked at how pleasant it was to sail on a happy ship.

Gabe noticed that the admiral had not eaten all of his noodles. "Damn Chinaman," Buck snorted. "Chen Lee is a great little servant, but thinks every meal has to have noodles or rice. Some of his concoctions are so blame hot and spicy, sweat breaks out on my head before I can eat it."

"Well, don't eat it," Cornish replied.

"There lays the problem," Buck countered. "It's too damn tasty to let set."

"Well damme," Gabe declared with a chuckle.

Cigars were brought out and each of the men was given a splash of bourbon. Topside, the music changed.

"That's Hex's mandolin," Gabe announced.

"A talented musician," Cornish said, after listening for a minute. The three had stopped talking as Hex played.

"That and more," Gabe said acknowledging the doctor's comments.

After a couple of up-tempo shanties, the tempo slowed and Hex began to sing:

Baby, come to me while I'm in Portsmouth
The ships gonna be here a month or so
We can get us a room over a tavern
And love away the hours, while I'm ashore
Baby, come to me.

She said you're the only man I've ever loved
But a sailor's life is just too hard to live
All the sea does is take away...and
I have given all I have to give
Baby, come to me.

Baby come to me as the snow falls
We'd move up so high you can't see the sea
You can build us a little cabin

And every night you can make love to me
Baby, come to me.
He said I'd love to be with you in the mountains
But the sea is the only life I've ever known
Now it's time for us to weigh anchor
By the time you get this letter I'll be gone
I wish you'd come to me...
She cried I wish you'd come to me.

"I say that boy is too talented for the sea," Cornish stated after finishing off his drink.

"Nay," Buck replied. "He's too good not to be at sea."

"I don't know what I'd do if he wasn't," Gabe said as he stood and left without saying goodnight.

"Our captain is in a bad way," Cornish said. He then added, "Speaking professionally of course."

"Aye," Buck's voice was hardly above a whisper, "I've known him since he was a young middy, and I've never seen him like this. Dagan says there are brighter days ahead, though."

"Admiral," Cornish said, "would I be imposing if I asked you to tell me about Dagan? I can hardly believe the whispers I hear."

Buck rose and a smile lit up his face, "Chen Lee...recharge our glasses please."

CHAPTER TWENTY-ONE

"CAP'N...CAP'N, WAKE UP CAP'N."

"Hex."

"Aye, cap'n."

"What is it, Hex?"

"The lookout has spied a light in the water, sir. He's not sure if it is a boat or what. Says it's too low down in the water to be a ship, even a small one."

Rising up, Gabe could hear the normal sounds of a ship: the sound of water sluicing by the rudder, the groan of the timbers, and the occasional slap of a wave against the hull. How long had he been asleep? Only minutes it felt like. After putting on his britches, Gabe leaned over to put on his boots. As he did so, he felt a pain in his upper stomach and a burning sour taste as bile came up in his mouth. *Chen Lee's dinner*, he thought. *What was it Buck had said? Damn tasty but hard on the digestion*. With nowhere to spit, Gabe swallowed, which caused him to cough.

Finally he wheezed out, "Give me something to drink, Hex." He could hear his cox'n fumbling around and the clink of glass on glass.

"Here is a bit of something, sir."

Gabe took note of the "of something". Hex had grabbed the first decanter he'd found in the semi-darkness. The only light in the cabin was the one lantern that Hex had set down on the small table beside Gabe's cot. *Brandy*, Gabe thought as he took a big swallow. Well, that beat the sour taste that had filled his mouth and burned so.

Stepping over the coaming and out onto the deck, Gabe could feel a cool breeze. It was a full moon, and so the deck was lit up well. Lieutenant Wiley must have the watch, as he was telling the first lieutenant he'd sent Midshipman Michael to the tops to see if he could make out whatever it was the lookout had spotted.

"Seaman Rogers has a keen eye," Wiley was explaining, "but his descriptive ability is thin as a sailor's purse after a night on shore."

This made Gabe chuckle, which alerted the men around the wheel that the captain was on deck. "Captain," the group greeted in unison.

"We are waiting on Mr. Michael's report, are we not?" Gabe asked after nodding his greeting.

Hayes quickly advised, "We are south-southeast with a steady wind, sir, almost directly astern."

Before Gabe could thank the master, they heard a thump as Michael hit the deck harder than planned.

"I bet his hands are burning," Campbell volunteered.

Michael had taken the faster route down to the deck by sliding down a backstay. Indeed, he was blowing on his palms as he approached the wheel.

"You break that glass, young sir, and you'll spend the rest of the voyage in the tops," said Campbell, but his voice held no real threat. It was just his way of telling Michael to be careful. Looking up from his palms, Michael was smiling until he saw the captain.

When the youth didn't speak, Gabe asked, "Are we to wait until surgeon sees to your hands, or are you able to report now?"

"Sorry sir, it's much as the lookout says. A light, sir. Must be a lantern tied up high on a small boat. You can see it and then it disappears. Kind of like a cork on a fishing line when you are getting a nibble."

"Damme, sir," Wiley snorted. "But that is as useless a description as I've heard."

"No, not really," Gabe said, saving the mid's pride, "a small boat, say a longboat, adrift with a lantern lashed to an oar. It's somebody's attempt to bring attention to themselves. Fire off a flare, Mr. Campbell. If it's a boat as I imagine, and if there are people still alive in the boat it will give them encouragement. Mr. Michael."

"Aye, Captain."

"Good description. Now be so kind as to wake the admiral. Give him my compliments and tell him about our...er nibble."

"Aye, Captain," a smiling Michael replied as he turned to do as ordered.

Light was visble through the open skylight, so Gabe was sure the admiral was already awake and dressed, waiting to be alerted. Would he have the patience to wait below, Gabe wondered? A flash and suddenly the sky was bright as the flare was set off. That should let those in the boat know they'd been spotted. Those on watch on the other ships in the squadron as well. A smile came to Gabe as he thought of all the captains being rousted out by the sight of the flare.

"That will wake a few." This was from Dagan.

"I didn't know you were awake," Gabe said.

"Aye, had the feeling something was amiss."

"Amiss!?" It was the admiral.

Gabe quickly explained their sighting and added that whatever it was...wasn't yet visible from the deck.

Off to the side, Hex was speaking to Dagan and Crowe, the admiral's cox'n, "Wouldn't it be great if we could come up with the ability to communicate better with other ships at night? Better than the limited system we have now."

Overhearing the conversation, Buck said, "What was that, Hex?"

"I was saying, sir, it would be nice to set-up a system to communicate with the other ships even if we had to use colored lanterns to do so."

Crowe then joined the conversation, "Sort of like we did in Deal."

"I want to hear about this," Buck said. "Let's go below. Captain, if your duties allow it you may want to hear this."

"Aye, sir," Gabe replied.

Quite possibly these two smugglers were about to reveal a trick or two. They were well organized and rarely caught. If they were, it was usually due to bad luck or a tip by a competitor out to get them.

Turning to Lieutenant Campbell and Lieutenant Wiley, Gabe spoke, "Send for me once we get a better idea of what our light is." With that, Gabe went thru the companionway into the admiral's cabin, passing a sleepy looking sentry.

Once in the cabin, the admiral greeted him and stated he'd sent Chen Lee to get some coffee. With coffee poured and everyone settled down, Hex looked around sheepishly. He was uneasy about what he was about to say.

Seeing his cox'n's unease, Gabe volunteered, "Hex, I think I speak not only for myself but for the admiral as well when I tell you any information you share with us will not be disclosed to the Revenue Service."

"Thank you, sir. It's very simple really and you must understand, sir, our signals were mainly to alert other boats we were in company with as to dangers or changes. A lantern with a green glass would be hoisted to larboard and a regular lantern to starboard. If a revenue cutter or danger was spotted we'd hoist a lantern with a red glass below either the starboard or larboard lantern to show the direction for caution. A red glassed lantern between the two meant dead ahead."

"Where did you get different colored glass?" Buck asked.

Before Hex could answer, Crowe blurted, "Out of churches."

"Most churches of any size have stained glass windows," Hex explained. "It doesn't take much for a good man to take a bit of lead and a hot iron to fashion lanterns with colored glass."

"The navy has a rudimentary system with lanterns," Buck said. "You usually have to fire a flare before they are noticed, however.

"Well, sir, our boats sail close together, but the signal could be passed on so to speak. Now, the color of lantern could be changed by the captain of the lead boat before we went out if the captain was worried about treachery. We would dip a lantern to either side if it was desired for the other boats to come alongside," Hex said.

"Wouldn't the lanterns alert the customs boats you were about?" Buck asked.

"Aye," Hex replied. "But they didn't know what the signals meant. Remember the codes could be changed each time before putting off. Even if one of the boats were caught, the signals would usually allow the others to escape."

"When were the lanterns lit?" Buck inquired.

"Only when necessary, sir, remember we didn't even burn a stern light."

"Aye," Crowe spoke up, "our success depended on not being seen. Most of the time it was when we returned that we'd have to worry. At times we'd cast our cargo over the side with a barrel or some type of buoy attached."

"Wouldn't that be spotted?" Gabe asked.

"Not usually," Hex replied. "Not unless you knew where to look. The buoy was usually on a short rope and so it was just under the surface. We would come back in a fishing boat later. We'd grapple the buoy and haul our cargo aboard."

"Course, we'd have a couple on board making a show of fishing," Crowe added.

Gabe looked at Dagan. As a midshipman, he had spent time aboard a customs boat with Dagan.

"We catch the odd smuggler now and then, as they let us," the lieutenant in charge of the revenue cutter had told Gabe and Dagan. "They usually get fined and a little vacation time in the gaol. Course, his mates would pay the fine and the magistrate would get his cut. It's all a show if you ask me."

The lieutenant had continued, "If they really wanted to stop the smuggling they'd send out a fleet of customs cutters then send a few up the halter."

Gabe's train of thought was broken as the sentry announced, "Midshipman of the watch, sir."

"Lieutenant Wiley's compliments, sir. It's just as you thought, Captain, a long boat."

"Well, damme," Buck said.

CHAPTER TWENTY-TWO

THE BOAT HAD INDEED been bobbing like a cork on a fishing line. Three men sat in the boat. "Look like drowned rats, they do," Hayes volunteered.

Campbell, seeing that the men had no control of the boat, had sent a boat to tow it to the flagship. The men did look like drowned rats, soaked through to the skin and shivering. They were in a bad way.

"Bond, sir," a man spoke as he was helped through the entry port. "I was formerly a lieutenant aboard *HMS Raven* of eighteen guns."

"What happened to your ship, Lieutenant?" Buck asked.

"We were taken, sir, yesterday at dawn. A group of privateers, sir, but only two had been spotted when the captain decided to fight. When the third joined, a small frigate that looked to be British, the captain decided to surrender. He was wounded and the first lieutenant was already dead. The captain had sent me below to cast our papers and dispatches over the side. When I returned on deck the captain was dead. We were given a choice by the captain in charge of the privateers. A boat or join the Americans."

"Only three took the boats?" Buck asked incredibly.

"There were more," the lieutenant stated. "Two boats in fact. However, the wind got up and a rogue wave almost swamped us. Three men out of our boat went over the side along with the water cask, a case of food, all but one oar, and the lantern. As dark came on I had the oar put up and the lantern lashed to it."

"What happened to the other boat?"

"I don't know, sir. The master was in it. He was a good man. My men, sir, they're in a bad way."

"They've been taken to the surgeon," Gabe advised the lieutenant.

"Good men they are, sir. Laqua is a master's mate, and Sizemore is a gunner's mate."

"We will make sure they are cared for, Lieutenant," Buck said. "Now, before you go down to be checked out yourself, tell me: did you hear or learn anything from the rogues that took your ship."

The shivering man thought for a minute. He'd been given a blanket when he came aboard and now Crowe handed him a glass.

"This will warm you a bit, sir," Crowe then turned to the admiral. "With your permission, sir?"

"Yes, yes," Buck responded. "I'm glad someone is thinking."

"Experience," Crowe replied. "Been in an open boat once myself."

After downing the glass of fiery liquid, the lieutenant shook involuntarily and said, "Thank you." Handing the empty glass back to Crowe, Bond said, "The privateer who boarded us said he was Captain Horne."

This caused Gabe and Buck to look at each other. The same bloody privateer they were chasing, and his ship was probably the *Foxfire*.

As the lieutenant was led to the surgeon, he stopped. Turning to the admiral, he said, "I believe Laqua mentioned he overheard one of the privateers say something about Trinidad or Tobago, sir. But you'd have to ask him to be sure."

"Thank you," Buck said. "Now, go see the surgeon." Buck watched the lieutenant disappear through the companionway. As he was led below, Buck seemed deep in thought. After a moment he seemed to have made a decision. "Captain Anthony."

"Aye, sir."

"Have the master get what charts he may have of Trinidad and Tobago and bring them down to my cabin. You and the first lieutenant come as well."

"Aye, aye, sir," Gabe replied.

Wine was poured by Chen Lee as the group met in the great cabin. "No hot water for coffee," Chen Lee said in his broken English.

The master laid out his chart on the table. Using a couple of decanters to hold the map open, he began, "The island of Tobago lies here, sir, just a few miles north of Trinidad. It was governed by us when this chart was made. Course it's probably changed hands a hundred times." This created a chuckle as Hayes figured it would. "Trinidad is the island lying south of Tobago and to the north of Venezuela. It's held by the Dons."

"If you were a privateer, Mr. Hayes, where would you choose to anchor?" Buck asked.

"Well, Admiral, there's a good many. On the Caribbean side, either Port of Spain, which lies off this peninsula," Hayes said pointing with a caliper. "Fullarton is more southerly about here." Again he was pointing to a spot on the map. "Moruga lies here to the south as well. Being on the southern end of Trinidad and just off the northern coast of Venezuela, it would be a good, sheltered anchorage, as well."

Looking over the master's shoulder, Gabe asked, "What's this passage here?"

Hayes responded with a smile, "That's called the Serpent's Mouth. It lays off Icacos Point here," this time he was pointing with his index finger, "and Venezuela."

Lieutenant Campbell, who'd been silent thus far said, "So, if I was a pirate anchored here in Moruga and spotted a warship I'd have a choice of trying to escape into the Atlantic Ocean or go through the Serpent's Mouth into this..."

"Gulf of Paria," Hayes filled in for the first lieutenant.

"Thank you," Campbell said, and then continued, "and out into the Caribbean Sea where I could go in any direction I desired."

"You are right, Mr. Campbell," the admiral agreed. "We'd have to guard both entrances."

"Might be on station until the war is over," Gabe said.

"Oh?" Buck inquired.

"Spain is supposed to be neutral, sir, but we know where their allegiance lies. American privateers frequently take their prizes to Havana or San Juan in spite of their neutral status, much as the Danes did at St. Croix. Horne, if he's there, could probably stay as long as he desired. If you recall, Admiral, Lord Skalla said that with the French out on the side of the Americans, the Dons would likely follow suit. If they've not already done so."

"Aye, Gabe. I remember our foreign office man's concerns."

"Would it not be wise to call on the governor at Tobago?" Campbell asked. "Hopefully, he'd have a better grasp of both the political arena and a likely anchorage for the privateers."

"I think our first lieutenant is right," Gabe said as he gazed at the predawn light through the cabin's stern window.

Seeing Gabe's gaze, Buck spoke, "I've kept you too long from your duties, Captain, so I'll detain you no longer. After quarters, see if you can find out any more from our new volunteers. Maybe they can add a touch more light on the matter."

Gabe didn't miss the double meaning in his use of the word light. Campbell was also quick to pick up on new recruits, and thought new hands were always welcome, regardless of from where they're plucked.

***

ADMIRAL BUCK WAS GREETED by Tobago's Lieutenant-Governor General, Peter Campbell, who explained that the island's governor had been killed in a duel. Thus far, a replacement had not been furnished by London. So Campbell continued as the acting governor. Without being asked, the man volunteered, "We are a small island, Admiral, with limited resources, but we will be glad to accommodate your squadron as much as possible."

"Thank you," Buck replied. "You are most gracious. Having not long ago been in Barbados, our needs are few."

The governor general then invited Buck and his captains to dine with him that evening.

***

AT EIGHT P.M., DINNER was served after the governor general introduced his wife. Buck in turn introduced Gabe as his flag captain, and then the captains of the other ships in his squadron.

"Someone so young for such an important position," Mrs. Campbell said, speaking of Gabe.

Gabe smiled, not sure how to respond, but Buck came to his rescue. "A lifetime of experience packed into a few years of war, Madam."

"I understand," the woman replied sincerely. "This is a peaceful island, yet we are under constant fear of the French or even Colonial invaders. We are occasional guests...political guests...of the Spanish on Trinidad. Yet who can say what tomorrow will bring."

"I see there's work going on at the fort," Gabe mentioned.

"Humph."

This drew a sharp look from Campbell at his wife's grunt. "We are now putting the finishing touches on Fort King George," Campbell said defensively.

"Peter has to be the politician, but I don't." It was apparent the lieutenant governor's wife had a mind of her own, which Gabe had found was not uncommon among the island women.

"Charlotteville has the fort to protect it from the enemy," Mrs. Campbell was saying. "But it does nothing to help or defend the island's other towns, especially those on the eastern side. What will the fort do to protect the people of Scarborough or Canaan, or even Plymouth for that matter?"

"As you see, gentlemen, my wife is very passionate in some areas."

Thinking how Mrs. Campbell reminded him of Faith, Gabe responded, "I have a wife made of the same fiber, sir. I often find it easier to make a hasty retreat."

Everyone laughed but Mrs. Campbell, who mouthed, "Smart man."

CHAPTER TWENTY-THREE

ADMIRAL BUCK'S OFFICERS GATHERED around a large mahogany table in one of the meeting rooms at Government House. A sweet lime juice was offered as refreshment. It was good but would have been better had there been ice. Gabe watched as John Jenkins looked at the thin slice of lime floating on top of the juice. After a moment, he reached in with his finger and caught the slice. Tearing it in half, he devoured the piece of fruit, letting the peel fall back into the glass. Leaning over to his friend, Peter Parkinson of the *Fortune*, he explained, "It'd be better with salt."

Joseph Taylor was leaning back in his chair with his eyes closed. *He must have had a long night,* Gabe thought. He knew several of the officers had left the governor's house and enjoyed a few wets at one of Charlotteville's few taverns. Admiral Buck had spent the night ashore, as the Campbells' guest. He and Gabe had talked with the governor general after the other officers had thanked the Campbells for their hospitality and departed. Cuban cigars were passed around as Campbell informed his guests that they were a gift from the governor of Trinidad.

"I pass them out sparingly," he said, as he held a candle so that Buck could light his.

"You could give them all away and not hurt my feelings," Mrs. Campbell volunteered. "The stinking things."

Buck stopped puffing, not sure what to do.

"Go ahead, Admiral, light your cigar. I just wanted to take a moment to say it's good to have someone from the outside world stop in. Captain Anthony, congratulations on your son."

The fact that Gabe had a new son had come up during dinner. As Mrs. Campbell left, the governor general handed the candle to Buck to finish lighting his cigar. He spoke to a servant who left the room but quickly returned with a decanter and three glasses. Brandy was poured and the servant departed. *Out of sight but close at hand*, Gabe thought. Admiral Buck, with a glass in one hand and a cigar in the other, filled in Campbell on the taking of the *Foxfire*, its cargo of gold and silver, and the likelihood that they would join up with the French preying on British convoys.

"We've had a few raids here," Campbell admitted. "Usually they've taken no more than could be carried in a long boat, but on a couple of occasions they've taken ships. One was a planter's vessel that was loaded down with cargo to be sent to England."

"Do you think Horne and his cohorts could be using Trinidad for a base?" Buck asked.

Campbell thought for a minute, taking a draw on his cigar and exhaling, he said, "It's possible. Not in Port of Spain, that would be flaunting the neutrality too much. But it'd not surprise me if he's found a small village along one of the many beaches or in some inlet. As to which one, I couldn't guess."

***

A HUSH FELL OVER the group of officers as Admiral Buck and the governor general walked into the meeting room at Government House. After a quick greeting, Buck got right to business. "We have every reason to believe the American, Horne, and his raiders may be using Trinidad as a base of operation."

William Peckham, of the frigate *Venus*, raised his hand. "Captain Peckham," Buck called on him.

"Is this as opposed to what we were led to believe in regards to St. Mary's, Admiral?"

"In truth, we don't know," Buck admitted. "The Dons are still neutral, as far as we know, so I doubt they'd risk international attention by openly breaking the neutrality. Therefore, I believe this is just a stopping point where they can replenish before going on to their rendezvous. But remember, gentlemen, it's a long way to either Madrid or London. It would take a year or more before one government could complain to another."

All of the squadron's officers knew well what their admiral meant. Anything could happen.

"What I intend to do is pay my respects to the Spanish governor at Port of Spain," Buck said. "I will do so in one of our sloops. Captain Anthony will decide which one."

Thanks a lot, Gabe thought.

"After paying my respects, if allowed, we will make our way through the Gulf of Paria, through to Serpent's Mouth. and out into the Atlantic, sailing as close to the coast as possible. If we spot anything we will make our way back here and make plans accordingly."

"Sir," Captain Lamb spoke. "Wouldn't it be good to have the squadron patrol the eastern coast while you're at Port of Spain?"

"I've thought about that," Buck answered. "Captain Anthony has already made that recommendation. However, the knowledge of a British squadron patrolling off the coast of their island might mean a different reception by the Dons. No, I'll go in one ship. The rest of you will remain here. Captain Anthony will be in command until my return. Unless there are any more questions you are free to go about your duties."

Gabe stood and asked the three sloop commanders to remain. After everyone had filed out, Gabe saw a servant with a broom. He called to the servant who was surprised to see this naval officer snatch a straw from her broom. Smiling, he thanked her then walked away. Gabe broke the straw into three pieces, two relatively the same length and one shorter.

Placing them in his fist, he smiled at the three commanders and said, "Draw straws, gentlemen. The short straw, the unlucky one, gets to ferry the admiral about while the other two get to laze about the island until our admiral returns."

John Jenkins drew the short straw. "We'll be thinking about you, John, while we consort with the island ladies," the other sloop captains joked.

Gabe knew it was nothing but talk. In truth, Taylor and Parkinson were envious. Having the admiral on your ship would get your name in a report at the least and possibly earn a man an early promotion if the situation arose.

***

DAGAN SAT ACROSS FROM Gabe. He'd been trying to assure Gabe that all would be well with Faith when they returned. 'Trying' was the key word, as he really didn't have a good feel. Too many things seemed to be crowding his mind: his sister back in Portsmouth, Betsy in the colonies, and the mission ahead. *Squalls*, he kept thinking. Squalls, and Gabe's mind elsewhere. Hex had a done a good job, actually better than good, but now...now Dagan felt he would be needed, and before too long. *Gabe...well, Gabe isn't the only one who needs to clear his mind*, Dagan thought.

A knock at the door and Hex entered. The marine sentries had long since learned that Dagan and Hex came and went as they pleased. There was no need to announce either.

"*Zebra* has been spotted," Hex said, confirming Gabe's suspicion when he'd heard the lookout's cry. "I told the first lieutenant that I'd bring word, sir, so the young gentleman could continue his lessons with the master."

Gabe could just hear Hayes as he patiently tried to teach the middies how to go about the noontime sights. Gabe could remember his first master. "Pay attention, Mr. Anthony, I'll not have the admiral say I was remiss in teaching his son the proper technique." A rap across his backside with a bosun's starter once when he'd been daydreaming during a lesson assured the master he had young Anthony's full attention in the future.

Admiral Buck's head had just broken the entry port when the shrill of the bosun's pipe and honours were rendered. Buck bowed and quickly doffed his hat. As he shook hands with Gabe, he said, "Have the captains repair on board, and then come down to my cabin."

"Aye," Gabe said, and then turned to the first lieutenant.

"I've sent for the signal midshipman, sir," he said.

"Damn, but that was quick," Gabe quipped.

"I was expecting it, sir," Campbell replied, and then added, "I also overheard the admiral." Gabe clapped his first lieutenant on the shoulder, and then turned to go below.

The officers gathered in the cramped space of the great cabin. Seeing the officers so close, Buck felt a pang of guilt at taking the sixty-four as a flagship. She was not meant to be utilized so. No need to dwell on it now, though.

After a quick greeting, Buck got down to business. "I am sure Captain Jenkins will be glad to have his ship back," he began which caused the officers to laugh. Once they quieted down, Buck continued, "The Dons were cordial, but cool and closed mouthed when I tried to bring up the possibility of American privateers on the island. The only real response was, 'I've not been informed of such'. However, Captain Jenkins took the opportunity to talk with a fisherman who'd brought his catch to the city's market. Telling the man how much he liked fish but alas had no opportunity to do much fishing, he asked if he might purchase enough for his crew to enjoy a good meal. It would be a delightful change from the routine ship's fare. The old man was glad to make such a sell and was even happier when our good captain invited the man aboard for a glass to seal the deal."

Buck paused and said, "Should any of you like to add fish to your evening meal, I'm sure Captain Jenkins has plenty to share." The men smiled and then broke out in laughter when Buck said, "But if Chen Lee hears that, I'll have the informant flogged around the squadron."

Crowe, who was standing in the back of the cabin, swallowed hard and wondered if he could intercept the admiral's servant.

Buck continued on, "Aside from the addition of fish to our diet, the other benefit of Jenkins' time with the fisherman is that the man told our good captain the Americans don't care for fish as much as the British do. It seems there are several ships anchored just off the beach from his fishing village. Moruga, gentlemen, is where our foe is spending his days. We purposely avoided the area when we departed, going back through the Caribbean rather than taking the Serpent's Mouth. Now, here is what I plan."

CHAPTER TWENTY-FOUR

UNDER TOPSAILS AND CLOSE-HAULED, Jenkins' sloop was jammed full of men and towed two of *Trident's* boats, a launch and a cutter. Buck sat in the sloop's tiny cabin, which was sparsely furnished. No extra trimmings or extravagance. The cabin was like the man, nothing false or flashy.

Jenkins was a confident captain and had a thoroughly trained and seasoned crew. His subordinates were reliable and showed confidence in their handling of the ship. Another testament to their captain, who had no doubt, trained them well.

Making his way into the dimly lit cabin, Jenkins informed the admiral, "We are about a mile off the coast, sir. The wind is picking up and will make for a hard pull in the boats."

Buck went to stand and remembered just in time to duck the overhead beam. Jenkins handed him a cup, "A bit of something to warm you up, sir." A cup of lukewarm coffee, but laced liberally with brandy.

I wonder if he knows Silas, Buck thought, thinking of Lord Anthony's man. Once on deck, Buck was met by Lieutenant Campbell. *Trident's* first lieutenant would lead the cutting out. Buck could also see the marines as they stood by, waiting for *Zebra* to lower two of her long boats.

Blocks squeaked and the ship's boats made their way from the boat tiers and down alongside the ship. Soon, sailors and marines were going over the side and down into the waiting boats.

Buck walked up to Lieutenant Campbell and said, "It's your party, Lieutenant, so act as you see fit. If you can cut out one of our ships so be it, if not, try to fire a cannon through the bottom or set it afire. I don't want that bloody Horne to use any more of our ships against us, if at all possible."

"I understand," Campbell said.

Campbell was to send the cutter ashore. Jenkins' first lieutenant was in charge of that party. "Gunter is a good man," Jenkins said. *He'd better be*, thought Campbell.

After a steady row for what seemed like an eternity, the master's mate, Laqua, made his way aft to the stern sheets. "I can see light from ashore, sir. Looks like campfires, several of them."

"Cease rowing," Campbell ordered.

The other boats, which had been directly astern following in the launch's wake, pulled alongside. The seamen were all tired from the long pull into the wind. Gunter was to take a party and create a diversion ashore. Once that was done, Campbell's party would see about the ships.

"Remember, Gunter, a diversion," Campbell cautioned. "We don't want to needlessly risk any life or kill any of the islanders. That would cause problems with the Dons. Otherwise, Admiral Buck would have sailed in with the squadron and given the rogues a broadside or two. We will give you a ten...no, fifteen minute head start, and then make our way to the anchored ships. Remember – create a diversion, then pull back. If a man falls, bring him with you."

"Aye," Gunter said, acknowledging his instructions.

"Now, everyone put on your armbands and you be off." Campbell watched as the cutter pulled off. A hard row going ashore but the wind would be at their backs for the return trip.

As the three boats bobbed about, Campbell frequently checked his watch. The men were silent, each deep in his own thoughts, most of them hoping the pre-dawn expedition would result in a bit of prize money. Finally, he ordered the men back at their oars. After ten minutes of steady pulling, Laqua passed the word he could make out two ships anchored dead ahead and another off to larboard.

"Pass the word for Laqua to come aft," Campbell whispered to the closest seaman. Soon the stout figure was in the stern sheets hovering over Campbell.

"Let's pull in between the two ships and hook onto the main chains. Keep the men quiet but ready," Campbell said. "If there appears to be no anchor watch, up you go. I'd like to be on board, if possible, by the time Gunter creates the diversion."

"If there's no opposition do we cut the cable and try to get underway?" Laqua asked.

"Yes, the wind and the tide is right but if she runs aground, hole her and get a fire started."

"If there are prisoners, sir?" Laqua inquired.

"Cast them over the side if you have to. We don't have enough men to hold a proper guard over the whoresons."

Finding no watch, the cutting out party swarmed up the sides of the unsuspecting ships. What passed for an anchor watch was asleep, lying on the deck by the ship's wheel on the ship Laqua's men boarded. A rap with a belaying pin made sure he stayed asleep.

"Bugger will wake with the worst headache 'e ever 'ad," a seaman whispered.

"If 'e wakes," his mate answered.

Laqua's ship had only a few of its crew aboard. They were all asleep in their hammocks and were quickly dealt with.

"Time to cut the cable, lads," Laqua whispered as he came back on deck.

The sky was starting to brighten, almost dawn. Looking across to the other ship, Laqua could see Campbell walking across its deck. On shore a dog barked, was silent a minute and then started barking again. This time other dogs joined in. *Damn*, Campbell thought, *I hope Gunter hasn't got himself into some fix.*

Laqua spoke to Pittman, a bosun's mate in his party. "Cut the forward cable. With the flood tide and the wind from shore she should swing around."

Thuds were heard forward as the cable was cut to the ship's best bower. As expected, the bow swung around until the ship was pointing out to sea. Laqua put a seaman on the wheel and took a group to set the head sails.

Back at the wheel, Pittman said, "She's tugging at her aft cable."

"Cut her loose," Laqua ordered.

Once that cable was cut, the brig surged forward like a racehorse out of the gate. "She answers her helm," the seaman at the wheel volunteered.

Looking aft, Laqua could see Campbell swing around.

Soon a fire appeared ashore; a big roaring blaze lighting up the little fishing village. Shouts could be heard coming from the beach. At first, everyone's attention was on the fire and nobody seemed to notice the ships drifting out to sea. Then someone on the third ship fired a musket. They had been spotted, but too late; they were underway.

As Campbell's ship began to make headway, he had the two stern guns loaded and run out. Once they were brought to bear, Campbell had a round fired from each into the hull of the third ship of the privateers.

"That should wake them," a marine sergeant commented.

"I think Mr. Gunter has taken care of that for us," Campbell replied. "We just added the fireworks."

This caused the men to laugh. The laughter was cut short, however, when a cannon was fired and the shot landed alongside, splashing the men on the small quarterdeck.

"Upset the buggers you did," a seaman volunteered.

Where had that come from? Trident's first lieutenant wondered. Looking to the men at the wheel, Campbell ordered, "Two points to larboard." He then called to a bosun's mate, "See if we can get more sail on her, Moore."

Campbell quickly took a glass and looked astern, *another ship, how had they missed it?* They had not intended to cut out two ships, but by doing so they were vastly undermanned trying to sail them both out. Hopefully, Gunter would be where he could be picked up without having to reduce sail. The sound of another cannon firing echoed over the water and a hole opened in the mainsail. *Trying to bring down our rigging,* Campbell thought. Horne wants his ship back without too much damage, if it is the American.

"Sir, Laqua 'as veered to larboard."

Looking through his glass, Campbell could just see Laqua was changing course to pick up Gunter's group. A grappling hook was thrown to the cutter, and with little effort the boat was pulled alongside. Gunter's party was up the battens and through the entry port in nothing flat.

BOOM!...Damned if the rascal didn't seem closer. **BOOM!**...*He's got two forward chase guns,* Campbell thought. That can't be the same ship he'd fired into. It had to be another one from further down the beach. One they hadn't spotted. It should be only a mile or so, and then they'd be up to *Zebra* and beyond that the rest of the squadron.

***

ON BOARD *ZEBRA*, BUCK felt like an animal in a cage as he paced the cramped quarters of Jenkins' cabin. He'd been on deck but felt it'd do no good for the men to see how nervous he was. Shadows danced across the cabin as the sun came up.

Jenkins had just come about and was closing in on the rendezvous area when he heard a shout and the sound of feet running across the deck.

Unable to stand it any longer, Buck was rising to go topside when Jenkins rushed into the cabin. "Gunfire, sir, my master is sure of it."

On deck, a shout called down, "Sail ho!" Then after a moment, he added, "Two ships being chased by a third ship, sir."

The unmistakable sound of cannon fire could now plainly be heard.

"Set a course to intercept those ships, Captain."

"Aye, aye, Admiral."

The small ship seemed to take off as Jenkins called for more sail and adjusted his course to intercept the fleeing ships. On board Campbell's ship, the balls were now finding their mark. Tired of trying to disable the ship's riggings, the cannon's fire was now directed to the ship's deck. Just forward the larboard bulwark had been blasted away and two men impaled with large splinters.

Campbell sent a trusted seaman down to the captain's cabin for something that might ease their pain. He returned with a bottle of wine.

"It ain't rum, sir, but maybe it'll take the edge off their pain temporarily like."

BOOM!...Another crash, this one hit the aft rail. Thankfully, nobody appeared injured.

"Take her two points to starboard," Campbell ordered. He'd been zigzagging but not so the privateer captain could detect a pattern.

Up forward a cheer was heard. "It's the *Zebra*, Mr. Campbell," a seaman shouted. "The admiral 'as come to get us."

Another crash was heard and the hull shook where a ball had hit it. *Hopefully, there will be something left for the admiral to rescue*, the lieutenant thought. Soon, *Zebra* had passed Laqua's ship and was bearing down on Campbell and the enemy.

A cheer went up as *Zebra* passed Campbell's ship. Men shouting, "Huzza, the admiral will show 'em proper like."

Jenkins had fired his forward guns to let the Yankee know he now had a ship with teeth to take on.

"A hit," the lookout called down.

"Reduce sail, Captain," Buck ordered. "I want you to put a broadside into yonder ship as we come about."

"Aye, Admiral, but those are twelve pounders with greater range and weight than what *Zebra* carries," Jenkins advised.

BOOM!...**BOOM!**...**BOOM**...*Zebra's* six-pounders spat forth her entire broadside.

"You hit 'em, sir, you hit 'em," the lookout called down.

Zebra had completed her turn and was now sailing under full canvas in retreat when the privateer's cannons found their mark. The first ball hit the mast, which shuddered but didn't come down. The second ball hit the small quarterdeck, tearing the wheel away and leaving a bloody spot where the helmsman had been. Suddenly, the ship slewed out of control and the damaged mast came down. Several men were flung to the deck as the enemy balls tore into *Zebra*. Before the men had a chance to recover, much of the overhead rigging toppled down on them.

Captain Jenkins tried to clear his head as he got to his feet. As his vision cleared, the first thing he saw was that the admiral was down; down and bleeding from several wounds made by splinters. His arm lay in an odd angle and he was unconscious. "Dear God," Jenkins prayed. "Don't let him be dead."

Stunned men started to gather around their captain and the admiral. Jenkins called to his bosun, "Quick man, see what we can do to regain steering."

The gunner was down but rising, determined to get the crew back to working the guns. A bosun's mate and a midshipman had a party hacking away at the downed mast. Jenkins then realized the ship had a terrible list and would capsize should a wave of any size crash into them before the mast was hacked away.

BOOM!...**BOOM!**...*Damme,* Jenkins thought, *cannot the rogue see we cannot fight*. After a moment, it dawned on him that not only had they not been hit, but the sound of those shots was from a much bigger gun, a twenty-four pounder at least. Looking forward, Jenkins could see the flagship, her forward guns blazing. Captain Anthony had disobeyed orders and closed with the coast. Hearing gunfire, he'd chosen to risk international outrage, and come to the aid of his admiral. *Would I have done the same*? Jenkins wondered.

"Look," someone shouted. "They's come about and hauled their wind, the bloody cowards. No match for *Trident*, they ain't."

***

Gabe had *Trident* hove to and sent several boats over to *Zebra*. The surgeon, Cornish, was in Gabe's gig.

"I was afraid to move the admiral when I saw you crossing over with the surgeon, sir," Jenkins explained. "I knew the surgeon would want to see him in the light."

Cornish did a quick evaluation of Admiral Buck, and then came over to Gabe. "He's in a bad way, Captain. He has broken the upper bone in his arm, which will require surgery to fix, and it still might have to come off. He's been impaled with at least three splinters, maybe more. I won't know until I can remove his uniform."

"I'll have him taken to *Trident*," Gabe said.

"I'd rather not," Cornish argued. "I'll do what I can for him here on deck and once we return to Charlottesville...we are returning to Charlottesville?" he asked.

"Aye," Gabe replied.

"Good, when we get there I will have the admiral taken ashore where I can take care of him properly."

"He's not going to die, is he?" Gabe stuttered.

"That's in God's hands," Cornish answered. "But I will do all I can to prevent it. Of course, any help you may offer up in the way of prayer would be appreciated." Then looking at the captain, Cornish continued, "Are you in good standing with the Almighty, Captain?"

"Not as good as I should be," Gabe replied, his mind suddenly on his mother and her church in Portsmouth. "But I will seek to improve that standing immediately, doctor."

"Good," Cornish replied.

***

AT CHARLOTTESVILLE, THE ADMIRAL was taken to a room at Government House, where he was given a tumbler full of brandy. As the alcohol took effect, he was strapped down and the broken bone in his upper arm was set. Thankfully, he passed out as Cornish applied traction to pull the bones in place. The leather thong holding the arm was held by a strong seaman while the wound where the bone had broken through the skin was cleansed and sutured up. Barrel staves were then fixed around the arm to immobilize it, with the staves held in place by leather straps. The splinters were then removed, wounds were cleansed, and a few drains were inserted to allow suppuration of any contagion.

"I wish we had opium or laudanum," Cornish had said once the surgery was finished. "It would help the admiral rest."

"Hemp would also help," Gabe volunteered, recalling how Bart had been treated when he'd suffered from his appendix and hemp was used before the surgery.

"Something we must discuss," Cornish said, upon hearing Gabe's comments. "But first let's do what we can to make the admiral comfortable."

CHAPTER TWENTY-FIVE

THE AFTERNOON SUN BLAZED down on the ships at anchor in Charlottesville. Gulls seemed to float on the air, then they would suddenly dive down into the Caribbean waters as some small fish or scrap of food that had been thrown over the side of a ship drew their attention. There was very little breeze, and Lieutenant Hawks wondered for the hundredth time if putting up the wind sails had been worth the effort. The trees on shore looked as still as the limp flag hanging from the fort.

In the great cabin, Captain Anthony was talking with the first lieutenant. The skylight was open, but when Hawks ambled over toward it the master caught his eye with a look that said, "Your duties are more forward."

Seeing the prizes, the *Bulldog* and the *Raven*, off to starboard, Hawks thought either would be a fine ship for some lucky devil's first command. That was exactly the topic of conversation in the great cabin. Sipping from a fresh glass of lime juice, Gabe looked at Donald Campbell.

"Don, I've decided to send the prizes back to Barbados. They will carry the admiral back with them. By all rights, you should be given the choice of commanding one of the two," Gabe said looking his first lieutenant in the eye. "But," Gabe sighed then continued, "I can't spare you. You are the next senior and should something happen to me it would fall on your shoulders to command the ship."

"Have you decided who to give the ships to?" Campbell spoke with no hint of bitterness in his voice.

"I have a name," Gabe replied. "But I wanted to know your thoughts first."

"Wiley," Campbell said without hesitation. "The *Raven* had been Lieutenant Bond's ship, so I'd put him in temporary command. But *Bulldog* I'd send back with Wiley."

"Your thoughts and mine are as one about *Bulldog*," Gabe said. "But I've another to talk to about *Raven*."

A smile lit up Campbell's face. "He'll never take it, sir, if it means leaving you."

"You may well be right," Gabe said. "Although it's an offer that has to be made."

"I'll tell Bond to get his chest together," Campbell said.

"That sure are you, Don?"

"Never been more sure of anything, sir."

"Sail ho!"

Rising, Campbell said, "Probably one of your patrols returning."

Gabe had taken a page from Lord Anthony's book and had been sending patrols out, a pair of ships at a time. *Venus* and *Thorn* should be returning about now; then *Brilliant* and *Fortune* would go out.

"Is the surgeon going with the Admiral?" Campbell asked.

"No, we are going to send Wright. Cornish has full trust in the man and says while he's a surgeon's mate, he has more knowledge than most of the surgeons he's met."

"I see," Campbell replied. "Should I send Hex down, sir?"

"Aye," Gabe replied.

***

A KNOCK AND THEN the thud as the musket butt pounded against the deck. The marine sentry called, "Midshipman of the watch, sir."

"Very well," Gabe said.

"What can I do for you, Mr. Caed?" Gabe asked as the boy stared at the pitcher and glasses on the table.

Seeing the direction of the boy's eyes, Gabe spoke to his cox'n, "Do you think the first lieutenant would think it amiss if a glass was offered to our young gentleman?"

Hex appeared deep in thought for a second and then answered, "Not if he thought it was to quench the young man's thirst so he could repeat the message he was sent to deliver."

Young Caed turned red and then blurted out, "It's not our patrol returning, sir. The first lieutenant said it was Captain Jepson in *Revenant*."

"Well, damme," Gabe exclaimed. "Hand the boy a glass, Jake."

The middy downed the glass of lime juice in a single gulp. "Thank you, Captain," Caed said as he fled from the cabin with a grin on his face.

"Likely bend everyone's ears in his mess tonight, telling them how he'd shared a wet with the captain today while on watch," Jake said.

Dagan was on the taffrail smoking his pipe when Gabe came on deck. "Guess Jep is bringing Lord Skalla for a visit," Dagan volunteered.

"Did you see him?" Gabe asked.

Dagan shook his head no as he tapped his pipe in the palm of his hand and let the ash fall down into the water. Straightening up, he said, "Be more comfortable if Jep took the admiral back. That way you could keep one of the prizes, was you a mind to."

Gabe nodded but didn't say anything. Then taking his glass from under his arm he peered at the approaching ship then said, "I don't see Lord Skalla."

"He's there."

"You sure?" When Gabe didn't hear a reply, he looked to Dagan and asked again, "You sure?"

This time he caught Dagan's look, which said, "He's there."

Walking over to Campbell, Gabe said, "Signal 'captain repair on board' and be ready to receive our foreign office friend."

"Lord Skalla?" Campbell asked. Gabe nodded. Campbell took his glass and peered at the approaching ship and said, "You sure, Captain?"

Seeing the look, Campbell said, "Aye, sir. You are sure. Mr. Hawks."

"Aye."

"Prepare to receive Captain Jepson and Lord Skalla."

Gabe had just gotten back to the great cabin when the sound of the cannons firing the salute echoed across the water.

***

LORD SKALLA, JEPSON, AND Dagan sat in *Trident's* cabin, each with two fingers of bourbon in a glass.

"Drink it quick before the cox'n comes down," Dagan joked. "Otherwise, Hex will feel left out."

Jep roared with laughter and Lord Skalla smiled his broad smile. Gabe had already told the two about the cutting out of the *Bulldog* and *Raven*.

"Most would say it's a small price for the two ships," Jepson said. "Of course, we know how you feel about the admiral. I will pay him a visit if the doctor will allow it," he quickly added.

"He will appreciate that," Gabe responded.

"And I as well, as soon as I've met with the governor general," added Lord Skalla.

"Is the doctor sure he can make the trip back to Barbados?" Jepson asked, realizing the responsibility he would be undertaking in transporting a wounded admiral.

"Dr. Cornish believes it may take upwards a year before the admiral is ready to return to duty. He feels he will be better off on Barbados where there's a better hospital and doctors able to care for him than here."

"And Livi," Jep threw out.

This time Gabe smiled. "Aye, the widow, Livi. The doctor is also concerned about the fevers and ill humours on this island," Gabe added.

"And the French," Lord Skalla said.

"The French!" Gabe exclaimed.

"Aye," Skalla responded, using his learned naval lingo. "We didn't expect to find you here. We came to warn the governor about the probability the island would be attacked."

"Then you think the squadron should stay here?" Gabe asked.

"No, the squadron's mission has not changed. You will proceed as acting commodore."

Gabe sat as if in a trance. "I thought they'd send another admiral or senior captain to take the squadron," he admitted.

"There is no one else, nor the time to get anyone else," Skalla said as he stood and stretched. "Admiral Buck had every faith in your abilities when he chose you as flag captain, Gabe." Lord Skalla placed his hand on Gabe's shoulder. "Nothing has happened that I know of to change that. No, Captain, we will proceed."

"Does that mean you're coming with us?" Gabe asked.

"It means I'm sailing with you," Lord Skalla answered. "Although, I can think of damn little good it will do."

Gabe was not sure either, but for whatever reason he felt better about proceeding; a damn sight better than at any time since Admiral Buck had been wounded.

"I'd planned on giving *Bulldog* to Wiley and sending her to Barbados," Gabe told Jepson. "He understands Gil...Lord Anthony will have to confirm the appointment." Gabe gave a sigh. "I'm also sending my report back, I will give them to you directly," Gabe said to Jepson, who nodded.

"I disobeyed orders when I closed with the coast and fired on the privateer," Gabe volunteered, sounding downtrodden.

"And we are all damn glad you did, Captain Anthony," Lord Skalla responded. "Not the least, our admiral."

CHAPTER TWENTY-SIX

STEPPING OUTSIDE GOVERNMENT HOUSE, Gabe noticed a brisk wind that almost took his hat. The marine sentry standing at the door made to grab it, but Gabe recovered it first. Snapping back to attention the marine was surprised when Gabe offered his thanks.

"You're welcome, zur, but I'd keep a tight 'old on 'er."

Hex fell in beside his captain as he passed the marine. Gabe noticed the man's shaggy mane blowing in the breeze. *Probably tired of holding his hat on*, Gabe thought.

"The admiral ready?" Hex asked.

Thinking of the admiral's pale, empty eyes and ghastly pallor, Gabe nodded his answer as he recalled his early morning visit with the admiral.

"I was wrong, Gabe," Buck had whispered. "I should have had *Trident* or at least *Stag* standing by. They would have been more than a match for the bloody raiders."

Trying to salve his admiral's self incriminations, Gabe answered, "No sir, Admiral, I beg to disagree. *Trident's* draught was far too great to work that close inshore, and *Stag's* would have been suspect. No sir, the sloops were the only choice and you made it. Fact is, Admiral, the expedition was a total success. We took two ships and holed another. We had no way of knowing the other ship had come in after dark and buoyed as it had. The cutting out party never saw it."

"You are kind, Gabe." The admiral winced in pain as he made to adjust the way he was laying. Gabe made to help but was waved away. "Think I'll ever raise my flag again?" he asked weakly.

"I've no doubt we'll see blue at the mizzen in no time at all," Gabe reassured his friend.

"I'll want you as my flag captain," Buck said.

The door creaked open and Jepson, with his surgeon and two seamen entered Buck's room. "It's time to board the ship, sir," Jepson said.

"Aye," Buck replied. Turning to Gabe, he said, "Give 'em hell, Gabe, give 'em hell."

"Aye, Admiral, we will make the bloody bastards pay." With that, Gabe turned and walked away, pausing only to thank the governor general and his wife for their hospitality and their care for the admiral.

As he walked away, Mrs. Campbell leaned on her husband's shoulder and whispered, "So young...and so much responsibility. What is this war doing to our young men, Peter?"

Hex had kept silent, realizing Gabe's mood. As they neared the beach, he spoke, "Ebb tide, sir."

The captain's gig was there waiting. Oars were tossed and a seaman was standing at the bow, ready to shove off once the captain was ready. Stepping into the boat, Gabe felt a chill. Was it an omen? Settling down in the stern sheets, he looked at Hex, who took hold of the tiller.

With the briefest of nods from Gabe, Hex called, "Out oars, give way together now, lads."

It was an easy pull with the wind at their backs. Gabe found himself concentrating on *Trident*. It was almost like she was a new ship; a new beginning. Was it because the admiral was no longer on board? Gabe could see the ship's cable was taut as the wind freshened. A glint of copper showed itself as the sun rose and gleamed down on the ocean. Would copper be the answer, he wondered, thinking of his old *Merlin*. Her hull had been eaten away by shipworms.

Dover, *Merlin's* carpenter, had said the teredo worms loved the warm waters and that he'd demand they copper the bottom of ships going to the Indies. *Well, I hope it works*, Gabe thought.

Looking up to the main deck, Gabe could see the marines making ready for him to come aboard, their scarlet uniforms standing out. The *Trident* figurehead needed a coating of gold leaf. That would come from his pocket, when time and elements permitted. The commission pendant flew in the early morning breeze.

Gabe's mind seemed to be a jumble of thoughts. He was thinking of his new relationship with the ship, the squadron, Lord Skalla, the mission, and Faith...Faith and their son.

"Boat ahoy!" the cry brought Gabe's mind back to focus.

"*Trident*," Hex replied in his booming voice. He moved the tiller over and the oarsmen expertly maneuvered the boat toward the entry port. A wave caused the boat to lurch as Gabe stood, but Hex's steady hand was there.

"Wouldn't want the sea water to dull your gold lace," Hex said with a grin.

Gabe couldn't help but grin back at his cox'n. As the boat neared, Gabe leaped over the gunwale and, grasping the rope, made his way up the battens and through the entry port. The shrilling of the bosun's pipes and the slap of muskets as the marines presented arms always caused a stir. A chill of sorts ran through him as he came aboard his ship. Would a landsman understand this, would Faith understand this calling of the sea? Could he give it up?

Campbell was there smiling, "Was the admiral in good spirits, sir?"

"As could be hoped for," Gabe replied.

"We could see him being rowed out. Jepson had his flag raised already."

"A thoughtful gesture," Gabe said. "Are we ready to get underway, Mr. Campbell?"

"Aye, sir, waiting on your orders."

Looking about the ship, Gabe saw the men were already at their stations. "Very well, Lieutenant, signal the squadron. I will change and return on deck."

"Captain."

"Yes, Mr. Campbell."

"We had the rest of your things moved to the great cabin and most of the admiral's belongings ferried over to *Revenant*."

Gabe had started to make his way to his quarters when a thought entered his mind. "Did Chen Lee go as well, Mr. Campbell?"

"Aye, Captain, both he and the admiral's cox'n."

Turning, Gabe felt relieved. He'd always heard two cooks in a kitchen were sure to bring trouble. Nesbit would be grateful, but Hex...Hex would miss Crowe. As he stepped over the coaming, Gabe caught a glimpse of Laqua, now acting-Lieutenant Laqua. *He should pass the lieutenant's examination*, Gabe thought...*I did*.

With Wiley and Bond taking *Raven* and *Bulldog* back to Barbados, there had been a change in the watch. Holton had moved up as the second lieutenant. Hawks was now the third. Turner was made acting lieutenant and was now fourth, with Laqua being fifth.

"Turner should have already taken the exam," Campbell had said. "If we could stay in port long enough for a board to be assembled."

Something that would have to be remedied once they got back to Barbados...*if we get back*, Gabe thought.

By the time Gabe was back on deck he could see men at the capstan bars. A group of petty officers waited with a group of men below the mainmast. One petty officer was nervously slapping a starter against his leg. Aloft, the masthead pendant was streaming out to sea.

Without thinking, Gabe looked toward the mizzen. The admiral's flag was gone. Would it ever fly again? Pray God, let it be so. Seeing the first lieutenant, Gabe ordered, "Get the ship underway if you please, Mr. Campbell."

"Hands aloft," Campbell ordered and the cry was repeated. "Hands aloft, loose topsail."

Men swarmed up the rigging and shrouds. Gabe had no doubt the bets had been made as the topmen raced aloft.

Rap...some laggard had felt the business end of some petty officer's starter. Was it the nervous one?

"Mr. Holton, break out the anchor."

"Aye, sir."

Without waiting for the lieutenant to pass the order, Adams' baritone voice could be heard clear to the quarterdeck. "Man the capstan, man the bars. Heave round, heave you lubbers. Heave, Jackson, no wonder your wife left you for a soldier if you can't put more into it than that."

Crack...the bosun's cane came down, "I see you shirking, Martin, you lazy bilge rat."

Overhead gulls squawked as the men heaved, the sun beating down on sweaty backs. The men kept at it steadily causing a clank, clank, clank, and soon water dripped from the cable onto the deck.

"Anchors have short," Adams bellowed.

"Loose headsails," Campbell ordered.

Above the deck the loosened canvas flapped and tackles banged about in the wind as barefooted men went about bringing things in order.

Adams voice boomed again as he shouted, "Anchors aweigh."

Trident paid off into the wind, like a dog released from a chain, and charged forward, causing the ship to heel sharply.

"Man the braces," Campbell yelled. "Lively now, look alive. Don't you know the governor is watching?"

Gabe couldn't help but smile. "Not likely," Dagan whispered. *When had he come on deck*? Gabe wondered.

As the men pulled, the yards creaked and groaned as they were pulled round. The sails flapped back and forth, and then snapped out hard and full.

As the ship made headway, one of the helmsmen advised the master, "Answers her helm, Mr. Hayes."

Forward, Adams had his party scrambling as ordered, "Hook the cat. That's it, you're learning, mates. Hook the fish, haul taut. Walk away...away blast you, walk away. Belay, that's it, my lovelies. Now unrig the fish. You're finally earning your keep Martin, you laggard. Ring up the anchor." Satisfied with the men's work, Adams watched as the topmen who had completed their task slid down the stays and helped the men with pulling on the braces.

Walking toward the taffrail, Dagan pulled his pipe from his pocket. The small island of Tobago with its one fort was getting smaller and smaller on the horizon. Would the French come as Lord Skalla predicted? Would the Campbells be safe if they did? *Everything has a season*, Dagan thought. Hopefully, this one wouldn't be too harsh. He'd seen Gabe give a letter to Jepson to carry to Faith. Would seeing Buck wounded and on the verge of death make her see how fragile life was? It could have been Gabe lying there. A shiver shook Dagan to the depths of his soul. *It still might be, but it'll have to come through me*, Dagan thought as he squatted to light his pipe.

The Battle Won

The men listened quietly
To their captain speak
It had been a hard voyage
The mission now complete

Gone were some mates
Cut down by the guns
A savage battle fought
Outnumbered still they won

We're headed for home lads
The butcher's bill I fear
A double tot for every man
The crew gave a cheer

Michael Aye

CHAPTER TWENTY-SEVEN

THE CARIBBEAN'S WARM WATERS were left on the horizon like the small island of Tobago, replaced by the dark heavy seas of the Atlantic Ocean. Once at sea, Lord Skalla came down to Gabe's cabin and informed him he needed to call on a man in Cape Town, South Africa. This had been the second part of his journey with Jepson, prior to learning about Admiral Buck's accident.

"This is one of our agents?" Gabe asked.

Smiling, Lord Skalla replied, "He works in the office of the Dutch East India Company."

That was a yes, or as close as Skalla would come to a yes, Gabe decided. Sending for the master and first lieutenant, Gabe informed them of their change of course.

Sail drill was alternated with gun drill and at any given hour the hands were rousted out for fire drill. This was done with the captain declaring one or more of the officers, warrant officers, or key petty officers dead. By doing this a man had to know not only his job, but also those above and below him in rank.

When a senior bosun's mate said he didn't know what orders needed to be given when his team leader was declared dead, Gabe responded, "As far as I know, a fire has no respect for rank or position. Therefore, you better know what actions to take in case of a fire. Otherwise, you may only have two choices: burn or drown."

This brought a lot of chuckles and ribbing from the man's mates. Two days later, Gabe played the same scenario and the bosun's mate sailed through the drill.

"Put it to them where they can understand it and more often than not they'll get it right," Gabe explained to the surgeon as they observed the drill. "If they don't, you change the man's station. You never know when one man's actions may be the difference in saving or losing a ship."

Cornish stated he'd never seen Captain Brian become involved in any of the ship's drills. "He actually only took part in punishment, as I recall," Cornish admitted.

"See where it got him?" Dagan volunteered, hearing the surgeon's comments.

***

GABE STOOD AT THE quarterdeck rail and watched as the sun started to descend. Lieutenant Taylor and *Thorn* were closing with *Trident.* While no longer officially considered the flagship, the rest of the squadron continued as if nothing had changed. Part of this was due to Lord Skalla's presence. Gabe was, however, still the senior captain.

The squadron was just to the west of Cape Verde. Taylor, in *Thorn*, had stopped an island coaster. He had no intention of trusting his news to signals. He closed with *Trident* and then had himself pulled across to the two decker. *Thorn* lay hove-to and rolled in the heavy waves of the Atlantic, waiting on her captain. Hooking on to the main chains, Taylor nimbly scaled the slippery battens and pulled himself through the entry port. Once in the captain's cabin, Nesbit poured a glass for Gabe, Taylor, Lord Skalla, and Dagan.

"Taking a page out of Jenkins' book," Taylor said, pausing momentarily after taking a sip of wine and then eyeing the dark red liquid appreciatively. Obviously, his own stock didn't measure up to that left by Admiral Buck. "I stopped a coaster and asked if they had any fresh vegetables or fruit." Taylor continued. "No vegetables the master said, but they had plenty of bananas. In talking over a fair price the fellow said, 'A large number of American ships had went past just a few days ago'. He remembered one particularly, as it had a fox with a torch in its mouth painted across the stern."

"The *Foxfire*," Lord Skalla threw out.

"Aye, my Lord, that was my thinking."

"They were headed south," Gabe said, as much a question as a statement.

"They were when the trader saw them. The trader said there were four ships, all about the same size except for the ship with the fox, which is probably a small frigate."

"Or even a captured corvette," Gabe thought aloud.

"Are they headed in the direction of St. Mary's?" Lord Skalla asked.

"Aye, at least in that direction," Gabe replied. "Does that change our orders in regards to Cape Town?"

Lord Skalla seemed to ponder the question a minute while he took another sip of his wine. "I think not, Captain. The short time we are in Cape Town will not make any difference, I'm thinking. The potential information received about the American privateers and the French could be well worth the short delay."

Like I was thinking, Dagan thought to himself. Lord Skalla has a spy working for the Danes. Wonder what they'd think if they knew about the attack on the Fort at St. Croix.

"*Foxfire*," Lord Skalla said, thinking aloud. "What a name for a ship. Is that not the luminescence you see on wood rotting in the forest?"

"Aye," Gabe answered, "but Dagan told me it was called fairy fire in Scotland and Ireland."

"Nonsense folklore," Skalla said.

Gabe just shrugged. "The Indians in the colonies call it 'Cold Fire'. Dagan got that from a family friend, Kawliga. There is also a tale of a fox carrying a torch or firewall in its mouth."

"The Americans must have someone in their company with a sense for the dramatic, someone with a hand for painting," said Hex, who spoke for the first time.

"What makes you think that?" Gabe asked.

"The *Tomahawk* had an Indian war ax painted on the stern. Now, we have a fox with a torch in his mouth. Have you seen such before?" Hex replied.

"Come to think of it, I haven't," Gabe admitted.

"Reckon what he'd come up with for a ship named *Nymph*?" Hex asked, a grin on his face.

"Damme, Jake, but you're a sly one," Lord Skalla exclaimed. "All tales," he continued on.

"What about *Thorn* and *Trident*?" Gabe said.

"Point taken," Skalla replied and helped himself to another glass.

After the laughter died down, Gabe saw Taylor over the side and watched as the ship sailed back to its station.

***

GABE STARED AT THE chart lying on his table. The air was warm inside his cabin. He'd had Hex open a stern window and now a slight breeze blew at the chart, requiring it to be anchored down. He had never sailed this deep into the Atlantic before and wanted to familiarize himself with the area.

Hayes had brought the charts down, and when asked if he'd ever sailed around the Cape of Good Hope he answered very frankly, "Aye, Captain, and it can be a nightmare. Not like the Horn, mind you, but I'd not like to get washed up on the rocks either."

"Is this a good bay to anchor while Lord Skalla goes ashore?" Gabe asked, talking about Cape Town.

"Aye, Table Bay lies here," the master said pointing to his chart. "Good anchorage between here and Moville Point. That's actually before we get to the Cape. Once around the Cape of Good Hope and Cape Point there's another good anchorage here on this side of the peninsula. It's called False Bay and is actually much bigger than Table Bay. Small town there, not much more than a village last time I was here. It's called Simon's Town."

The charts did little to ease Gabe's tensions about either the east side of the peninsula or any other part of the Cape. What Gabe read was only words to some, but would cause a seaman to want plenty of sea room: a rocky peninsula, a sheer cliff rising eight hundred fifty feet above the ocean, hazardous winds and currents. No wonder the master called it a nightmare. *It could prove to be a challenge,* Gabe thought as he rolled up the chart, glad he had Hayes around for his experience and advice.

Overhead, the shrill call of the bosun's pipe was followed by the soft thuds of bare feet as one watch replaced the other. It was eight p.m., the first watch. Gabe could never rationalize why the particular upcoming watch coming would be called the first watch. Why not call the middle watch, which started at midnight, the first watch? That's when it went from one day to another. *Oh, well.* He always thought the admiral, who was in charge of naming each watch, was either in his cups or in bed with some wench, and when asked said the first thing that came to mind.

Once when he'd told Gil his theory, his brother had said, "I'd not deny either of those distinct possibilities but I'd not go spreading it around. I don't see how it would do your naval career any good were it to be heard in the wrong circle."

What he'd give to have those carefree days back. *Ah...well.*

Dagan rose from where he was sitting and said, "It would not be amiss for the captain to take a stroll on the quarterdeck and pause long enough to smoke a bowl of tobacco with his uncle."

"By damn, you are right," Gabe said with a smile. "Let me find a pipe."

"No need," Dagan replied, holding one of Gabe's father's pipes in his hand. Together, they walked on deck and past the quarterdeck watch.

On deck, Turner was enjoying the rise to acting lieutenant. While on watch he made it a point to examine everything he could: the standing riggings, a line that needed splicing, a spot that needed a touch up of paint. He listened to the groan of tackles, a squeak that might need grease. He was so intent on his inspections that when the sound of laughter was heard from aft he couldn't figure what would cause such an outburst. Nor did he hear Mr. Mark, the midshipman of the watch, whisper, "Captain is on deck," as he rushed pass.

"What's going on here," the acting lieutenant snapped as he came upon two men passing a bottle and smoking pipes. Too late he realized his mistake.

Still smiling from some joke or tale, the captain looked up and said, "Nothing to keep you from your duties, Mr. Turner."

CHAPTER TWENTY-EIGHT

A LOW, HEAVING ROLLING OF thunder that grew with intensity boomed from the southeastern horizon. Standing by the fife rail, Gabe looked to the master.

Catching Gabe's look, Hayes replied, "Aye, Captain. Someone's in for a blow. Should have blown itself out before we close, however."

Not one to doubt the master, Gabe nevertheless felt a pang of anxiety as the heavy Atlantic rollers crashed into *Trident's* hull on the larboard side, occasionally sending spray on board.

The smell of cooked beef drifted along the deck. Looking forward, Gabe could see a small plume of smoke from the galley funnel dissipate on the wind. The smell of food caused his stomach to growl.

"What's that, sir?"

Smiling Gabe said, "Just thinking, other than coffee I've not broken my fast today."

"That'll do you no good, Captain," Hayes replied in a fatherly manner. "Eats when you can, I says. You never know when the fires have to be put out. Then it's cold beef and beer...or rum."

"Good advice," Gabe answered. "Hex."

"Aye, Captain."

"Tell Nesbit I think I'll eat within the hour."

"Aye, Captain, within the hour."

Walking over to acting-Lieutenant Laqua, Gabe asked, "Settling down to the wardroom, Lieutenant?"

Laqua smiled at being addressed as lieutenant. "The other officers have made it a warm and easy transition, sir, one that will be hard to give up."

"No reason that you should. As soon as we get back to Barbados you can sit for the lieutenant's exam. You can study when off duty, though I've little doubt you could pass the exam now."

"I've heard that they can ask some mighty difficult questions," Laqua said.

"Aye, there's always one or two that will do his best to stomp you. Somebody always wants to know how you'd go about box-hauling in a blow on a treacherous coast."

For the next hour, Gabe and Laqua talked about the exam and different aspects of handling a ship in all types of conditions. Seeing the new lieutenant and captain in deep conversation, Adams took it upon himself to handle things normally done by the officer of the watch.

Laqua was a likable sort and hadn't put on airs since he'd been bumped up to the wardroom, like some. He'd likely make a good officer. He'd do the sod a favor or two. You never knew when you might need one in return. Besides Laqua didn't seem like the sort to forget.

"Captain...captain." Gabe had been so intent in his conversation that it took a moment for him to realize he was being spoken to. Looking up, Gabe spied his cox'n who had been speaking. "Nesbit has everything ready, sir."

Gabe nodded and then turned back to Laqua. "Some good points, Lieutenant, we will continue this conversation later."

***

THAT EVENING, DAGAN AND the surgeon were playing cribbage. The whalebone board had been intricately decorated with scrimshaw work. It didn't take but a glance to see who was ahead in the game. Dagan was leaning back, arms crossed and smiling, while Cornish was scowling. Hex sat on an upholstered cushion under *Trident's* stern window tuning his mandolin. Gabe had feasted on roast chicken, potatoes, buttered peas, carrots, and apple pie with a sweet whipped cream poured over the top.

Nesbit had poured a cool glass of sweetened tea. This he'd picked up from Nanny. A jug of tea rested in the bilges to keep cool, as the captain was not much for hot tea. Following the meal, coffee was served with the apple pie. Gabe now sipped on a glass of brandy as he watched the others in the cabin; his belly felt so tight he considered loosening his trousers.

Hearing Hex strum his mandolin, Gabe was reminded of some of the shanties he and Stephen Earl used to sing back on *Drakkar*. It's amazing how things changed with the responsibility of command, he thought.

"Play me a tune, Hex," Gabe called.

"A fast tune or a slow one?" Hex asked.

Gabe took a sip of his brandy then replied, "One of each."

He cleared his throat, and then struck up a bawdy little tune.

There's poker there's whist
All games that people play
But for me the cards
Has done seen their day
So if my bed is a squeaking
Don't you come a peeping
Don't look so shocked
At what I have to say
Met a blonde-haired beauty
She came right to me
And gave me a list
Of games we can play.

"Damme Hex, but ain't you a rowdy one," said Cornish, who had given up on beating Dagan in cribbage and turned his attention to the music and song.

Gabe had gotten up and recharged Hex's glass and then filled Dagan and the surgeon's glasses. *I wonder what Butcher Brian would have thought, seeing a captain fill a seaman's glass, even his cox'n*, Cornish thought. *Such different styles, such different men. Thank God for men like our captain,* he decided.

"Still want a slow one, Captain?" Hex was saying.

"Aye."

Another swallow of the brandy and then Hex started again.

The day is dark and dreary
I can smell the rain
The ships set for sailing
Will I stand the pain
What's it like to be along
I worry what she'll do
I been taken by the press gang
Will she find someone new?

The cabin was very quiet as Hex sang. It seemed that even the ship was suddenly still as the mournful ballad was sung. With the skylight open the men on deck gathered around and listened. No doubt the song struck home to more than a few.

Lieutenant Holton had the watch. *No wonder the cap'n likes Hex*, he thought. *Bugger's got a voice that would make the angels cry.*

***

GABE ROSE FROM HIS cot. He'd not undressed, had not even taken off his boots. He'd just lain back for a moment and fell asleep. Now it was several hours later and he was thirsty. *A glass of lime juice or Nesbit's cool tea would be good about now*, Gabe thought. But a small glass of wine would have to do. There was no reason to wake his servant. Not wanting to sit in the darkened cabin, Gabe went topside. Out of habit he peered at the compass.

Acting-Lieutenant Turner was on deck. "Morning, sir, the wind has backed a bit and the rain has been falling off and on for the last hour or so." Gabe could see water dripping from the shrouds and stays onto the deck. "It will be dawn soon," Turner was saying.

The dawn of a new day, one never knew what dawn's early light would bring. Hatless, Gabe could feel the breeze blow his hair. They should make Cape Town in another day...two at the most. Around the Cape of Good Hope and two-hundred-fifty miles off the east coast of Africa lay Madagascar and the enemy. He was ready; ready to meet these raiders and go home...home to Faith and his new son. If he survived.

CHAPTER TWENTY-NINE

"LAND HO." THE CRY created a wave of excitement among the crew as men looked up and those more brave than others rushed to the rails. However, it would likely be an hour before land was visible from the deck. Hearing the patter of feet on deck, Gabe was not surprised to see young Mr. Caed and Mr. Brayden scamper across the deck and up the shrouds like monkeys.

Mr. Caed was a couple of ratlines ahead but Mr. Brayden was catching up fast. It was only the duty that kept Mr. Sebastian on the deck.

"Any wager on who will reach the tops first?"

Turning, Gabe smiled and spoke, "Damned, Dagan, if you ain't taking on Bart's bad habits more-n-more." Walking forward they could see Lord Skalla.

"Morning Gabe," Lord Skalla said as the two approached. He had been leaning on the forecastle rail.

"Good morning," the two answered. "You are liable to get wet up here," Gabe said.

"A welcome reprieve I'd think," Skalla replied. "I never did like Africa. It seems everything around will bite you, sting you, or eat you alive. That's if the heat and ill humours don't kill you first. How the Danes have survived so well is beyond me."

Gabe turned and leaned his back against the rail. As he did so, he saw a group waiting patiently to speak with him. The cry of "land ho" was like sugar to ants. They all came out of their holes. The carpenter, the sail maker, the purser, and the bosun, each with a list of things they needed once they reached port. They'd be surprised, because even he didn't know how long they'd be in port, and time might not avail itself so their lists could be acted upon. Even Lord Skalla had no idea.

"I can only promise to send a message back with my intentions as soon as possible, Captain," he had said. "I would think it prudent to anchor in such a way we would not be impeded and have to be towed out to sea if a speedy departure proves necessary."

Gabe had decided to send Lord Skalla ashore with Hex and Lieutenant Laqua. Both of them were savvy enough to recognize trouble and avoid it if possible, but deal with it if need be. Dagan would go if asked but Gabe didn't feel like asking. He'd done enough for king and country already. Gabe would send Midshipman Mark along to stay with the boatmen and keep things in order and act as messenger if needed.

They still had ample time before entering port, but Gabe decided to go below and change his shirt. He stepped past the marine sentry, who snapped to attention and greeted him with the familiar, "Cap'n, zuh."

Entering the cabin, it felt like a twenty-degree drop in temperature. Nesbit had cracked the stern windows and the skylight was open, causing a gentle breeze to funnel through the cabin. Nesbit entered with a dripping bottle. "Lime juice, sir. It's been cooling in the bilges. Would a glass by satisfying?"

"Aye, Josh, it would."

Sir Gabe is in a good mood to address me as such, Nesbit thought as he hurriedly wiped the bottle down and poured his captain a glass. Gabe drank half the tangy liquid down in one swallow. He then sat down in one of the upholstered chairs next to his desk. The cool cabin and juice seem to relax him so Gabe laid his head back. He'd not been sleeping well and the fatigue was starting to set in. Hopefully, if they stayed in port he'd get a good night's rest tonight. Soon the shipboard noises grew muffled and distant. Without meaning to, Gabe dozed off.

"Sail ho." The cry startled Gabe from his dozing. As he jumped up from his chair he'd forgotten about the half empty glass of lime juice propped in his lap. The consequence was a wet uniform and lap.

"Damn," Gabe shouted, slamming the glass down on the table.

Oh dear, Sir Gabe has lost his pleasant mood, Nesbit thought. Not taking time to change his britches nor his shirt, Gabe came on deck in time to hear the lookout telling the first lieutenant the sails were merchant vessels. He walked to the larboard side of the quarterdeck.

A swell caused *Trident's* deck to cant slightly, so he gripped the sun-warmed wood of the rail. The heat seemed more intense than that in Barbados. At the wheel, the master was in a whispered conversation with the helmsman; giving last minute instructions about coming into a foreign port and anchoring, no doubt.

Lord Skalla appeared on deck, hatless as usual, but with a white ruffled silk shirt. Seeing Gabe's gaze, Skalla said, "I've already changed for the trip ashore, but with this sun blazing down I could not bear the thought of my dress coat just now. These pants are too hot by themselves." Shaking his head, in disgust, over the thick, hot pants, Skalla spoke again, "Tell me, Gabe, have you ever wondered if any London tailor has had thoughts on using materials that would be convenient anywhere else but London? It'd do one or two a world of good to spend a few months in the Caribbean or India. We would find ourselves with a choice of cloth that would prove a damn sight cooler, I believe."

"No doubt," Gabe replied. "I'm sure the tailor on Antigua knows this as well and that explains his claim to turn out a suitable wardrobe in a week. Of course, the service comes with a pricey fee."

A cry from overhead was heard again. "More merchant ships departing Cape Town."

Robben Island was now off the starboard beam, about two miles south-southwest. Hayes called to the helmsman, "We'll steer a course for Green Point."

In less than an hour, *Trident* was ready to shorten sail in preparation to enter Table Bay. The master was pointing out Blaauwberg or Blue Hill. This was a dark round hill that rose up seven hundred and forty-five feet. It sat at the northern boundary of Table Bay.

Gabe said, "Once we shorten sail, Mr. Campbell, I want a good man in the chains. In reading the master's charts, it seems the bottom is foul and rocky."

"Aye, Captain." Without waiting for further orders, Campbell ordered, "Prepare to shorten sail." With the shrill of the bosun's pipe, men went to their duties.

Hayes spoke to the helmsman again, and then turned to Gabe. "That's Green Point, Captain, and there is Moville Point. The greatest depth is mid-channel between Green Point and Whale Rock...about twenty fathoms. I would suggest we anchor after passing Moville Point in ten to twelve fathoms so as to not run afoul of all these grocery captains." Gabe nodded his agreement.

The breeze was from the southeast, a land breeze. The men of the anchor party in the fo'c'sle would appreciate it, but still it would be hot work preparing the ship for anchoring. Dagan decided he did not miss those days as a common seaman. By the quarterdeck, Gabe stood next to the first lieutenant. When he dropped his hand, the anchor party let *Trident's* best bower slip. Hex was standing by with his crew as the captain's barge was being hoisted over the side to take Lord Skalla into Cape Town. It would be a long pull, but that was better than having to worry about being crowded in by some of the merchant vessels. It was doubtful many of the bumboats would make the long pull to hawk their wares.

Fresh vegetables would be good, but you could bet that was the only thing that they carried that wouldn't land a seaman at the surgeon's door, poxed by some doxy, or before the captain for smuggled alcohol. Whether the men realized it or not, they would be better off if the bumboats stayed closer inshore.

***

ANOTHER HOUR AND IT'LL be sunset, Hayes reflected as he gazed toward Cape Town. Lord Skalla had promised to send word back if he intended to stay for any length of time. Dagan could tell Gabe was worried as he paced the deck. He'd been down in his cabin for an hour but then returned to the deck. *Is his mind on Lord Skalla, or Faith? Probably both*, Dagan thought.

Dagan decided to approach Gabe and engage him in conversation, if for no other reason than to get his mind off his worries. No sooner had he made the decision than a cry from overhead rang out.

"Deck thar! Barge is returning."

Damn the man, Gabe thought, but before he could say anything the first lieutenant spoke, "Damn it man, am I to wonder who may be in the barge?"

More than a few of those on deck smiled at Campbell's remarks. He was a fair man, the first lieutenant was, but he'd brook no slackness.

"It's the government man with Mr. Laqua and the cap'n's cox'n."

"Government man," Campbell spat. "He's been aboard off and on for months and you still don't know he's Lord Skalla? Maybe some additional instruction might help. Mr. Adams!"

"Aye, Lieutenant Campbell, educated he'll be."

Once on board, Lord Skalla approached Gabe. He was fuming as he spoke, "Made to wait an hour only to find my man is at Simon's Town. But we'll discuss that later. Is there any chance we can weigh anchor now, Captain? We can rendezvous with the other ships once we are outside the bay."

"The breeze is a land breeze and the tide is on the ebb. However, I trust our master can see us safely out of the bay," Gabe said. This brought a snicker from those within hearing. "Mr. Campbell, prepare to weigh anchor and get underway. Mr. Sebastian, if you will signal the squadron, please."

"Aye, Captain."

Once underway, Gabe went down to his cabin where Lord Skalla had helped himself to a glass of hock.

"Well," Skalla snorted in an irritated voice. "I would not be surprised to hear the Danes have thrown in with the French on the side of the Americans."

"Did someone say that?" Gabe asked.

"No, it was attitude and behavior more than what was said. Did you see that Dutch sixty-four...of course you didn't? You couldn't have from where we were anchored," Skalla said, after draining his glass and taking a moment to think. "She was anchored much closer inshore."

Lord Skalla gazed at the empty glass and set it down. Gabe called for Nesbit, and while Skalla was pacing, he ordered something a bit stronger. Fresh glasses were brought out and two fingers of the amber bourbon were poured into each one. Skalla paused in his pacing to accept the glass. Experience had taught him the fiery liquid was to be sipped, not gulped.

After taking a sip, Skalla started again, "Bet you can't guess where the Dutch warship just came from?" Before Gabe could speak, Skalla answered his own question. "St. Croix. Seems they've had some type of a raid on a fort there. While no evidence was found or flags flown to identify the culprits, they spoke English."

"Could have been Americans," Gabe responded glibly.

"Damme, sir, but we think alike. Those were my exact words when I heard the story. Of course, I was properly enraged that anyone should attack one of our friends and politely asked if any reason for the attack had been discovered. When none was given, I explained how American privateers had on several occasions attacked and raided our small island of Tobago, from whence we just came."

"Did you have to give a reason for looking for your man?" Gabe asked.

"Oh yes, I volunteered it." Seeing the confusion on Gabe's face, Lord Skalla continued, "We have always had agents of trade between us and the Dutch. I was merely calling on the fellow, who is a lifelong family friend, on my way to the Indian Ocean, where I will speak to the Honest Johns about the American and French raiders. Did you know, Captain, our squadron is to serve as convoy protection for the East India trade ships sailing home."

"I do now," Gabe acknowledged. "I doubt anyone else in the squadron knows that...except maybe Dagan."

"Aye," Lord Skalla agreed with a laugh. "Except Dagan."

CHAPTER THIRTY

DAGAN AND HEX STOOD by the stern looking back at Table Mountain. "You'd have to see it to believe it," Hex was saying. "The master says the base is granite, while the top is sandstone and rises to about 3,500 feet at the south part of the bay.

"He'd know...his kind usually does," Dagan responded.

"He also said," Hex continued trying to make conversation, "That even though the Cape Peninsula is rocky and barren with stunted trees here and there, the inland ground is rich and fertile." When Dagan didn't respond, Hex gave up and kept silent.

After a minute or so, Dagan grasped his friend's upper arm. "Forgive me, Jake, I'm poor company this afternoon. I think I'll go down and write a few letters."

Hex watched as Dagan walked away. His demeanor spoke volumes. *He thinks we are in for a fight*, Hex decided. *Well, at least he's got someone to write to. That's more than I can say. Were it not for Sir Gabe, I'd be as much adrift as anyone.* Thinking back to England, Hex sighed and then smiled to himself. Well, there was a lass or two who'd not soon forget old Jake Hex, he bet. *Wonder if Katie remembers our coach ride? Probably not, but then again maybe...*

In the great cabin Gabe, the master, and the first lieutenant were going over the charts again.

"Simon's Town lies at the foot of these hills," the master was saying. "Last time I was there, they only had a single street. Of course, there are lots of little fishing villages all along here," he said pointing to little beaches on the map. "To get to Simon's Town we have to enter False

Bay. Since it's near night I'd say lets sail out to sea and make our approach in the morning."

Lord Skalla, who'd been lounging in one of Gabe's upholstered chairs, rose up on hearing this. "Is there no way to enter tonight? I need to speak with my man as early tomorrow as possible."

Hayes stared at the 'government man' for a second. Clearing his throat, he said, "We need plenty of sea room when we round the cape. Three to five miles, I'd say. More if the wind picks up."

"Once around the cape," Hayes continued with emphasis, "and with a fair wind, we steer north-northeast into False Bay. According to my charts, Simon's Bay lies but eleven miles northward of Cape Point, near the northwest corner of False Bay. The ordinary channel into Simon's Bay lies between Noah's Ark here and the Roman Rocks here, a width of seven cables. My recommendation, Captain, with time being a factor, is I'd round the cape but anchor once we are in False Bay and enter Simon's Bay upon the morrow." Lord Skalla didn't miss the "captain."

"Very well," Gabe replied. His answer was direct with finality.

Hearing this, Lord Skalla seated himself. He was no sailor. If entering the bay at night might jeopardize the ship there'd be no mission. The mission had to come first.

***

ENTERING FALSE BAY PROVED no problem at all. Dawn came with a fair breeze, causing wavelets that lapped against *Trident's* hull. Now the squadron had weighed anchor yet again and were making their way into Simon's Bay.

Campbell greeted Gabe, "The anchor party is getting plenty of practice, Captain. Before you know it they'll be able to do it in their sleep."

"Hopefully, they will be able to add to their practice today," Gabe replied. "After that, I hope the next time we break out the bower will be in Carlisle Bay."

"Aye, I'm ready for a break, as I know you are, Captain."

Did the first lieutenant know about his fight with Faith, Gabe wondered. Somehow word always seemed to get out aboard a ship.

Hayes ambled up. He was about to speak but paused as the lead man called out, "By the mark, fourteen and a half." Not liking the sounding, Hayes turned towards the man in the chains.

"By the mark, sixteen." A look of relief flooded over the master with the new sounding. Plenty of water under the keel and it should remain so into the anchorage.

He turned back to Gabe and spoke, "That flat rock is called Noah's Ark, Captain. Not sure who named it. On the other side, you will see Roman Rock. See the white water as the waves crash on it? That's a picture I'd love to paint. We were in Simon's Bay once when from the southwest a wind rose that not only brought rain, but the cold as well. I was later told it's called the kloof wind." Handing Gabe his glass, the master then pointed out a conspicuous mountain in to the northeast. "That is Hangklip Berg, Captain. It rises over Cape Hangklip. From anywhere in Simon's Bay it's a true bearing of S.71°E. No matter what position the ship is in. More than one captain has anchored here and found the ship's compass in need of adjustment."

"Sounds like a good exercise for the young gentlemen," Gabe said.

"It's already in the plans, Captain. Time permitting, it is in the plan," the master said.

***

LORD SKALLA WENT ASHORE as he had done the previous day. Only this time the barge with Hex and Laqua was back within the hour. Gabe called his professional men together and gave them permission to go ashore. A signal had been sent to the rest of the squadron and soon ship's boats were plying back and forth from ship to shore.

Hearing the water in Simon's Town was excellent, barrels were brought up from the hold, emptied, scoured and made ready for the water hoy.

Nesbit, Hex, and Dagan had all found reason to go ashore. Gabe had considered inviting all the captains to dine that evening when the sentry announced, "First Lieutenant, zur."

Gabe rose to greet Campbell, "All I have to offer is a glass of lukewarm lime juice, Don, but if it fits your taste, pour yourself a glass."

"Thank you, sir, I believe I will." Campbell then handed an envelope to Gabe. "Boat is alongside waiting for your reply," the first lieutenant added.

Reading the note, Gabe spoke, "We are invited to dine with Lord Skalla's man tonight and afterward a captain's conference."

"So it is not a social occasion," Campbell said.

"Not that it would appear." Then having a thought, Gabe walked over to his desk and took his writing quill out, dipped it into the ink bottle and scribbled a few lines. He returned to where Campbell sat. "Finish your glass, Mr. Campbell, and then have the boat take you ashore. Deliver this to Lord Skalla personally."

"Am I to wait for a reply, sir?"

"Yes, but have Hex or Lieutenant Laqua return to the ship with it."

"Am I to know what's in the note, Captain?"

"I suggested if this was to be a council of war, it might be good if each of the ships' first lieutenants and masters were to attend also. Lord Skalla is a good man, but he's not a sailor...yet. The dinner is not until eight o'clock tonight. It is not yet noon and I'd think it amiss, Lieutenant, if you didn't find something that would amuse you until which time you have to get ready for the dinner. You deserve a few hours away from the ship. That, and more. I don't know what I'd have done without you."

Campbell made to protest but Gabe waved it away. "I understand you are not a married man, Don."

"No sir."

"Well, I am. Now go see if you can charm some lovely Dutch maiden. Tell her you are an admiral and you are in charge of the British fleet."

Smiling, Campbell responded, "Damme sir, but that sounds rehearsed. Have you used it?"

"There was a time," Gabe admitted with a grin. "There was a time."

CHAPTER THIRTY-ONE

HAVING NEVER TASTED A South African dinner, Gabe had nothing to compare it with, but it did not stand up to what he was accustomed to. Those dinners at Government House on both Antigua and Barbados were much more traditional in regards to etiquette and the fare. Most of the food served that evening was cooked over an open fire in a three-legged pot called a potjie. Gabe did not attempt to identify the meat in the pot, which was cooked together with several other ingredients so as to make a stew...a damn spicy stew. He did recognize a type of corn, rice, carrots, and cabbage in it.

There was also a dish called bredie. It was cooked sweet potatoes mashed with butter and sprinkled with a nut and topped off with a drizzle of honey. Tripe was also served, perhaps as a nod to the guests' culture,. Roasted kid was also available, but the sauce on the goat caused Gabe's forehead to sweat.

"Damned if this is not worse than some of Chen Lee's concoctions," Gabe whispered to Dagan.

"Aye," Dagan whispered back. "They do not hold back with the chili peppers and spicy curries."

Gabe saw Hayes, the master, appear to be playing it safe, eating the tripe and pickled fish along with a helping of mieliepap, a porridge made from maize and meal served with butter. A South African wine from the Constantia Estate, and which was reportedly from the first vines planted in South Africa, was particularly appeasing to the palate.

Campbell, whose taste for the wine was less than enthusiastic, was drinking a cloudy beer that was said to be made by the native women.

Lord Skalla had been seated to the right of their host, Mr. Bridges, with Gabe on the left.

Getting Gabe's attention, Lord Skalla said, "Bridges here is going to give us a supply of droëwors." Realizing Gabe had no idea what he was talking about, Skalla explained, "Droëwors is a dried sausage. It provides a quick, between meals bite that will stay with you. I always get a case when possible. If we were going to be here longer," he continued, "I would impose upon our host to have his cooks prepare us a dish called Bobotie. You would love it."

Little did either one of them know the opportunity would arise. After the business had been completed and the latest scouting reports gone over, Hayes said, "It will be a dangerous bit of navigation. Ambodifotatra is where you say the rebels are likely anchored. I don't even have a chart that shows the place and only a couple that list St. Mary's. We know nothing about the depths close in, what the bottom is like, sandy or rocks or how quickly it shoals. All we have is your scout's theory that we should be able to get close enough to the blasted enemy for our guns to be in range. We are told Ambodifotatra lies just southerly to here," the master said, pointing to a spot on a chart that jutted out. "Depending on the direction of the wind, we may only be able to attack from the north and then have to sail around the island for another pass."

"Why so?" Bridges asked.

Seeing the man was truly interested, Hayes answered, "St. Mary's is wide about the middle but narrows considerably where we think the anchorage lies. If we came from the south steering northerly we'd have to be ready to go about quickly, else chance running aground where the island juts out. If we knew for certain the island's defenses, would it not behoove us to heave to?"

"We could put a spring on the cable and thereby shift our fire," Lieutenant Campbell said.

"A good thought, Mr. Campbell. I feel we need to know more about the channel, how deep it is, and then discuss how to attack the place," Captain Peckham of *Venus* volunteered.

"Well, you can't sail in with a man in the chains," Chatham, the captain of *Brilliant* said.

"No," Gabe said. "You can't, but a couple of men doing a little night fishing might be able to take a few soundings."

"Aye," Hayes said, taking up the idea. "Should someone become suspicious and investigate, the lead could always be dropped over the side."

Looking to Bridges, Gabe said, "Can you get a couple of men in close?"

Nodding his head in the affirmative, the man spoke softly, "It can be arranged."

The following morning, Bridges sent out his coaster to do some trading on the eastern coast of Madagascar. From there, a few men in one of the island's many fishing boats should rouse no alarm. Three of *Trident's* men went along: Harper, who once earned a living fishing; Thorpe, the poacher, and to Gabe's astonishment, Dagan.

"I feel the need to get away a few days," was Dagan's only explanation; a reprieve from the day to day on board *Trident* or to get a feel of where they'd likely do battle…and possibly die?

A sudden thought came to Gabe that made him shiver. He'd never for once considered that Dagan might die. Now, it was like a ghost ran through his soul. Did Dagan have some premonition? Did death await him or Dagan or even Hex? The odds were not in their favor: a hostile enemy, an uncharted coast…and the looks of nasty weather. Not a damn thing was on their side.

Certainly not the island cuisine. In fact, Hex had had to see the ship's surgeon, as his innards were in such a mess. He still looked pale as he sat checking Gabe's weapons for rust.

"Feel better, Jake?"

"Aye, cap'n. It was like a broadside from both ends at once. But I drank the surgeon's pickle juice and now I feel some better." A grin broke out on the cox'n's face. "At least now I can fart without fear." A chuckle came from the pantry. Even Nesbit was amused by Hex's comments.

***

THE SUN WAS GOING down. Nesbit lit a lantern so his captain could see to sign the last of the papers the purser had brought down. Gabe had been so intent to get through the purser's pile that he hadn't noticed that the wind had picked up until it blew through the stern windows, causing some of the papers to fly about, scattering across the desk. The hanging lantern had started to sway, casting shadows across the cabin.

Hearing the captain swear got Nesbit's attention. He approached Gabe and asked, "Should I go ahead and prepare your evening meal, sir?"

"Yes," Gabe replied.

Gabe, the first lieutenant, and the master were to dine with the young gentlemen that evening. Would it have to be postponed?

"Captain, sir, midshipman of the watch."

Seeing Mr. Brayden, Gabe beckoned the boy to come forward. "How may I help you, young sir?"

"The first lieutenant's compliments, sir, and you may wish to come on deck."

Typically, the master and first lieutenant were quick to go topside should anything arouse their suspicion that something amiss was in the offering. Therefore, something must be brewing for Gabe to be summoned.

"A dirty night I'm thinking," Hayes volunteered. "Barometer has already dropped to 30-30. Wind is already stronger than usual and is from the south-southeast."

"Are we in for a blow?"

"Aye, Captain, that's what I'm thinking. I noticed heavy white clouds over Muizenberg earlier but the wind had not picked up then."

"Do we lay out another anchor?" Campbell asked.

"I think so, Don, before it gets any worse." Looking across the anchorage, Gabe could see the other ships in the squadron were busy breaking out second anchors. Would *Trident* drag her anchor? Maybe not, but why chance it. It was full dark when the task was done.

On shore, lanterns and candles were being lit so that it created a flickering appearance. Not unlike the lightning bugs Gabe had seen in South Carolina when he'd met Faith. A patter of rain started to fall. *Big drops turning the deck dark, like spots on a leopard's back*, Gabe thought. Bridges had one of the big cats on a chain in his backyard.

"Better than a watch dog," Bridges had said as he walked up, offering the big cat a morsel of meat from the palm of his hand. Gabe wasn't sure he was any better, thinking of Sampson, but he was scarier.

The watch had just been changed and Holton had the deck. *Good. He was a good officer and would not hesitate to sound the alarm if need be*, Gabe thought. The wind was now gusty. The rain picked up and the shower was replaced by a hard driving rain. Waves had turned from heavy rollers to churning white caps that crashed into the ship and onto the shore.

Hex had brought Gabe his tarpaulin and handed him one of the African sausages. "Good time to try one of these droëwors, Captain."

Biting into the dried sausage, Gabe was amazed at how flavorful it was. "Tried one?" Gabe asked.

"No sir." Breaking his in half, Gabe gave his cox'n part of the sausage to try.

"A little spicy, but not hot like the curry," Hex said. "A little salty though. We'll need a wet before long."

"Is there any of that Shebeen beer left?" Gabe asked.

"A pint or so I'd think," Hex replied.

"Might go good with this," Gabe said, holding up the sausage.

"I'll go check," Hex said, knowing the captain would not leave the deck in a blow.

CHAPTER THIRTY-TWO

THE CRY OF "SAIL ho" caused a momentary bit of excitement. However, when the ship was identified as Bridges' coastal ship, the hands went back to their make and mend. It was Sunday, but being in port, Gabe had allowed the first lieutenant to declare Sunday afternoon make and mend, as had the other ships in the squadron that were at anchor.

In spite of Bridges' and Lord Skalla's assurance that they had little to fear from the enemy in a neutral port, Gabe's years at sea had taught him to always expect the unexpected. Right now, *Venus* and *Thorn* were patrolling. The frigate was always in sight of the bay and the brig. Should the enemy approach signals could be relayed and the rest of the ships would be ready.

The enemy had not showed up, nor had any other ship for that matter. It was like Simon's Bay was deserted except for the British ships and a few fishing boats. It had been eleven days since Dagan's group had set sail. They were overdue and anxiety was causing Gabe to be snappish. Madagascar was said to be two hundred fifty or sixty miles away. St. Mary's lay about five miles off the western coast of Madagascar. If the coaster averaged five knots, they should have been there in three days at most. A day or so for sounding, then they should have been back in a week. Add a day or so for bad weather, and they still should have been back in nine days. Hopefully, the trip was fruitful.

The coastal tied up at its usual mooring and a boat was put over the side to row the three men from *Trident* home. The men's return was met with a warm welcome. The first lieutenant waited a while and then escorted Thorpe and Harper down to the great cabin, having given Dagan and the Captain a few minutes alone.

Once the men were brought down, Gabe asked their preference in drink, "Straight rum, hock, or a glass of wine?" He knew lime juice was not acceptable. Gabe winced as he also offered them the choice of bourbon.

"We'll take what that 'un be drinking," Harper said, speaking of Hex.

"Aye," Thorpe added. "If it be to Jake's liking, it'll be to ours."

"We...ah...confiscated a few cases of Cruzan rum from St. Croix," Hex said. "To my way of thinking that be a man's drink." Looking at Gabe, his cox'n added, "No offense meant, Cap'n."

"None taken," Gabe responded, all the while thinking, *you silver-tongued devil, Jake Hex.*

Catching Dagan's eye, he realized Dagan must be thinking the same thought. Both of them knew Hex preferred the bourbon, but with it in short supply, he'd taken steps to see it lasted a while longer.

The men began their story with the storm that hit them the first night at sea. Gabe remembered it well. He'd spent the entire night on deck, eating those sausages that gave him a bad case of dyspepsia. The surgeon had promptly recommended the pickle juice and damned if it hadn't done the trick.

Smacking his lips then eyeing the rum appreciatively, Harper spoke, "Once at Madagascar, the ship pulled into a couple of ports, setting up our, ah..."

"Alibi," Dagan added for the man.

"Then we pulled right over to where the bloody buggers were anchored. Greeted the cap'n like 'e was a mate," Thorpe added.

Gabe looked at Dagan, who nodded his affirmative.

"We were fishing off the ship's stern when this bloke in a boat says there's better fishing just off shore. We waited until it was dark and out we went. Dagan there, 'e did the soundings, while me and Thorpe fished."

"Gave a right smart of our catch to the bloody buggers," Thorpe added. "But it was worth it, as taking the fish ashore we got a peek at their defenses. Not so much there, but on the little island there be."

"Little island?"

"Aye," Dagan said. "Ilot Madame, it is located at the mouth of the harbour. This creates a narrow approach to the harbour making the island easy to defend. It has a fort of sorts, more a palisade with a few cannons on each side. There's also a similar defense on Ile Ste.-Marie and they have a guard boat of sorts that patrols the harbour at night. There are enough ships in the small harbour to make maneuvering difficult. However, we did see a ship that was beached on Ilot Madame. They were careening the sides, so the bottom there must be sandy. In truth, it would be a tricky piece of work even if the rebels were all we had to worry about."

"All?" Gabe asked, his mind still trying to digest all he'd been told.

"Aye," Dagan replied. "There's also the French."

"Well, damme," Gabe responded. "Aren't you all full of good news?"

"It's possible they won't be there when we attack," Campbell volunteered.

"Not with my luck," Gabe said, running his hand through his hair.

"It were a squadron of the Frogs, Cap'n," said Harper. "Had a big eighty gun with a commodore's pennant, they did. Rowed right under the big ship's stern we did."

"Aye," Thorpe said, adding, "Friendly sort of bloke, howsoever. Tossed us a bottle of wine 'e did. They may be frog eaters but 'e didn't want no fish, did 'e, 'arper?"

"Nay, mate, 'e didn't."

"You talked to them?" Gabe asked incredibly.

"Why not?" Dagan replied. "We heard several different accents and languages among the privateers."

"No one country 'as a monopoly on rogues, Cap'n," Thorpe said.

He's heard that somewhere, Gabe thought. Thorpe is a good man but he didn't put that sentence together. Seeing Dagan smile it was obvious where Thorpe had heard the phrase.

"How many ships were there?" Gabe asked.

Before Dagan could respond, Thorpe replied, "Eight at least. The big two decker what flew a commodore's pennant, and several smaller ships. One was a small frigate."

Gabe felt like he'd been hit in the midsection with a belaying pin. After a few more minutes and another glass of rum, it was obvious there was nothing more to be gained. Thorpe and Harper were dismissed.

"We need a captain's conference and I need some fresh air," Gabe said. "Jake, go ashore and see if it's convenient for Lord Skalla to return to the ship. I'm sure Bridges' captain has filled him in already. Mr. Campbell, see if the master has any charts with this Ilot Madame on it. If not, Dagan and he need to get together and draw it on the charts he has."

"Aye, Captain."

Once on deck Gabe and Dagan walked toward the stern where the signals midshipman was working at something in the flag locker.

"Mr. Sebastian!"

Startled, the young man whirled around and, seeing the captain, he smiled. "Yes sir, Captain."

"Make a signal, 'Captains Repair on Board.'"

Dagan and Gabe stood by the taffrail. Both were taking in the surroundings but neither was speaking. Boats were being shoved off from the squadron's ships. Hex had made it to the beach. The bargemen were sitting easy until his return with Lord Skalla. Dagan busied himself lighting his pipe.

When he spoke it was little more than a whisper. "I've letters in my sea chest."

Hearing this, Gabe looked up shocked, "Uncle...surely nothing will happen to you."

"No one is promised tomorrow, Gabe. It is best to be prepared. I set up things with Hugh as you did while we were in Portsmouth. Maria will be taken care of until she passes if I were to fall. When she passes, you are to get that which is left."

"Uncle, don't talk like this."

"We must, Gabe. I want you to know you've been more than a nephew to me. I remember when you were small and I promised your Grandfather Dupree that I would watch over you until you were a man. I often wondered what I'd gotten myself into. You are a man now, Gabe, and I have to say it has been a journey I wouldn't have changed for the world."

The cry of "boat ahoy" interrupted the conversation. Hurrying, Dagan said, "There is a letter to Betsy. I would ask that this be delivered personally, even if it has to wait until the war is over."

"You have my word," Gabe almost cried, the anguish on his face and in his voice.

"Go below now so you'll be ready to meet your captains," Dagan said.

Gabe looked into his uncle's face. It was weathered with crow's feet at the corners of his eyes. A sprinkling of gray was at his temples. Dagan had aged right before Gabe's eyes and he hadn't even noticed. *Damn this war, damn it to hell for taking everything a man had. Maybe Faith was right*. Not caring who was on deck or who might see it, Gabe hugged Dagan and whispered, "I love you, uncle...and I may be a man but I still need you. More than ever, I need you."

***

LORD SKALLA AND ALL the captains, except those on patrol, gathered in the great cabin. Beer, African beer, wine, and lime juice were all offered. To Gabe's surprise, most chose the African beer.

"Gentlemen, our scouting party has returned. I'm sure most of you witnessed Bridges' coaster when she returned to port. The reason I've...asked you here," Gabe said, choosing his words carefully, still not comfortable being in overall command of the squadron. Pausing he started again, "The reason I've asked you here, gentlemen, is that we have a problem."

CHAPTER THIRTY-THREE

"A FINE SIGHT, IS IT not, Captain?"

"Aye, my Lord. Even a single ship under full sail is something to behold, but an entire squadron is even more so. It's...magnificent."

"You are right, Captain."

The squadron was indeed looking magnificent. The wind was from the west-southwest, making it almost dead astern. The last check of the log showed eleven knots. It was probable that with a few hours at this speed they'd reach Madagascar a half-day sooner than expected.

The squadron had sailed from False Bay on a southerly course. Gabe doubted anyone in Simon's Town much cared, but you never knew who the Danes had watching from one of the cliffs along the cape peninsula. Dagan and Gabe had talked at length as to whether Bridges' man, the captain of the coaster, was trustworthy.

"He did nothing to make me suspicious," Dagan had said, but still the man was ashore without Dagan being present on several occasions. "My concerns are not with the privateers, Gabe. They are no match for the squadron. It's the damnable French that have me concerned."

"Aye," Gabe answered.

The French were definitely the major source of concern. Lord Skalla had been given reliable information that the French were putting together a fleet under the command of Admiral Pierre-André de Suffren. It was expected he would sail to Ile de France, which was a major French port in the Indian Ocean. Lord Skalla told Gabe that Bridges had informed him that French diplomats had been visiting Cape Town. It was very probable that the Danes would side with the

French and Americans, thereby virtually ending all trade in the Indian Ocean.

Ile de France was east of Madagascar. Were the French ships that Dagan, Thorpe, and Harper had seen *en route* back to Ile de France? Were they part of Suffren's fleet or another squadron sailing under a commodore with a different assignment? So many ifs. However, they must sail on. The mission had not changed. *Would he fight*, Gabe wondered. What if the French had an entire squadron in addition to the big eighty-gun man of war? The British squadron would have no chance against such a force, but would he give battle? There was only one answer. One damnable answer...yes.

No wonder Dagan had been so down, so demoralized. Would any of them survive such a one-sided battle? Gabe had talked privately with Lord Skalla and, holding nothing back, he had stressed the battle Lord Skalla had witnessed with Jepson in his fight with the corvette would be nothing in comparison to what they had in store if the French were there in force.

Lord Skalla thanked Gabe for being forthright but had said, using Gabe's title, "Sir Gabe, the mission was of my doing. I've put you in harm's way. I will see you through it. It may be to death or to glory we steer, but either way we will do it together."

The two shook hands, and then Lord Skalla went ashore to collect a few belongings he'd left at Bridges' house. No doubt he had a few letters to write as well.

The group sat around the table in Gabe's cabin: Lord Skalla, Dagan, Lieutenant Campbell, Lieutenant Holton, and the master Mr. Hayes, Dr. Cornish, and two midshipmen, Mr. Michael and Mr. Sebastian. The meal had been one of Nesbit's finest. The dessert was so good, the young gentlemen didn't hesitate to take seconds. The conversation was light, no one wishing to bring up the impending battle.

With a knock on the door the sentry announced, "Mr. Mark, sir, midshipman of the watch." Hawks was the lieutenant on duty. If he sent the midshipman down, there was a good reason. Mark looked at the crumbs on the dessert plates, envy in his eyes, sure he'd hear about it later.

"Addressing the captain," he reported smartly. "Mr. Hawks' compliments, sir, but the barometer is falling and he can see lightning on the horizon. He thinks we are in for a blow."

"Well, damme!" Gabe exclaimed. "What else can we expect? Tell Mr. Hawks I will be there directly."

"Aye, Cap'n."

As soon as Mark left, the master scraped back his chair and said, "With your permission I will go on deck."

"I will join Mr. Hayes if you don't mind, Captain," Lieutenant Campbell said.

"Very well, Mr. Campbell, I will be up directly."

Hearing this, Cornish finished his wine in a gulp and said, "Shoo, shoo, you young gentlemen. Duty calls our captain."

When everyone had left, Dagan said, "We'll see the sun." That was the second time in a few days span that he had uttered the same words.

Relieved, Gabe finished his glass and then went topside.

"I didn't want to warn you unnecessarily, Captain, but that's quite a display on the horizon; like a Chinese fireworks show."

Indeed, bolts of lightning could be seen on the distant horizon. After several bolts zigzagged across the sky, the whole horizon would light up like someone had set off a flare.

"Never regret calling me, Mr. Hawks," Gabe said, clapping his lieutenant on the back. "I'd rather know of possible danger sooner than later. Besides, I'd think something amiss if you didn't call me to share in witnessing such a display of nature."

"Thank you, Captain. Mr. Campbell and Mr. Hayes said much the same."

Hayes walked over and said, "The barometer is at twenty-nine. We are in for a squall, I'm thinking."

"It seems the Almighty is in league with the Frogs," Gabe said jokingly. "All we have had from the start is one blow after another." Turning to the master, he added, "Put two of your best helmsmen at the wheel, Mr. Hayes. We have too much at stake to perform poorly and succumb to the elements."

Soon there was thunder and rain along with the lightning, hour after hour of a driving rain. The winds were brisk, with the sea breaking over the starboard bow. Campbell, without waiting to be ordered, had lifelines rigged. The crescendo of wind through the riggings picked up until there was a constant whistle.

Men sat silent in their messes...waiting. All of them had stories where ships caught up in a desperate storm suddenly vanished. Would that be their fate?

The wind changed just before dawn, dropping from a full blow to a few gusts and then to a slight breeze. The rain slowed to a mild shower and then as the sun came up, it stopped altogether. The lookout called down that all the ships in the squadron were on station.

As the sun rose further and men were dismissed from quarters, the sky lit up a brilliant new day. The whole stretch of sea was clear as far as one could see to the horizon.

At breakfast, Dagan blew at his cup of hot coffee. "A beautiful sunrise, was it not?"

CHAPTER THIRTY-FOUR

"LAND HO!" YONDER LAY their foe, their destiny. To larboard Madagascar, to starboard St. Mary's, or as Dagan called it, Ile Ste.-Marie.

"Do you think the rascals will be up, Mr. Campbell?"

"I'm not sure, Captain."

"If they're like you, they aren't," Dagan chimed in, smiling.

It had been decided that *Trident* would enter the harbour first, passing Ilot Madame on the wider passage, while *Stag* passed through the narrow of the two passages with *Venus* and *Brilliant* following. The three smaller ships would not join in the attack.

Jenkins was to take *Zebra* to the northern tip of the island to prevent any of the smaller ships from escaping and to keep a weather eye out for the French. *Thorn* would keep watch to the south. *Fortune* would heave-to off Ilot Madame and be ready to send boats or aid where needed.

Campbell called up to the lookout, "Do you see anything?"

"Not a sail on the horizon, sir."

"Damme man, the island, the blasted island. Do you see anything of the island?"

Not waiting for a reply, Campbell called to Midshipman Caed, "Take my glass and up you go."

The ships had closed to between three and four miles when Caed called down. "Smoke from both the big and little islands, sir. Otherwise, there is no other movement about the island or the bay."

A fresh breeze blew against Gabe's shirt. Hex was there with his weapons, so Gabe lifted his arms slightly and whispered to his cox'n. "Have a care, Jake."

"Aye, Captain. I'll be by you."

"That's not what I said," Gabe snorted, receiving a smile from Hex.

"The crew might feel better with a word from you, Captain," Campbell said in a quiet voice.

Gabe had already gone around the ship speaking to the men. They had been at quarters since breakfast. The ship was in every way as ready for battle as could be. Taking a trumpet, Gabe addressed the men, "Our first lieutenant has asked if I might like to give you men a few words. What you'd like, I'm thinking, is a double measure of grog and a bit of prize money." This brought a cheer, as Gabe knew it would. "I promise you all the double measure after the villains yonder are put to rights, and if any prize money is to be had we'll share in it as well."

"Huzza, huzza the captain, huzza Sir Gabe," cried the men

"That was well said, Captain."

Turning, Gabe found Lord Skalla there in formal dress with his sword on and two pistols in his sash.

"Be sure to walk about, Lord Skalla," Hex volunteered. "Otherwise, you'll likely be taken as a ship's officer and used as a target by the rebels." This brought several laughs.

***

THE SHIPS WERE ALMOST to Ilot Madame when a bugle blared from somewhere on the island. Campbell had a man in the chains, and the sounds of the bugle drowned out his calls.

From overhead, Caed called down in an excited voice, "Warship, sir, a French warship inside the bay."

"Damn," Gabe shouted. It was too late now, they were committed. "Mr. Sebastian," he called to the signals midshipman. "Make signal, 'enemy in sight'."

"Aye, Captain."

That had been the planned signal if warships were in harbour. Mr. Hawks and Mr. Laqua were on the gun decks with Midshipmen Brayden and Michael at their sides. The gun crews were stripped down to the waist with rags tied over their ears.

"Mr. Hawks, concentrate the forward guns on the island's defenses. Save the rest and the other deck for the Frenchie."

"Aye, Captain."

"Mr. Campbell...reduce to fighting sail, if you please."

"Aye, sir."

From overhead, Caed called down again, "'Pears to be an eighty-gun ship, Captain."

Was this a setup? Gabe wondered. *Was Bridges' man a turncoat*?

Slowly, *Trident* approached the mouth of the channel. Seconds felt like hours to the men as they watched and waited.

BOOM!..BOOM!...BOOM... Cannon fire from the defenses on the small island. Gabe felt *Trident* shudder as the balls slammed into the hull but he could see no damage.

"Make a note," Gabe ordered. "Fired on by the enemy."

"Aye, sir."

Following his captain's orders the forward cannons fired at the flashes from the shore as the ship's guns came to bear.

"That ought to wake the Frogs," Campbell shouted.

"Indeed, sir," Gabe replied. "Let's hope they are still breaking their fast and were not at quarters."

"Deck thar," Caed was calling down again. "Corvette to larboard, sir, looks like she is slipping her cable."

"Mr. Thomas," Gabe called to the midshipman. "My compliments to Mr. Renfrow. Have him concentrate the bow chasers on yonder ship. I don't want the brigs to have to deal with it unless we fail."

"We'll not fail you, Captain," Thomas promised as he ran to pass the captain's orders on to the gunner.

The French warship was firing her guns now but few could bear.

"Two points to larboard, Mr. Hayes."

"Aye, Captain."

"Mr. Mark, go tell Mr. Laqua and Mr. Hawks to fire the starboard guns as we pass, and then prepare to fire the larboard guns once we come about."

"Aye, sir," the midshipman said as he ran to do as ordered.

"Harbour is full of ships," Dagan swore. "Far more than would be expected."

Down on the gun decks, the lieutenants were talking to the gun crews. "Pick your targets men, and then fire as you bear. Gun captain, keep your wits and keep the gun firing. It promises to be a hot day, but remember the captain has promised a double tot."

All the guns were double-shotted and the upper deck guns had a measure of grape as well. As *Trident* swung, gun after gun fired, belching orange flames of death. Gabe saw *Trident's* balls slamming home against the big French warship. Broadside to broadside the ships' cannons roared. Almost the entire starboard rail was gone on *Trident* as the French balls returned the same death and destruction as the British balls.

"The frigates will never hold up under such," Campbell shouted to be heard.

"Not a lot can be done about that now," Gabe replied, the smoke from the broadsides making him cough.

The plan had been for the frigates to concentrate on the privateers if the French were there and *Trident* would deal with the French. But nobody had bargained for an eighty-gun ship when the mission was assigned. *Stag* had now passed through the narrow passage. *Trident* sheltered her from the Frenchman but *Venus* would be behind her and have no protection.

Trident's guns continued to fire until they passed the French ship and prepared to come about. Now *Stag* was firing into the anchored privateers.

"Mr. Sebastian, signal *Venus* to luff until we come about. Possibly, we can offer her a bit of protection if we can come between her and the Frenchman. Mr. Hayes, prepare to come about."

"Aye, Captain, but we've not got the best wind."

Gabe either didn't hear or chose to ignore the advice. Either way he had little choice. "Helms a-lee," he ordered.

Trident came up into the wind. The big ship was momentarily in stays and Gabe questioned himself. *Have I misjudged it*?

The helmsman was holding the wheel, and then after what seemed like an eternity, she began to answer.

"Mainsail haul." The men hurriedly went about their task, knowing their lives depended on it. 'Round the bow came until her sails filled.

A sigh of relief came from the master, "I was about to say, Captain, this ain't no frigate but damned if you don't sail her like one."

Looking about, Gabe felt his body tremble. Dead and wounded men were scattered across the deck. It suddenly dawned on him that the repetitive splash he heard was dead bodies being cast over the side. Wright had his loblolly boys working among the downed men. Some were receiving attention where they lay while others were being taken below to the surgeon.

Cries of pain, anguish, and fear could be heard as the men were treated. Looking beyond the men, the deck was in shambles. Guns were overturned and dismounted, bloodstains spotted the deck but *Trident* could still fight.

"Ready, Mr. Hawks, Mr. Laqua?" The latter had a bandage on his arm.

"Aye," they said in unison.

"Captain?" It was Mr. Thomas.

"Yes."

"Mr. Holton believes the big Frenchie is slipping her cable, sir."

Trident was almost in position to fire into their foe again. Yes, he could see the bow swinging toward the shore. Had a lucky shot parted her anchor cables? Was the Frenchman trying to get underway? If so, he'd slipped the wrong cable first. The privateers also had activity as ships were trying to get underway.

"*Stag* needs help," Campbell volunteered.

"She'll have to wait," Gabe responded. "One broadside and *Venus* will never sail again."

"Frenchie's firing," someone shouted from forward.

Again, they'd fired too early, before all the guns could bear, but damage was inflicted nevertheless.

"The jib boom is dangling, Captain. She'll not take much."

"Once we pass the Frenchman, do what you can," Gabe ordered the bosun.

"As you bear, fire."

Gabe heard Hawks calling to his men. In steady succession, gun after gun fired until the entire broadside had been delivered, a deliberate fire that caused a cheer to go up as when the smoke cleared and the gunners could see the results of their gunnery. The mizzenmast was down, gaping holes were now seen where gun ports had been, but the French continued to return fire. *Venus* took advantage of *Trident's* position and sailed past without fear of the French warship. She was now well on her way to aid *Stag*.

"We can't stand another broadside like the last one, Captain." This came from the carpenter, Mr. Bufford. "We got two feet in the well and more coming. We have stove in planks everywhere. Likely need to fother a sail soon."

Gabe looked across at the French's ship. Her flag had been run up the mainmast now that the mizzen mast was down. Her position seemed changed…she was…yes by all that was holy, her bow had swung around until it was facing the shore and the stern was facing them.

"Mr. Campbell, have the Lieutenant Turner put together a party to help Mr. Bufford while we make another pass."

"Aye, sir."

"Captain," Bufford pleaded. "I don't know if she will float long enough for another pass."

"She'll have to, Mr. Bufford. Mr. Hayes."

"Yes sir."

"I'm going to take advantage of the Frenchman's position. We may not get another chance so I intend to close within musket shot range and give her every ball we've got up her backside."

"Aye, Captain."

"Mr. Mark, if you will please go tell Lieutenant Hawks and Laqua my intentions."

"I'll go with him," Dagan volunteered.

Trident passed through the narrow channel but the guns of Ilot Madame were silent. Between *Trident* and the frigates, the small fort had been reduced to a shambles. Once clear of the channel, Gabe gave the order to come about. No doubt about it, *Trident* was sluggish but she answered. With the cannons temporarily silent, the sound of the pumps could be heard. No time to worry about that now.

"*Brilliant* has boarded the corvette," Lieutenant Holton called. Gabe had lost track of the enemy ship.

Renfroe had not failed. His forward gunners had brought down the corvette's mast and now they had at least one prize.

One of the topmen spoke to Mr. Thomas, who then approached Gabe. "Captain, sir, this is Lewis. He says that yonder ship, the one *Stag* is alongside, is the old *Foxfire*. He said he'd know her anywhere."

"Thank you, Mr.Thomas. Wonder if Horne is on board," Gabe said to Campbell, who'd overheard the conversation.

"I wouldn't guess, Captain, but seeing our ships bearing down on him, I'd make a hasty retreat ashore and hide, were I him."

In the time it took to come about and make their way through the channel, the Frenchmen had put boats over the side and were attempting to haul the bow around.

"Wasted effort," Hayes swore.

"Do you offer them surrender?" Campbell asked.

A cannon was fired from the enemy's stern, followed by two more in rapid succession. "There's your answer, sir."

"Captain Schoggins," Gabe called to the marine. "I would think they'll have men on the upper deck firing down on us. They might prove good target practice for your marines." Other than standing guard at the hatches, they'd had little to do thus far.

"Aye, Captain. There's a few who could use the practice."

"Not likely," Hex muttered, hearing the marine's reply. "Any of them could probably shoot a flea off a cat's arse."

Adam's party was still working on the jib boom. They had used lines and tackles to support it but how long would it last? The enemy must have moved more guns as cannons continued to fire from the stern. A crash was heard amidships and several men were down. Gabe wondered how the men stood at their stations with the piercing screams and crash of cannon balls all about. Smoke drifted from the French ship, cutting down on visibility. It stung the eyes, burned the nose, and made men cough. He could hear Mr. Michael and Mr. Brayden encouraging the surviving gunners as they closed with the Frenchie.

Closer and closer *Trident* closed. His poor ship was taking a pounding, Gabe realized, but now it was payback time.

"Steady as you go, Mr. Hayes, steady as you go." Taking the speaking trumpet, Gabe called down, "Be prepared. Fire as you bear. Now, Mr. Hayes, to larboard."

Trident swung to larboard and the starboard guns fired from both decks. *Trident's* guns were sweeping the stern as they passed. Double-shotted balls slammed home, decimating the intricate stern work, the galley, and the rudder. Splinters and huge hunks of wood filled the air as one ball after another slammed into the once mighty French battle ship. A cheer went up as the French flag came down and a white flag went up.

The cheer died suddenly as someone shouted, "She's on fire, the Frogs on fire."

"Damn," Gabe said aloud. Friend or foe, there was no pleasure in seeing a ship burn.

"Not your fault, Captain. They gave you no choice."

"Move away," Gabe told Hayes. "Mr. Campbell, get some boats in the water."

However, before the order could be carried out the air was rent with a great explosion. A ball of flame rising above the mast...even above the tree tops on shore. A sudden silence, it was over. He'd survived... they'd survived.

"Sir Gabe! I congratulate you, sir. I've never seen anything like it. It's no wonder Admiral Buck chose you to be his flag captain. Had I the power, sir, I'd make you an admiral on the spot." Lord Skalla was giddy. He was happy to be alive. *As he should be*, Gabe thought, already wondering what the butcher's bill would be.

"Make signals, Mr. Campbell, take charge of prizes and prepare to make sail." Looking across the harbour, Gabe was amazed at the ships destroyed. They had the corvette, a sloop, and the *Foxfire* as prizes.

Another dozen ships were destroyed; some had been sunk but were so close inshore the masts were sticking out of the water. One ship had drifted ashore and was now on its side with cannon holes through the bottom. It looked like a ship graveyard.

"Do we go ashore, Captain?" Campbell asked.

"No," Gabe answered. "We've carried the day so far. There's no reason to tempt fate."

"Aye," they all agreed.

Trident had just made its way past Ilot Madame on its way out to sea when the lookout called down, "Signal from *Thorn*, sir."

Seeing Mr. Sebastian take overly long to answer, Campbell bellowed, "Must the captain wait, young sir?"

Sebastian was visibly shaken when he answered, "No, sir. Enemy in sight."

CHAPTER THIRTY-FIVE

HEARING SEBASTIAN ADVISE GABE of *Thorn's* signal was like a wicked blow to the midsection by a prizefighter. A collective 'humph' was heard from all on the quarterdeck.

"If it's the French seventy-four we've had it," Hayes volunteered. "*Trident* has stood more than she was built for already, Captain."

Gabe was silent as he stared at Dagan. Fate...was it their destiny to die today? What was it Lord Skalla had said, "Tis to death or glory we steer." Just about the time he thought they'd won...this.

"A fine day for it," Dagan said in a solemn voice.

"Mr. Sebastian."

"Aye, Captain."

"Make general signal, 'close with fl...'" Gabe hesitated. He'd almost said, 'Close with flag'. "Close with *Trident*," he corrected himself. Looking across the water to the captured corvette a plan came to mind. "Mr. Campbell."

"Aye, Captain."

"Go to the corvette yonder. Set the French aboard her adrift, then close with *Trident* for orders."

"The corvette?" Campbell asked.

"Aye," Gabe replied. "Only I don't see a corvette, I see a Trojan horse. Quickly now, while we have time. Captain Schoggins!"

"Yes sir, Captain."

"Prepare your marines to transfer to the corvette once Mr. Campbell closes."

In half an hour's time the ships of the squadron had hove to around *Trident* and the captains came on board. Gabe gave quick orders, as time was short. The sloops would transfer twenty men each to the corvette in addition to Schoggins' marines.

"We will keep enough men aboard *Trident* to put on a good show. The rest will go aboard *Foxfire*. Captain Jenkins, put your first lieutenant in charge of *Zebra* and you take command of the prize. We will pursue the corvette with Mr. Renfroe putting on a good show of trying to sink her. Hopefully, the French will recognize her as one of their own and concentrate their fire on *Trident*. As soon as possible, Mr. Campbell will close and board the seventy-four if she's there. If not, then the lead vessel."

"You think the seventy-four will not be in company with the squadron?" Lord Skalla asked.

"I'm not that lucky," Gabe replied. "I don't aim to stand off and trade broadsides," he continued. "If she floats long enough I will put *Trident* alongside the Frenchie and board as well. The rest of the French squadron I leave to our frigate captains. This brought a chuckle, as Gabe knew it would.

"What about us?" *Thorn's* Captain Taylor asked.

"I leave it up to you, gentlemen, to act as you think fit. I don't want any heroics, but if you can within reason lend assistance then so be it. Remember...someone has to carry word to Barbados." No one chuckled at this sad but important comment.

Back aboard their ships, the captains watched as sea water was pumped over *Trident's* side. The carpenter and a party sent by Lieutenant Turner were able to fother a sail, which slowed the intake of sea water. Would it last once the sails were on her?

A cannon fired by Campbell was the signal the French were sighted. Two cannons in rapid succession would mean the seventy-four was with the convoy. The British squadron appeared to be bearing down on a lone French ship when the little ship fired its feisty little cannons. Two cannons fired one after another.

"Did you expect any different?" Dagan asked.

Gabe only shook his head. "Look alive, Mr. Renfroe. Put one to either side of the escaping prize."

"Aye, Captain."

The forward guns boomed. Renfroe straddled the corvette, then one astern then one off the larboard bow. And then, for effect, as the ship closed with the Frogs, he put one through the sails before dropping another between the corvette and the lead Frenchie.

"Guns firing from the big Frog, sir," the lookout called down. "Mr. Campbell is up with them now, sir," the lookout continued.

"Come down now," Gabe called to the man. "Mr. Renfroe, if you will assist the lieutenants on the gun deck and direct our fire towards the seventy-four. We need to keep his mind on us. Mr. Hayes, bring her up another point or two, please."

"Aye, Captain."

In spite of himself, Gabe jumped as *Trident's* main battery on the larboard side began to fire. Gun after gun fired and a cheer went up as part of the enemy's bulwark exploded, sending splinters high into the air. A whistling noise was heard from overhead as the enemy's balls punched holes in the sails as they passed over.

"Fired too high," Hayes muttered. "Not had the practice that we've had, huh; Captain?"

The guns continued to fire when Hayes pointed out, "She's changing course just enough to get more of her guns to bear."

Suddenly ball after ball slammed into *Trident*, overturning one of the forward guns and killing its entire crew. Lord Skalla wiped his eyes as smoke drifted toward the quarterdeck. He blinked several times against the brilliant sunlight as it reflected off the water. His skin was grimy and blackened from all the cannon fire.

"It appears they've decided to try their luck," he said calmly. The helmsmen both burst out in laughter.

"Mr. Adams," Gabe called to the bosun. "Take every available man except for the gunners and shorten sail."

"Aye, sir."

Another crash was heard forward; screams and cries could be heard above the crash, followed by a muffled explosion. A splash caused Hex to look over the side. Debris and bodies were floating on the surface as the ship slid past. *No time for niceties*, he thought. Turning to Gabe, he whispered, "Mr. Turner has been done for, sir."

Gabe shook his head in acknowledgment, no time to talk now. The Frenchman fired an entire broadside just as *Trident* was closing. The deck was a shambles. Both of the helmsmen were dead as their blood turned the deck black.

"Quick," Gabe shouted at Hex. "Help the master lay us alongside. Grapnels, Mr. Adams," he shouted. "Mr. Michael, tell Mr. Renfroe to bring the gunners topside."

"He's gone, Captain," Michael replied.

It was then that Gabe saw the boy's arm was bleeding. Seeing his captain's gaze, Michael volunteered, "It's nothing, Captain," as he ran to do as ordered.

Thuds were heard as the grapnel hooks bit into the wooden rails on the French ship. The French captain sent men to hack away at the lines, but they were cut down by the marksmen Schoggins had assigned. The hatred was felt in every ball as the men's aim was true.

Gabe recognized Thorpe with a smoking musket in his hand. The former poacher was determined to prevent the Frogs from cutting the lines that held to ships together. As the lines were pulled taut the hulls of ships came together with a bump and loud groan.

Adams could be heard cheering on the marksmen as his men made fast the lines, "That's it, men. Damn the whoresons and the whores that bore 'em. Send 'em to hell, lads."

"Prepare to board," Gabe shouted.

His men had lined up along what was left of the bulwark. "Prepare to board" was the signal for the marksmen to fire the swivel guns into the French. The guns were loaded with canister and hopefully would cut down on the defenders standing by to repel boarders. The French, Gabe realized, had not strung up boarding nets; too late now...he hoped.

Gabe kneeled with only his head above the rail and watched as French crewmen rushed to the sides. Suddenly, the swivel guns fired, the shot tearing through the enemy crew, turning prime seamen into a bloody gore. It was now, before the French recovered.

"Boarders away, *Trident's* with me," Gabe ordered.

With a bloodcurdling yell the men on *Trident* crossed over in a rush. Yelling, cursing, and screaming over they went. It was now defeat the enemy or death, and every jack tar knew it.

CHAPTER THIRTY-SIX

THE SUDDEN ONSLAUGHT OF attackers caused the French to give way. Men were down, dead and dying. The sun was hellish hot but paled in comparison to the heated battle engaged below it. The battle was without mercy: swivel guns, pistols and muskets were being fired all around. The clang of steel was heard as blade hit blade. Men were downed by boarding axes, pikes, and belaying pins. Combatants frequently picked up a vanquished foe's weapon to continue on the battle. The harrowing screams of death intermingled with shouts of anger and curses.

A man with rotten teeth and bluish gums breathed his foul breath upon Lord Skalla as he tried to wrestle away his pistol. Lord Skalla gave it to him, ball first; the man's rotten teeth blown away as his face turned to pulp.

Hex fought like a madman, swinging a boarding axe left and right, opening a path toward the Frenchie's quarterdeck. Gabe followed behind him, but as they neared he found himself to be a target.

He was attacked by a French lieutenant. The attack came from the side and a full swing knocked Gabe's sword loose, the lanyard slipping over a wet and bloody wrist before he could recover it. Gabe quickly snatched his remaining pistol from his sash and shot the lieutenant, causing blood to gush from the man's wound. Bending over to retrieve his sword, Gabe was hit over the head and knocked to the deck. In a daze, he could see several men gather around him with blades and a pistol, ready to kill the British sea captain.

"Die, English dog," one of the men cursed.

A piercing yell was suddenly heard above the din of battle. Through his daze, Gabe could see Dagan swinging his cutlass. He swung with such might the blade went clean through the first foe's neck decapitating him. Dagan then spun with his blade, splitting the second man from his collarbone to his breast. He yanked his blade free and lunged forward, skewering the third man. This was the man with the pistol. As he fell backward he fingered the trigger, firing the pistol. The ball slammed into Dagan's chest. Forgetting Gabe, the fourth man, the French captain, lunged forward with his blade sinking it into the crazed English devil. It was like slow motion. Gabe watched as Dagan attacked the men who would have killed him. He watched the pistol ball slam into Dagan's chest and he watched, dazed, as the enemy captain tried to pull his blade from Dagan's body.

The daze was gone as Gabe rose. All the months of questioning himself whether he was ready for the responsibility as flag captain, the weeks of worrying about his marriage, of missing his son, of Dagan's sudden change, his premonitions...it all came to a head. The blood lust was on Gabe. He screamed "Dagannnn...uncle..." He stood, almost fell in the gore, then rose. Regaining his balance, Gabe spun his enemy around, the sword making a sucking noise as it was pulled from Dagan's body.

As Dagan slid to the deck, the Frenchman looked into the eyes of death. Hard, cold, fierce eyes that seemed to blaze with hate. The man raised his arm to swing his sword but his wrist was caught in a vice-like grip. The man watched in terror as Gabe grabbed the blade with his free hand and pushed the bloody steel down until the point was now at his stomach. Slowly and steadily Gabe pushed. The Frenchman was no match for the battle craze that engulfed his enemy. Then with a shove the blade penetrated. A burning sensation went through the man's innards. Gabe pushed in and down and then ripped the sword free, disemboweling his foe. A look of relief came upon the man just before he fell lifeless to the deck.

The French, seeing their captain fall, began to back away. Some threw down their weapons, and some tried to run below decks. Those that fought were given no quarter. Finally, the seventy-four had been taken.

The British sailors were all bone tired and weary when the last of the Frenchmen fell. Exhausted men leaned against rails that had been peppered with shot and masts that had been splattered with blood. Torn sails were used to cover the wounded until the surgeon's mate and loblolly boys could take them below to the surgeon.

Gabe watched as a surgeon's mate bound up Dagan's sword wound on deck and had him gently taken below to the surgeon. Holding Dagan's hand, he whispered, "I love you, uncle." A weak hand squeezed slightly, letting Gabe know he'd heard. "Lord, be with Dagan," Gabe prayed.

Gabe had lost track of Hex but found him washing blood from his face and arms using a bucket of sea water. Watching men throw broken planks, shattered rigging, and useless debris over the side, Gabe realized he hurt; his whole body hurt...his mind, body, and his soul. Making his way about the ship, Gabe looked over at *Trident*. He was appalled at what he saw. How she floated was beyond imagination. The battle cries, the rage of battle, the gun smoke, the smell of burnt flesh, it all seemed so distant now that the battle was over.

"It's amazing, so much devastation, and for what," Lord Skalla said as he walked up next to Gabe. "Must history repeat itself over and over again?" Splashes were heard as the wings and limbs tub was emptied over the side, punctuating Skalla's words.

Campbell came forward; he'd played his part perfectly. "I don't think the French even knew what we were about," he said.

The squadron had captured two of the French frigates as well as the corvette and sloop, in addition to the seventy-four; plus they'd retaken the *Foxfire*. Jenkins had given chase to another corvette, but gave up the chase when another French ship started firing on *Fortune*. However, that ship fled when Jenkins came about to give assistance to *Fortune*.

So much damage, so many dead, Gabe thought, shaking his head in disbelief.

"Do we head for St. Marys or Simon's Town?" Campbell asked.

"I think Simon's Town," Gabe said. "We can't get away from this place soon enough to suit me."

"Aye, sir."

"Mr. Campbell."

"Yes, sir."

"I do not feel comfortable with all the French prisoners we have in company. Keep enough to man the pumps on *Trident* and then send the rest ashore."

"Aye, Captain. What about the Americans?"

"Let them be. We got our frigate back and destroyed the rest of their ships. Maybe they will enjoy the French company until another ship comes along."

"Captain."

Seeing the surgeon's mate, Gabe's heart jumped a beat. "Yes."

"The surgeon wants to know if you could come below."

As Gabe descended the steps, he had a sinking sensation. What would he tell his mother? Cornish saw Gabe and indicated he'd be right with him. He was sewing up the stump of an amputation. Gabe looked about but didn't see Dagan. He was thinking the worst when Cornish finished and walked over, removing his bloodstained apron.

"I thought I should ask if you'd prefer Dagan be taken to your cabin or kept in a cot in the sick berth."

Not completely understanding, Gabe muttered, "He's alive?"

"Very much so. We will have to watch the sword wound to make sure it heals. A bloody blade can cause ill humours."

"Blade..." Gabe muttered. "What about the pistol shot? I saw him shot in the chest."

"Aye, that he was." Cornish reached into his pocket and pulled out a large gold coin that was bent and misshapen. "Lucky man he was. Had this not been in his coat pocket he'd be dead. Now all he's got is a cracked rib and a sore chest."

Looking at the coin, Gabe recalled taking a ship with a hoard of gold coins some years ago when they were on *Drakkar*. *Well,* he thought, *thanks to my uncle's larcenous ways he'll live to see another day. Thank the Lord.*

EPILOGUE

The British sailors worked steadily, making the ships as ready for sea as possible until the last red rays of the sun sank from the dark horizon. Now the seas and the sky were one. Other than the lanterns hanging from various places so that some small repair could be finished, there was no light.

Taking a note from the smuggler's handbook on lantern signals, the French were taken to within a short rowing distance from Ilot Madame in *Stag* and *Venus*. Upon the return trip, a green lantern would hang to starboard and red lantern to larboard. If a ship approached without the correct signal they would be fired upon.

Gabe sent Campbell across to take command of *Stag,* as Lamb had fallen. This was in spite of the lieutenant's argument that he was needed to oversee the repairs on *Trident* and the French seventy-four, *Le Cométe*. It was miraculous that *Trident* still floated. Her pumps were manned constantly, but she was still floating. After a quick survey of the French prize, Bufford, the carpenter, set his number one mate to supervising repairs while he went back aboard *Trident* with a working party.

Gabe had decided to keep twenty of the French seamen to man the pumps, watch on watch. Marine Captain Schoggins detailed a squad of marines under a corporal to guard the prisoners. This would free up jack tars for sailing the squadron home...and, if need be, be ready to fight the enemy if they appeared.

Gabe had decided to put Laqua in charge of *Trident*. Command of a ship, even a temporary command of a wounded ship, would look good in his record. The biggest deciding factor for the acting lieutenant, however, was that he spoke French.

Within the hour the frigates were back. Campbell had *Stag* hove-to close by and had himself rowed over. Gabe had to smile when the call "boat ahoy" was given, followed by the reply, "*Stag*." With there being a shortage of watch standing officers, Campbell recommended sending over the second lieutenants on *Stag* and *Venus*.

"Do you have any idea of the butcher's bill?" Gabe asked.

Campbell thought for a moment before he spoke, "Acting-Lieutenant Turner, Captain Lamb, his master, Mr. Saunders, *Fortune's* First Lieutenant Hamm."

"I knew Saunders," Hayes said, overhearing the conversation and joining in.

"Lieutenant Parkinson is wounded but should be able to maintain command. Captain Chatham may lose his arm," Campbell said.

This made Gabe think of the wings and limbs tub that had been emptied over the side. That was enough to pay, and still the number of dead and wounded sailors and marines had not been fully counted.

Seeing Gabe's gloom, Campbell spoke again, "I think the master will agree, Captain. The mission was a complete success. You've put paid the privateers by sinking their ships and recovering our frigate."

"Absolutely," Lord Skalla said, joining the group.

When he didn't speak further, Campbell continued, "You have destroyed an eighty gun ship of the line, taken a seventy-four, two frigates, a corvette, and a sloop. And that doesn't include the ships we took at Trinidad. Were I you, Captain, I'd be holding up my head and thinking of the prize money you will have in retirement."

"Aye, and all without losing a single ship," Lord Skalla said.

***

WHEN GABE WAS SATISFIED that as much as could be done had been done, he went down to his new roomy quarters. The seventy-four had quarters for both a captain and an admiral. The French captain must have been very well off, as the quarters Gabe inherited were very well furnished. Nesbit, Fleming, and House, Gabe's secretary, were moving his personal belongings to the captain's quarters. For some unexplainable reason, Gabe had Buck's furnishings, those that had survived, taken to the admiral's quarters, which had been sparsely furnished. The French commodore had used the eighty gun as his flagship. Gabe suddenly realized he'd forgotten, if he'd ever learned, the ship's name.

Dagan was lying down without a shirt on, pale as a sheet but breathing normally. Gabe could see the huge reddish purple spot on his chest where he had been shot.

"Thank God for the coin." Without realizing it, Gabe must have spoken aloud as Dagan opened his eyes.

Trying to rise, he felt a sharp pain so he lay back, but spoke in a hushed voice filled with pain. "I'm supposed to be your protector, not the other way around."

"You were and you are, Uncle. But for you, this tub would have a new captain."

Dagan managed a smile, and then spoke with a grimace, "No need for letters now."

Gabe shook his head, "For some unfortunately, but not for us." He made to rise but Dagan reached out and touched his arm. "Yes, Uncle."

"Faith will be waiting with little James when we get home."

APPENDIX

HISTORICAL NOTES

I have tried to be as accurate as possible in describing St. Croix, including the luminescence noted while paddling in the Salt River, the Mango Island, the landing, town, fort and harbour. There are a few pictures of the fort on my facebook page. The dungeon in the fort had low ceilings with very little light and was a cramped, musty, miserable place for prisoners to be held. While visiting St. Croix, I came upon an article in a paper, *The Virgin Island Daily News, July 74 – History Corner*, by Isidor Priewonsky, that was cut out and placed in a scrapbook. The article discussed how the Americans frequently visited the island during the Revolutionary War and how it was not uncommon for British ships to raid other ships in the harbour, almost with impunity, taking prizes, merchandise, and men. The practice was so great the Danish governor sent a request to Copenhagen for ships to be sent to help protect the harbour and St. Croix in general from these breaches of neutrality.

Thus far, the Caribbean has been the center for most of my stories. There are several reasons for this. The British maintained a significant force in the West Indies during the period in which I write, and this is vacation land for my wife and me. We have visited a large number of the islands, spending as much as a week at a time on some of them. However, I didn't want to get monotonous and so I was searching for another place in which to focus my main battle.

A few nights later, I was surfing through the television channels and came upon a documentary on National Geographic. It discussed how an underwater archaeologist was searching for a pirate ship just off St. Mary's. This stirred my interest.

After doing a bit of research I found that Ile Sainte-Marie, or St. Mary's, was at one time a pirate stronghold for such legendary pirates as Captain Kidd, Robert Culliford, Henry Every, and Thomas Tew, to name a few. Ambodifotatra was the main town for the island, and a pirate cemetery still exists near the town. It is said that several pirate vessels still lie just below the surface, one supposedly the Fiery Dragon. In 1698, Captain Kidd watched as his flagship sank in the harbour at Ile Ste.-Marie due to disrepair.

The pirates on the island were said to come from many different countries, including America and England.

During the pirate heyday of the seventeenth and eighteenth centuries, pirates patrolled the maritime routes used by merchant ships, most notably those of the East India Company as they returned home from trading in the Indian Ocean. After raiding the merchant ships, the pirates would sell or trade their booty and then return to their strongholds either on Madagascar or Ile Sainte-Marie/St. Mary's. After doing my research, I decided to revisit the "pirate round," only it would be the American privateers and French raiding the British shipping lines.

I did find that one of the channels between Îlot Madame and Ile Sainte-Marie has been closed and is now a causeway between the two islands. Anyone interested in the pirates on Madagascar and Ile Sainte-Marie can find some interesting articles written by Cindy Vallar.

While haze gray and underway during my active duty days, we always had someone playing a musical instrument and singing. It might have been in a sleeping compartment sitting on a locker under your rack, on a bench on the mess decks, or sitting on the fantail. Someone always seemed to be singing and playing with a crowd gathered around listening. Therefore, I've tried to include music and song into my stories. On the USS Newman K Perry, DD883; we had a first class machinist mate who could play a mandolin behind his head. He could also make a steel guitar talk. It's his memory that made me add the mandolin to this book. It should be noted that the mandolin as we know it dates back to the early eighteenth century.

Pickles – They didn't have Tums or Rolaids back in Gabe's day but they did have pickles. Cleopatra believed they enhanced her beauty. Julius Caesar and Napoleon rationed pickles to their soldiers to help prevent scurvy, and I read some years ago they were beneficial in the treatment of dyspepsia. I have a patient who swears they are good for hangovers. With so much positive data, I had to include a few lines about them. I'm sure Claussen will appreciate it.

In describing the approaches to Cape Town, Table Bay, False Bay, Simon's Bay, and Simon's Town, I found the *"Africa Pilot III*, 6th edition 1897 to be a great help. It discusses the rounding of the Cape of Good Hope and proved to be interesting reading.

The foods, beverages, and cookware discussed were all found on the web, researching South Africa during the American Revolutionary War and Early Danish rule of South Africa.

I recently was asked how I came upon what words and orders to use for various aspects of ship handling. First, I must say, having been a "Doc," sailing was not one of my strong points such as with James L. Nelson. He is a true tall ship sailor. Therefore, I have intentionally left out a lot to do with ship handling. I was told by a reader who is now a friend that when he got to the areas of a book that was heavy in ship handling, he'd skip pages.

However, I do feel that to add authenticity to my books, a degree of ship handling has to be included. For this I refer to the following:
Seamanship – Age of Sail by John Harland.
Arming and Fitting of English Ships of War 1600-1815 by Brian Lavery.
The Young Sea Officer's Sheet Anchor 1808 version by Darey Lever.

Age of Sail Glossary

aft: toward the stern (rear) of the ship.

ahead: in a forward direction

aloft: above the deck of the ship.

barque (bark): a three-masted vessel with the foremast and mainmast square-rigged and the mizzenmast fore-and-aft rigged.

belay: to make a rope fast to a belaying pin, cleat, or other such device. Also used as a general command to stop or cancel, e.g., "Belay that last order!"

belaying pin: a wooden pin, later made of metal, generally about twenty inches in length to which lines were made fast , or "belayed." They were arranged in pin rails along the inside of the bulwark and in fife rails around the masts.

binnacle: a large wooden box, just forward of the helm, housing the compass, half-hour glass for timing the watches, and candles to light the compass at night.

boatswain's chair (also "bosun's chair"): a wooden seat with a rope sling attached. Used for hoisting men aloft or over the side for work.

bosun: also boatswain, a crew member responsible for keeping the hull, rigging and sails in repair.

bow chaser: a cannon situated near the bow to fire as directly forward as possible.

bower anchor: the name of the two largest anchors carried at the bow of the ship. The best-bower to starboard and small-bower to larboard.

bowsprit: a large piece of timber which stands out from the bow of a ship.

breeching: rope used to secure a cannon to the side of a ship and prevent it from recoiling too far.

brig: a two masted vessel, square rigged on both masts.

bulwarks: the sides of a ship above the upper deck.

bumboat: privately owned boat used to carry out to anchored vessels vegetables, liquor, and other items for sale.

burgoo: mixture of coarse oatmeal and water, porridge.
cable: (a) a thick rope, (b) a measure of distance-1/10th of a sea mile, 100 fathoms (200yards approximately).
canister: musket-ball sized iron shot encased in a cylindrical metal cast. When fired from a cannon, the case breaks apart releasing the enclosed shot. (not unlike firing buckshot from a shotgun shell.)
Cat-O'-Nine Tails: a whip made from knotted ropes, used to punish crew-men. What was meant by being "flogged."
chase: a ship being pursued.
coxswain: (cox'n) The person in charge of the captain's personal boat.
cutter: a sailboat with one mast and a mainsail and two headsails.
dogwatch: the watches from four to six, and from six to eight, in the evening.
fathom: unit of measurement equal to six feet.
fife rail: the uppermost railing around the quarterdeck and poop
flotsam: Debris floating on the water surface.
forecastle: pronounced fo'c'sle. The forward part of the upper deck, forward of the foremast, in some vessels raised above the upper deck. Also, the space enclosed by this deck.
Fother: to seal a leak by lowering a sail over the side of the ship and positioning it to be sucked into the hole by the rushing sea.
founder: used to described a ship that is having difficulty remaining afloat.
frigate: a fast three masted fully rigged ship carrying anywhere from twenty to forty-eight guns.
full and by: a nautical term meaning proceed under full sail.
furl: to lower a sail.
futtock shrouds: short, heavy pieces of standing rigging connected on one end to the topmast shrouds at the outer edge of the top and on the other to the lower shrouds, designed to bear the pressure on the topmast shrouds. Often used by sailors to go aloft.

gaff: a spar or pole extending diagonally upward from the after side of a mast and supporting a fore-and-aft sail.
galley: the kitchen area of a ship.
gig: a light clinker-built ship's boat adapted for rowing or sailing and usually used for the captain.
glass: shipboard name for either the barometer, a sand-glass used for measuring time, or a telescope.
grapeshot: a cluster of round, iron shot, generally nine in all, and wrapped in canvas. Upon firing the grapeshot would spread out for a shotgun effect. Used against men and light hulls.
grating: hatch cover composed of perpendicular, interlocking wood pieces, much like a heavy wood screen. It allowed light and air below while still providing cover for the hatch. Gratings were covered with tarpaulins in rough or wet weather.
grog: British naval seaman received a portion of liquor every day. In 1740, Admiral Edward Vernon ordered the rum to be diluted with water. Vernon's nickname was Old Grogram, and the beverage was given the name grog in their disdain for Vernon.
gunwale: pronounced gun-el. The upper edge of a ship's side.
halyard: a line used to hoist a sail or spar. The tightness of the halyard can affect sail shape.
handsomely: slowly, gradually.
hard tack: ship's biscuit.
haul: pulling on a line.
hawse: the bows of a ship where the hawse-holes are cut for the anchor cables to pass through. The space between the stem of a vessel at anchor and the anchors or a little beyond.
heave to: arranging the sails in such a manner as to stop the forward motion of the ship.
heel: the tilt of a ship/boat to one side; a ship normally heels in the wind.
helm: the wheel of a ship or the tiller of a boat.

holystone: a block of sandstone used to scour the wooden decks of a ship.

idler: the name of those members of a ship's crew that did not stand night watch because of their work, example cook, carpenters.

jetty: a manmade structure projecting from the shore.

jib: a triangular sail attached to the headstay.

John Company: nickname for the Honourable East India Company

jolly boat: a small workboat.

jonathan: British nickname for an American.

keel: a flat surface (fin) built into the bottom of the ship to reduce the leeway caused by the wind pushing against the side of the ship.

ketch: a sailboat with two masts. The shorter mizzen mast is aft of the main, but forward of the rudder post.

knot: one knot equals one nautical mile per hour. This rate is equivalent to approximately 1.15 statute miles per hour.

larboard: the left side of a ship or boat.

lee: the direction toward which the wind is blowing. The direction sheltered from the wind.

leeward: pronounced loo-ard. Downwind.

Letter of Marque: a commission issued by the government authorizing seizure of enemy
property.

luff: the order to the steersman to put the helm towards the lee side of the ship, in order to sail nearer to the wind.

mainmast: the tallest (possibly only) mast on a ship.

mast: any vertical pole on the ship that sails are attached to.

mizzenmast: a smaller aft mast.

moor: to attach a ship to a mooring, dock, post, anchor.

nautical mile: one minute of latitude, approximately 6076 feet – about 1/8 longer than the statute mile of 5280 feet.

pitch: (1) a fore and aft rocking motion of a boat. (2) a material used to seal cracks in wooden planks.

privateer: a privateer is a captain of a privately owned ship with a Letter of Marque which allows a captain to plunder any ship of a given enemy nation. A privateer was *supposed* to be above being tried for piracy.

prize: an enemy vessel captured at sea by a warship or privateer. Technically these ships belonged to the crown, but after review by the Admiralty court and condemnation, they were sold and the prize money shared.

powder monkey: young boy (usually) who carried cartridges of gunpowder from the filling room up to the guns during battle.

quadrant: instrument used to take the altitude of the sun or other celestial bodies in order to determine the latitude of a place. Forerunner to the modern sextant.

quarterdeck: a term applied to the afterpart of the upper deck. The area is generally reserved for officers.

quarter gallery: a small, enclosed balcony with windows located on either side of the great cabin aft and projecting out slightly from the side of the ship. Traditionally contained the head, or toilet, for use by those occupying the great cabin.

rake: a) a measurement of the top of the mast's tilt toward the bow or stern. b) to fire along the length of a ship from bow to stern (or stern to bow). Raking a ship is particularly devastating, and limits return fire from the raked vessel.

rate: Ships were rated from first to sixth rates based on their size and armament:

First rate line of battle: 100 or more guns on 3 gundecks

Second rate line of battle: 90 to 98 guns on 3 gundecks

Third rate line of battle: 80, 74 or 64 guns on 2 gundecks

Fourth rate below the line: 50 guns on 1 or 2 gundecks

Fifth rate frigates: 32 to 44 guns on 1 gundeck

Sixth rate frigates: 20 to 28 guns on 1 gundeck

ratline: pronounced ratlin. Small lines tied between the shrouds, horizontal to the deck, forming a sort of rope ladder on which the men can climb aloft.
reef: to reduce the area of sail. This helps prevent too much sail from being in use when the wind gets stronger (a storm or gale).
roll: a side-to-side motion of the ship, usually caused by waves.
schooner: a North American (colonial) vessel with two masts the same size.
scuppers: Drain holes on deck, in the toe rail, or in bulwarks that allows water to run into the sea.
scuttle: any small, generally covered, hatchway through a ship's deck.
sextant: a navigational instrument used to determine the vertical position of an object such as the sun, moon or stars.
ship's bell: the progress of the watch was signaled by the ship's bells:

1 bell	½ hour	5 bells	2 ½ hours
2 bells	1 hour	6 bells	3 hours
3 bells	1 ½ hours	7 bells	3 ½ hours
4 bells	2 hours	8 bells	4 hours

ship's day: the ship's day at sea began at noon; the twenty-four day is divided into watches measured by a four-hour sandglass.

12:00 P.M. to 4:00 P.M. - Afternoon watch
4:00 P.M. to 8:00P.M. – Dog watch (this is broken into 2 separate sections called the first and last dog watch. This allows men on watch to eat their evening meal).
8:00 P.M. to 12:00 A.M. – First watch
12:00 A.M. to 4:00 A.M. – Middle watch
4:00 A.M. to 8:00 A.M. – Morning watch
8:00 A.M. to 12:00 P.M. – Forenoon watch

shoal: shallow, not deep.
shrouds: heavy ropes leading from a masthead aft and down to support the mast when the wind is from abeam or farther aft.
skiff: a small boat.
skylark: to frolic or play, especially up in the rigging.
skylight: a glazed window frame, usually in pairs set at an angle in the deck to give light and ventilation to the compartment below.
slew: to turn (something) around on its own axis; to swing around
spar: any lumber/pole used in rigging sails on a ship.
starboard: the right side of a ship or boat.
stern: the aft part of a boat or ship.
stern chasers: cannons directed aft to fire on a pursuing vessel.
tack: to turn a ship about from one tack to another, by bringing her head to the wind.
taffrail: the upper part of the ship's stern, usually ornamented with carved work or bolding.
thwart: seat or bench in a boat on which rowers sit.
topgallant: the mast above the topmast, also sometimes the yard and sail set on it.
transom: the stern cross-section/panel forming the after end of a ship's hull.
veer: a shifting of the wind direction.
waister: landsman or unskilled seaman who worked in the waist of the ship.
wear: to turn the vessel from one tack to another by turning the stern through the wind.
weigh: to raise, as in to weigh anchor.
windward: the side or direction from which the wind is blowing.
yard: a spar attached to the mast and used to hoist sails.
yard arm: the end of a yard.
yawl: a two-masted sailboat/fishing boat with the shorter mizzen mast placed aft of the rudder post. Similar to a ketch.

yellow admiral: a term used in Britian to denote a post-captain promoted to rear admiral and placed on the retired list on the following day. The yellow admiral was created after the Napoleonic War.
zephyr: a gentle breeze. The west wind.

CPSIA information can be obtained
at www.ICGtesting.com
Printed in the USA
LVHW081318160820
663325LV00002B/335